A Stroke of Good Fortune

Daughters of the Gentry, Book Two

JENNIE GOUTET

Development edit by Jolene Perry at Waypoint Authors

Proof edit by Theresa Schultz at Marginalia Editing

Illustration by Sally Dunne

Cover Design by Shaela Odd at Blue Water Books

This is dedicated to the downtrodden, the oppressed—the ones who feel that somehow they are not enough. You are.

CHAPTER 1

The afternoon sky above Penwood Estate was a dark purple that might have been ominous were it not for the broad beams of sunshine piercing it that painted the summer blossoms lining the gate in vivid pinks, whites, and yellows. Inspired by the sight, Arabella Northwick picked up her son and pointed across the courtyard.

"David, do you see the flowers?" Her feet crunched on the gravel as she approached the magnolia tree planted on the grass bordering the brick row that housed the unoccupied servants' quarters. Mrs. Billings, her son's nurse, hovered possessively behind, but Arabella would not be troubled by her today. There was too much to look forward to with Honoria's wedding, and being back in their Lincolnshire estate, to spare a thought for a nurse who did not know her place.

"Frahs." Eighteen-month-old David reached his hands out toward the fat magnolia blossoms, and Arabella granted his wish by lifting him up to the branch, where he could grab the large pink and white petals.

"That's right. Flowers." She pulled him away suddenly as a bee flew out of the one he was reaching for. He twisted in her arms to follow the bee's path, and she coaxed him back. "The bee is gone, but you can have this flower."

Little David clutched the velvety blossom in his fist, destroying its beauty, and waved his hand up and down in triumph. Arabella chuckled. Never mind that he had crushed the flower; there were many more where that came from. Nature was generous that way.

A drop of rain skimmed Arabella's cheek at the same time that Nurse called out a warning. "Mrs. Northwick!"

It was not needed. Arabella hurried toward the front entrance, David's form settling like a blessed weight in her arms. At the front entrance, she stood back for Mrs. Billings to open the door for her. Instead, the nurse reached for David, and Arabella handed him over reluctantly. She never seemed to have as much time with her son as she wished. And as the nurse was under the employ of Arabella's brother-in-law, she answered to no one but him.

In passing through the doorway, Mrs. Billings's gown caught on a sharp edge of metal on the door jamb that the servants had yet to repair, and it left a large rent in the cloth. She let something close to an oath slip from her lips, and Arabella held her hands out for David.

"Please allow me to take him. You will need to see to your gown."

Her tone was pleading, and it shamed her. Even if she was a widow and young, having reached her nineteenth birthday only the month prior, her place should unquestionably be that of mistress of Penwood. But when one had gone from the hands of an indifferent father into those of an authoritarian husband, and was now under the thumb of a...well, she could not think how to describe her brother-in-law. Surely cruel was too harsh a word... Her thoughts trailed away as Nurse handed David to her and went toward the servants' quarters.

Arabella looked down at her prize. It was a small miracle that Mrs. Billings had heeded her entreaty. She kissed David's head and went in the opposite direction through the open door of the drawing room. The sound of a carriage driving on the gravel path on its approach to the manor caused her to duck instinctively out of sight from the tall windows that held eighteen evenly glazed panes of glass. Her heart began to beat, and she tried not to allow her trembling to become apparent to her son. He must never know she was afraid. How often she was afraid.

It was Mr. Northwick arriving from London. She had been expecting him to come—had known he would appear as soon as the news of her whereabouts reached him, and he'd had time to pack and set off after her. Now he was here, and her first instinct was to hide. She ran to the servants' stairwell, hoping she would not meet any of them. Perhaps she could use the pretext of there being old toys stashed in the attic for a reason to remain out of sight when he came in search of her. All she knew was that she had to leave.

For no matter how much she tried to convince herself otherwise—underneath that polite veneer, George Northwick was indeed cruel.

Noiselessly, Arabella climbed the stairs to the second floor, then continued to where the servants' quarters were, the cloth of her gown whispering with every step. At the top of the stairwell, she peeked around the corner to see if any servants were there who would be loyal to their master. All was still, and David was blessedly quiet as though he knew silence was essential to the success of her mission.

She crossed the wooden herringbone of the second floor and rounded the corner to where a door led to the vast, neglected attic.

"Shall we see what toys we have upstairs, David?" she whispered, her breath reedy with nervousness. Her question released his frozen state and caused him to spin in her arms and shove his fingers into his mouth. She sent up a prayer of thanks that he had not yet made a sound, which would resonate in the echoing corridor. She grasped the thin metal latch and lifted it, slipping through the door to the attic with her precious charge.

Their surroundings changed drastically as she climbed a final set of stairs to the attic, located just underneath the rafters. Here, the wooden beams were all in evidence with thick cobwebs extending from several of them. The attic was on two levels, with centuries' worth of discarded furniture and clothing on the lower level and a sort of a bridge leading over the clutter to get from one side of the attic to the other. It would be amusing to go through the relics one day if she were ever granted the gift of freedom from having her every move watched. She had little confidence in such a thing.

A muted noise in some distant part of the house sent a wave of panic over her that knew no reason, and she hurried over the bridge to the opposite end of the attic. This led to another tier under the rafters, with a separate door leading to a different wing. That was not her destination, however. She intended to remain hidden in the attic for as long as she could to steal time with David.

It was such a rarity that she was allowed to spend time with her son. Her brother-in-law had been named David's sole guardian in her late husband's will, and he could remove her son from her if he so wished—a threat he did not hesitate to make. Mrs. Billings, like all of the servants, showed loyalty only to the man who paid her handsomely. Arabella had no one to take up her defense.

At the end of the wooden bridge, a rickety set of five stairs led to a lower level that was barely visible. There, a hiding spot presented itself, made up of a French commode on one side and a pile of stacked barrels forming a wall on the other. One barrel without a lid revealed an interior, empty of contents but made with wooden storage compartments perfectly contrived for concealment should one need such a thing. Her father and late husband had bought smuggled goods with no compunction, so this discovery held little surprise for her.

Having poked around in the attic while her husband was still alive, she knew she would find a brocaded doll that looked to be centuries old. There had not been enough time to make a thorough examination, but she was positive there must be other treasures stored there that she could entertain her son with. She slid to the floor, her strength ebbing under the weight of her growing son and the relief at having found hard-earned freedom, be it ever so brief.

David made a half-hearted attempt at playing with the doll she handed him, but his eyes soon grew heavy. He slumped against her chest, asleep at last, and she was able to contemplate his fair skin and breathe in his scent. She had never loved anyone the way she loved her son—had never known that such a depth of attachment could exist. It was as though she had spent her entire life as little more than a shadow, until a series of violent pains delivered an infant into her arms who was entirely dependent on her. That was when she discovered her reason for living. It was when she became slightly more than a shadow. How she wished she could spend more time with him; how she wished she could be sure he wouldn't ever be taken from her.

The door from the wing below opened, and she heard the sound of footsteps coming up the stairs behind her. She held her breath. The clip of Hessians could be none other than Mr. Northwick.

She was obliged to continue calling him George to his face, because they had taken on a brother-and-sister familiarity upon her marriage to Josiah. But she hated that he had been given such intimacy, when they were now nothing more to each other than two people joined by circumstances. She had begun calling him Mr. Northwick while in the company of others, and it was as close to rebellion as she dared.

"She will not be up here, I daresay." Mr. Northwick's voice carried, and Arabella instinctively put her hands over David's ears, fearful that he would make a sound and alert her brother-in-law to their presence.

"Arabella?"

His voice was commanding, and it resounded through the air around the wooden timbers. A servant gave a murmured response, and David stirred in her arms. Arabella's limbs shook, although Mr. Northwick had not yet done anything specific to cause her such fear. It was all in his innuendos and oblique threats, his way of keeping her dancing to his tune if she wished an unhindered relationship with her son.

He began to cross the bridge above her, and she saw the back of his coat and shiny boots, then tucked herself further into the shadows. If he turned back, he would spot her.

"Arabella? If you are here, you must stop this nonsense." His words echoed in the rafters, and when the string of a cobweb crossed his face, he muttered an oath from the far end of the attic.

The sound caused David to whimper in his sleep and Arabella's heart to thump violently. But Mr. Northwick's attempts to free himself from the cobwebs sent his arm crashing into a stack of empty gilded frames, which toppled to the floor. David jumped in her arms but did not make another sound as she whispered soothing words into his ear. After that, Mr. Northwick wasted no more time in the attic and soon disappeared down the stairwell on the opposite end. The door slammed shut, and she and David were alone.

Arabella breathed a sigh of relief. She was safe for now, but to what end? She had waited until the last possible minute before writing to inform her brother-in-law that she would be returning to the estate in Lincolnshire for her friend's wedding. Her weak hope that he would not trouble himself to come after her when he'd said he had pressing business to attend to had been in vain. His desire to keep her under his thumb was too strong for him to overlook such a show of independence.

She regarded her still-sleeping son and allowed her heart to fill with joy at having him in her arms. She would be given an hour more at most. David did not take long naps in the afternoons. But for that one hour, she would not be watched, or told to give the baby over, or that he needed to sleep in his bed lest he be coddled into ill health. Here, she could gaze at him and care for him in any way she pleased, and face the consequences of her flight later on.

This evening was the dinner at Farlow Manor, held for close friends the night before Honoria and Philip's wedding. She had been thrilled to receive the invitation to the wedding and even more so to have been invited to the dinner. Before coming to Lincolnshire, she had never had close friends who sent invitations for her own sake, rather than to oblige her father, or pander to her husband for his wealth. Here, everyone had been so kind from the beginning—Honoria and her mother in opening up their home to her, and Christine, too, in her own quiet way.

Only Christine's brother, Mr. Grey, caused her a degree of discomfort. He paid her an attention she supposed was flattering, but that she could not like. It felt too much like the focused regard her dead husband had paid her for selfish ends. A regard his brother now continued.

If there existed a man on this earth who treated her in a most exemplary manner, it must be Philip's cousin, Mr. Dawson. He had not stared at her or forced his conversation upon her. He made his presence felt in more subtle ways by directing a kind word her way or complimenting her on her son. She could scarcely remember what he looked like, except that he was fine to look upon and possessed impish brown locks at odds with his steadfastness.

It was the way about him that stayed with her. He was cheerful, steady, and unassuming. After returning to London last autumn, the number of times her thoughts turned in his direction had caught her by surprise. It was not like her to spare a thought for any man, except for how to make herself small enough not to be noticed. However, she had thought of Mr. Dawson in a way that could only be described as interest. Longing, even.

Pish. Arabella blushed all alone in the semi-darkness. As if Mr. Dawson had spared her a thought in all the months since she had seen him. He had not—of that, she was sure.

David breathed in deeply, then out again with a shuddering sigh. He began to shift in her arms, and she knew her hour of bliss was at an end. She would have to paste on a smile for Mr. Northwick and call him George and exclaim what a pleasant surprise that he should join her here in Lincolnshire. She would have to make up an excuse for hiding in the attic.

If she brought one of the dolls down, then she could use that as a pretext for her mission, or maybe claim to have fallen asleep with David in her arms, which would explain why she had not heard his voice when he'd entered the attic. She prayed God would forgive her for the perjury.

In the end, it seemed she had not only been forgiven but had received more than her fair share of grace, because something happened to distract Mr. Northwick from his principal mission of terrorizing her. When she crept down from the attic with David in tow, she crossed the path of a maid she'd met for the first time yesterday, who at once dipped into a curtsy.

"You are new to Penwood, aren't you?" Arabella asked her. "What is your name?"

"Rose, ma'am." The maid showed a rare mix of openness and deference that Arabella liked.

"Rose, have you seen Mr. Northwick?"

"Ay. He's in a rare temper, ma'am, that he is. One of the footmen left his things out o' doors and the rain wet 'em through." The maid darted a glance at Arabella and, apparently finding her new mistress to be not quite so terrifying, looked at her more frankly. "The footman was only following orders to find ye, ma'am, which is why he left the things out o'doors. But the master warn't happy."

"I see." Arabella's regret for the footman's trouble at her expense was swallowed up by her next problem. "And Nurse— Mrs. Billings? Have you seen her?"

Rose nodded. "She war also in a rare taking. She swore to the master that you'd hidden yerself a'purpose."

Of course Mrs. Billings would throw blame, even if it were entirely the truth. Arabella shifted David to her other arm. "Thank you for the information. What sort of maid are you?"

"A maid-of-all-work, ma'am. Mrs. Aster hired me as I'm Betty's sister and she war married."

Mrs. Aster was the housekeeper, but to Arabella's chagrin,

she did not know who Betty might be. The new maid was a sturdy young woman, barely out of girlhood, with ruddy cheeks and straight blonde hair pulled into a maid's cap. There was a sincere look in her brown eyes, and Arabella felt that the maid was someone in whom she could repose confidence. She hoped it proved true.

"You may return to your duties." Arabella smiled at her. Perhaps Rose could be trained one day to wait on her as a lady's maid.

She decided to go to the nursery rather than seek out Mr. Northwick, but she had no peace there. Mrs. Billings shot to her feet as soon as Arabella entered.

"You took David from me and went off without letting me know where you'd gone. I did not know what to tell Mr. Northwick." The nurse came forward and took David from Arabella, and for once she was able to let him go without too much of a pang. She had had over an hour with him, her sore arms reminded her.

"I am not answerable to you, Mrs. Billings, as well you know." Arabella spoke quietly, but Nurse answered as though it hadn't taken every ounce of courage for Arabella to stand up for herself.

"You are answerable to Mr. Northwick as the child's guardian. I did not know what to say to him when he asked where you were," she repeated, feeling the cloth under David's bottom. "He needs to be changed."

Arabella knew that and would have done so herself had Mrs. Billings not whisked her son out of her arms. "I will go see Mr. Northwick myself so he knows there is no danger to me or the child. Really, such a fuss about nothing."

Those parting words were more of Arabella's courage leaking out. She had so little of it, but she couldn't bear to be bullied by someone whose station was below hers.

After holding out her fingers for her son, she left, deciding she had better see Mr. Northwick and get the interview out of the way so she might ready herself for the dinner at the Greys' residence. The front of her dress was damp, evidence of her son's soiled linens. Fortunately, this dress was ready to be laundered anyway.

Upon hearing Mr. Northwick's voice in the drawing room, she entered it just as he dismissed the unfortunate footman who looked as though he were ready to crumple. Mr. Northwick turned to her, his face as disagreeable as she had ever seen it, and the vestige of her courage completely deserted her.

"Where have you been hiding?"

"I was not hiding," she replied, attempting to pull up her dignity with her thin shoulders. "I brought David up to see the toys in the attic, and he fell asleep. I must have too because when I awoke, the light had dimmed so I hurried down to bring him to Nurse."

She curtsied and turned toward the door. "I must change, for I was invited to dinner this evening."

He let her flimsy excuse go, but would have none of her attempt to flee. "Whose dinner party are you attending?"

Arabella tried to lift her chin but could not quite meet his eyes. "I don't believe my every movement is any of your affair, sir."

Mr. Northwick narrowed his eyes at her. "Perhaps not. After all, only your son's affairs are my concern. I could always take him with me and leave you to your own inclinations, if that is what you wish."

His threat worked, as he must have known it would. Arabella's heart beat with the alarm of losing her son. She clasped her hands in front of her. "If you must know, I am invited to Philip Townsend and Honoria Bassett's dinner at Farlow Manor. It is the evening before their wedding, as I am sure you are aware since I told you so in my letter."

"As long as David remains here, you may attend," Mr. Northwick said. Arabella had grown so accustomed to bearing his insolence, she was hardened to it. She merely nodded, prepared to walk past him.

He rested a hand on the back of an armchair as he faced her. "And I will be here when you return. With your increasing propensity to run off without giving notice, taking *my* heir with you, I find it more prudent to be close by and keep an eye on you."

His slight emphasis on the word "here" caught her attention, and she shot her gaze up, eyes wide.

"You are remaining in this house for the night?"

"Yes, I am staying in the manor house for as long as you remain in Lincolnshire," he replied. "I do not want to let my nephew so easily out of my sight, and I'm finding that even the dower house is too far."

"But...but it's not proper," she protested, every reason against the idea springing to her aid, but none providing her with any power.

"Well," he replied, with a grim smile that terrified her. "We both know how to sidestep public censure in that regard. You have only to marry me, Arabella."

CHAPTER 2

Theodore Dawson was, in general, a man of even temperament. It served him well when the yarn snapped on the spinning mule and got tangled in the machinery, requiring him to delay a shipment of cloth and send a conciliatory note. It served him when his mother and siblings requested coin as freely as though he were Midas, only to assume the gold came without any effort on his part, for surely he would also be available to run errands for them. It served him when his younger brother found himself in yet another scrape, causing Theo to wonder not only if Anthony would ever make something of himself, but also whether Theo would forever be required to bail his brother out. And it served him well when he saw the wistful looks the plainer maidens cast at the whirl of dancing partners on the floor of a ballroom. He could not remain hard-hearted at the sight of their longing.

It served Theo today as his cousin Philip called to him again from the foot of the stairs, urging him to hurry if they didn't want to be late for dinner, even if the fault for being late fell entirely on Philip. He had decided at quite the last minute to surprise Honoria by repainting the master bedroom in time for the wedding, even going so far as to force Theo to join him in donning a smock and taking up a brush on the last day, when the servants were all occupied with more urgent tasks. It had taken Theo more time than expected to wash the paint out of his hair. He would be gracious with his cousin, however. Allowances must be made for a man in love.

He tugged at his white cravat one last time, took a final look in the mirror, and strode out of the door to his bedroom and down the stairs, where Philip waited at the entrance. Theo grabbed Philip's hat from the side table and handed it to him before putting his own on his head and following his cousin outdoors. Philip walked with a brisk step, throwing over his shoulder the kindly expostulation, "You are worse than a lady. I've been waiting an age and more."

Theo didn't even remind Philip that *he* hadn't needed to wash his hair as he wasn't sent to paint the ceiling. He merely grinned and replied, "Tut, tut. I cannot fathom what has you all in a flutter," before climbing beside his cousin onto the tilbury. Philip flicked the reins and the carriage jerked forward, throwing Theo back in his seat, and they were off.

The conversation on the way to Farlow Manor was light, the silence comfortable for both of them, given their kinship and the strength of their ties. Theo was happy for Philip and content to let him rattle away over whatever errant thought took him, pertaining to his wedding on the morrow. Whenever pauses in speech arose, Theo could not help it if his mind flitted to whether Mrs. Northwick, the young widow he'd met on his last stay in Lincolnshire would be present this evening. He had no reason to think she would be, as Philip had not mentioned it to him, and Theo had not gotten wind of her returning to the area. But he knew that she and Honoria had corresponded, and he thought it likely that she would have been invited. Whether she would be at liberty to attend was another matter.

In the months since he'd met her, his thoughts had settled on her more than reason could account for. There was something about the widow that could not but leave a lasting impression. No, it was not her timid, sweet smile, her soft blue eyes, or those perfect blonde curls that framed the prettiest face he had ever had the pleasure to behold. Although those things certainly didn't hurt. It was that she seemed to have no one to defend her in all the world. She had seemed so alone, especially in the face of a brother-in-law who, Theo thought, took delight in humbling her and controlling her movements. This last bit brought out in him every instinct of chivalry. He wanted to be the one to stand in front of her and spare her from ill.

So he thought of her, all the while knowing there was no sense in aiming his hopes in that direction. For all he knew, he had completely misread the situation. Perhaps she even welcomed her brother-in-law's attention and submitted content-edly to his control. Or perhaps she was being pursued by some other worthy in London. She might even have married again, although he didn't think that was the case. Surely Honoria or Philip would have mentioned it if she had.

As they drove through the gates leading to Farlow Manor, Philip's mild remark about the repaired roof on the stables brought Theo out of the aimless wanderings of his mind— reminding him once again that he had spent an awful lot of energy these past months on a woman who was likely uninter-ested, remarried, or simply would not suit upon closer acquain-tance. Either she would not come, and he would be able to put her out of his mind as a chance-met woman, or she *would* attend, and he would see for himself that it had been nothing short of fanciful to have concocted an entire set of feelings based on a woman he scarcely knew. The spell would be broken, and he could continue on with his life.

The door at the Greys' house opened, and Theo took every-thing in at once: Christine's expression of delight, Honoria coming to greet Philip with eyes that shone, and a set of blonde curls deeper in the room, with only a view of her back as she spoke to Gus.

She turned and met Theo's gaze. Her eyes widened in recog-nition as a smile came unhindered to her lips, and he knew he had not been mistaken to have thought so much about her. Taken she might yet be, but he wasn't nobody to her.

"Mrs. Northwick!" he exclaimed over the crowd as he moved forward to meet her. The pleasure he felt at seeing her would be evident to anyone who listened, and he hardly knew what he or she said next. He only knew that Gus remained fixed at her side. So, Gus still had designs on the widow.

But this unkind thought was quickly replaced with something warmer when Gus reached out his hand and welcomed Theo back to Lincolnshire. He could hardly blame Gus for being as smitten with Mrs. Northwick as he was. He just hoped he wouldn't have to fight his friend over her.

In no time at all, Christine indicated for Gus to call the guests to order so they might enter the dining room. Her petite figure was as neat as a pin in a gold-colored evening dress with brown trim, and she had a way of quiet competence despite her reserve. Christine would make a fine mistress of an estate one day should she decide to marry. He had no doubt she would be asked by someone deserving.

He had further reason to appreciate the mistress of the house when they piled into the dining room, and he found he had been seated next to Mrs. Northwick. What a boon!

When they had begun their meal, Theo placed the dish of lamb cutlets beside Mrs. Northwick so she might serve herself. "How long have you been in Lincolnshire? Have you come up from London alone?"

His last question had been spontaneous, and he realized belatedly it was perhaps indiscreet of him to ask it. He was therefore relieved when she answered in a tone that showed no offense.

"I arrived three days ago, and my son David is with me."

She had not mentioned her brother-in-law, which must mean he was not here. Good! It had seemed to Theo, the last time he'd had the opportunity to observe the man, that Mr. Northwick was little better than a jailer. Perhaps if he were not around, Theo would have a chance at getting to know her better. He might even prolong his stay in the shire to that end. Surely the manager at the mill could carry on without him for another week or two.

These hopes had scarcely made themselves known to him before they were dashed by Mrs. Northwick adding, "However, today my brother-in-law arrived. It was only partially expected that he should do so."

The hesitation that followed made Theo wonder if she was disappointed at Mr. Northwick's arrival or pleased by it. He found himself trying to guess, trying to discern how she felt on the matter.

He was not any more enlightened when she added, "I was unsure if he would finish his London business in time, and apparently he has done so. When I mentioned it to Honoria this evening, she was agreeable enough to extend him an invitation to the wedding and breakfast tomorrow."

This gave him pause. It did not seem as though she were eager to escape Mr. Northwick's attention. Had he completely misunderstood the nature of their relationship?

"How old is your son now, and what sorts of antics is he up to?" Theo asked. It was safer, he decided, to keep to a subject he knew she loved well.

Indeed, the question caused Mrs. Northwick to smile with great warmth, and the guarded look left her eyes completely. The futile wonderings about her happiness and well-being came back in full force at the sight of it. He wished he could see her like this more often.

"David is now eighteen months, and he is quite determined to have his own way. He is walking and is only content to be carried when he is tired. If he reaches for an object, he throws such a fuss if he cannot have it. His nurse is able to keep him in line, but I suppose I indulge him too much." She smiled in nostalgia then flashed him a guilty look.

"I suppose a mother's love is so great she cannot resist coddling her son," he replied as he nodded to the footman who stepped up to refill his glass. "I say, let her indulge him. There will be plenty of other people in his life to say him nay. As long

17

as he is not in danger of being thoroughly spoilt, who else will give him such unconditional love, if it is not his mother?"

She cast a grateful look his way. "It is good to hear you say that, Mr. Dawson. As David grows, I have a great many doubts about whether I am carrying out my role as his mother well or not. With your blessing, I believe I shall coddle away." She laughed at herself and then began to eat with more vigor.

After a comfortable stretch where they both observed the occupants of the room and conversed with the neighbors on their other sides, she turned back to him. "And how are the affairs at your mill? Honoria has told me that Philip boasts about you often, saying what a great man you are for running things there—which I am very sure is the truth."

"Philip said such flattering things? I hardly believe it to be true."

Despite his jesting tone, warmth spread through to Theo's heart. So Mrs. Northwick thought him a great man. He didn't know why he sought her good opinion, but he did. It made him long to be more forthright than polite conversation usually permitted.

"My family is indeed in possession of one of the largest textile mills in Nottinghamshire, which my grandfather and father began on the heels of the Cromford Mill's success. Our finer cloth is sent to London, and we sell broadcloth to shops locally. The mill was bequeathed to me as the oldest son, and therefore it is my duty to run it in the best way I can, following in my father's footsteps."

Theo had kept his eyes on his plate as he spoke, cutting his meat for something to do, although he strangely had little appetite. Now he looked up to meet her gaze. "I have never desired to fill my father's place, but this is the lot that has been given to me. And so I attempt to find satisfaction in a mill well-run."

Arabella looked thoughtful and paused before answering, shaking her head when the same footman offered to refill her wine glass. "I understand what it is like to make the best of what fate has given you, or at least strive to do so. But Mr. Dawson, if you could do anything, what would you choose?"

Something eased a little in Theo's heart, although he could not say exactly what. Perhaps it was the relief that came from being open about how he truly felt. He fingered his napkin under the table as he contemplated her question.

"I suppose I would like to be doing what Philip does and oversee a portion of land. Please do not think I envy him, for I do not. Even in school we always knew his future would be at Boden and mine would be at the mill. But I suppose I like to get my hands dirty by working the soil. And I like to be outdoors with dogs at my heels, perhaps raising sheep rather than carding their wool. This is what I should aspire to if I'd had a choice in the matter. Alas"—he shrugged—"I had not one."

Mrs. Northwick sighed and replied softly. "How I understand you."

Theo suspected she was referring to her own situation, but he had no chance to ask her, for his attention was claimed on the other side by Mrs. Bassett, young Samuel's wife. They had little opportunity for any deeper conversation for the remainder of the night, but as they finished their meal and joined the other guests for an evening of games, his eyes were frequently drawn in her direction. The highlight of the evening was when Honoria's sister-in-law offered to play the piano, and he partnered Mrs. Northwick for a dance. She'd felt just as he'd imagined in his arms, and with such a heady sensation at last realized, he was amazed he was able to carry on a conversation with any degree of ease.

When the night was over, his thoughts were consumed with seeing her again at the wedding the next morning.

THE FOLLOWING DAY, although Theo entered fully into the excitement his cousin expressed over the upcoming nuptials, his own excitement stemmed from an entirely different cause.

Because he was keeping his eye out for Mrs. Northwick, he noticed the minute she entered the chapel. He watched her hesitate at the back, noting how well her pale blue gown became her.

Her brother-in-law entered the church next, stepping forward to grasp her elbow and guide her into the pew. Mrs. Northwick did not pull away or even flinch at his touch. Theo saw it all from his position next to Philip in front of the church. He straightened his lips and glanced away.

Philip and Honoria made a fair couple, each in crisp attire made from summer cloth a shade lighter than their hair. Theo was no judge of such things, but he thought Honoria looked particularly like a bride, with sprigs of white flowers tucked on each side of her chignon. Philip was as finely dressed as Theo had ever seen him—and uncharacteristically nervous. He didn't blame him. It was not every day a man took a wife. Until lately, Theo had not contemplated such a thing, thinking himself too young. But he was approaching his thirtieth year, and he did wish for children. Perhaps it was time.

As the rector droned on, Theo's attention was drawn back to Mrs. Northwick, who sat demurely in her pew facing forward. She kept her attention fixed on the rector.

Look at me. It was fanciful to wish for her regard to turn to him, but his heart urged again silently. *Look at me.*

She did not avert her eyes from the one performing the ceremony, even to turn them a few feet to the right. However, Mr. Northwick did turn his scrutiny in Theo's direction, his glance then slanting back to Mrs. Northwick. Theo looked quickly away.

At the end of the ceremony, after all the guests had filed out, Theo and Christine followed Philip and Honoria down the aisle as the two witnesses. Outside in the bright sunlight, he received some of the petals tossed in the way of the couple.

Gus stepped up to Theo's side and put his hand on his shoulder. "Coming with us, are you?"

Theo had not thought through what he would do following the ceremony, but of course he could not ride to the Bassetts' with Philip, the way he had come. Philip had his bride to look after now. Directly following the wedding breakfast, they would be leaving Weeton for a short honeymoon on the outskirts of Lincoln—a small cottage that Mr. Reid had offered to lend them. Neither wanted to travel far, and as Philip was to have a visit from another gentleman interested in looking over his stud horse in a week's time, it was necessary he return.

Any hopes Theo might have harbored for once again being placed next to Mrs. Northwick at the wedding breakfast were quickly dashed as he took his place between Mrs. Mercer and young Mrs. Bassett. He followed Mrs. Northwick's movements as she took her seat and was glad to see she was not placed next to her brother-in-law, either. Such a thing would have been irregular since one was not generally seated next to a family member —or considered a family member the way in-laws were. Instead, she was seated with Gus on one side and the older Mr. Bassett on the other.

Theo's relief in seeing Mr. Northwick on the far end of the table was tempered when he was forced to watch Gus lean in and carry on a seeming monologue meant for her ears only. He practically ignored Mrs. Goodall, seated on his other side. Occasionally, Gus's comments caused Mrs. Northwick to smile, but more often than not, she seemed distinctly uncomfortable as though such attention was too much for her.

Theo was careful to converse equally with the women on either side of him, and as he did so, he noticed Mr. Northwick's frequent study of Arabella. He began to form the conviction that it was a proprietary thing and not simply that the man was infatuated with her, although Mrs. Northwick was indeed lovely. In fact, it was difficult to take one's eyes off of her.

They could not marry anyway, Mr. Northwick and his widowed sister-in-law—at least not with any possibility of the union standing up under the scrutiny of the church, if someone chose to object to it. Any offspring they had would be considered illegitimate in that case. But he'd heard that people did sometimes wed under these circumstances, and when they had connections, the union was not necessarily challenged.

Mr. Northwick might be pursuing her simply because he loved her, or he might be doing it to gain more control over the estate. The widow could not have been given full guardianship over her son, which meant that she must share it with her brother-in-law. That might also cause a man of lesser morals to try to control her. Theo could not abide such scoundrels.

It was giving him a headache, the way his thoughts kept tying in knots over the issue of Mrs. Northwick and her brother-in-law.

At the end of the wedding breakfast, the crowd went to see the happy couple off. Theo managed to shake Philip's hand and kiss Honoria on the cheek before they closed the door to the carriage and rode off in the direction of Lincoln.

When Theo turned back, Mrs. Northwick had arrived at his side with Mr. Northwick nowhere in sight. "Where is your brother-in-law?"

Mrs. Northwick faced him with a smile as broad as he'd ever seen, her constraint appearing to lessen now that it was the two of them. For her to show such ease in his presence must surely be a promising sign of her interest in him.

"Mr. Northwick has gone to speak to Mr. Reid." She lifted her face to his more fully. "It was a beautiful ceremony, was it not?

"It was."

Theo paused, searching for the right thing to say next. Had today's ceremony brought her back to her own wedding to her first husband? Did she long to be married again? He wished he could ask her, but he could not. Not at this stage.

"And so what will you do now, Mrs. Northwick? Do you return to London or stay in Lincolnshire?"

"I..." Arabella darted a nervous look to her side as Mr. Northwick rounded the corner with Mr. Reid, and his penetrating gaze immediately sought her out. "I cannot say. It depends, in part, on what Mr. Northwick wishes to do. I truly enjoy the house and company here in Lincolnshire. But it is perhaps wiser to go back to London. Here, I find myself a little isolated."

Mr. Reid and Mr. Northwick had taken a few more steps in their direction, but they were not yet within earshot. Theo felt this was his chance to ask what had most been preoccupying his thoughts.

"I hope you will not take this amiss, but might I ask if you feel entirely safe in Mr. Northwick's company?"

"Oh." Mrs. Northwick's hand fluttered to her chest for a minute, before she dropped it to her side. "Mr. Northwick is very attentive. He is eager to see to my son's comfort and my own. It is just that in London he has a separate residence, and here I would not want anyone to have the wrong idea."

This brought up more questions, and Theo quickly pursued the most pressing before he would lose his chance. "Is he not staying in a separate residence here? I thought he was in the dower house. At least, I believe Honoria to have mentioned something along those lines."

"Oh, yes. He is. It is only..." Mrs. Northwick faltered as her brother-in-law finished his conversation and moved to join them. At his approach, she turned away from Theo and dropped his conversation entirely.

"Mr. Northwick, if you have had the carriage readied, I am at liberty to leave."

He held out his arm for her to take. "Very well. Let us go then." He bowed to Theo. "Mr. Dawson."

Mrs. Northwick dropped into a curtsy, and Theo thought he read something apologetic in her features for having ended their conversation abruptly, but he could not be sure. Everything in Mr. Northwick's demeanor toward her had appeared upright. But Theo's instinct left him uneasy.

The man might be as polite as his outward appearance gave one to believe, but if Theo were a betting man, he would stake his mill that Northwick's civility was merely a mask for something uglier.

CHAPTER 3

Arabella rode at Mr. Northwick's side, thankful to be returning home to David, but regretting not having told the entire truth to Mr. Dawson. She did not welcome her brother-in-law's presence or help. Not in any degree.

She was also disappointed to have lost the opportunity to speak with Mr. Dawson at length. He was an easy person to talk to. Not once in his presence had she ever felt a hint of judgment coming from him—toward her or anyone else. But she could not let him know openly how much she appreciated him. It was impossible to show too great an interest in anyone with Mr. Northwick's eyes constantly on her.

Even during the wedding ceremony, she had not dared to observe Mr. Dawson as he stood beside his cousin at the altar, despite the fact that a fleeting glimpse told her he cut a dashing figure. Nor did she dare to glance at him more than once or twice at the breakfast table, knowing Mr. Northwick was sitting in a position where he could see her easily, and that his eyes frequently sought her out. Her brother-in-law had never made any specific threats about repercussions she might face should she encourage other gentlemen. But she knew all the same she must not attempt it. He was easily jealous, and one wrong step might lead him to retaliate by restricting her time with her son.

"You are quiet," he observed. "What are you thinking about?"

Arabella took comfort in the fact that her thoughts, at least, were her own. "I was thinking of how beautiful Honoria looked on her wedding day." She strove for a light tone, free from the fear she felt, hoping that by treating him in a perfectly natural fashion, he might watch her less closely. "And what did you think of the ceremony and the wedding breakfast?"

"Mr. Dawson seems to stare at you a great deal."

That the subject of her thoughts was spoken aloud caused heat to rise immediately to Arabella's cheeks. It brought her pleasure to know he *did* stare—as she had wondered whether he enjoyed her company as much as she enjoyed his—but the knowledge brought as much trepidation as pleasure at Mr. Northwick's having noticed. That did not bode well.

"I do not think you can be right," she murmured. "In any case, I hardly noticed."

Mr. Northwick held the reins loosely, but Arabella knew this to be a deceptive posture. She had seen him go from a surprisingly relaxed stance to something more sinister in a matter of seconds.

"Yes, I am sure you did not notice, as you most purposefully did not look in his direction. This leads me to believe that you have as much interest in him as he does in you." His carefully controlled words confirmed that she had every right to be cautious.

Am I to be so hemmed in? After all, what was Mr. Northwick to her that he should have a say in her personal life? Arabella refused to be cowed.

"I believe you must have windmills in your head—"

Her words were cut off as he whipped to the side and pointed a finger in her face. "Do not *ever* tell me what is in my head. You, a mere woman, and not a particularly bright one at that, can be no judge."

Arabella's eyes widened instinctually as she glanced at him, then faced ahead. It was the first time that—rather than using veiled threats—he had openly shown his hostilities, and she feared it was only the beginning. Mr. Northwick waited, apparently expecting an answer, and she forced her voice not to shake as she replied with quiet dignity, "I beg your pardon."

She deemed it prudent not to say anything else, particularly about Mr. Dawson. Although her brother-in-law had cut off her impertinent words, she hoped that they'd been enough to instill some seeds of doubt.

And what she could scarcely admit, even to herself, was that Mr. Northwick was right. She had been deliberate in her attempts not to look at Mr. Dawson. She only knew him to be the kindest, most interesting man she'd ever met. And she found his appearance attractive. He was not short like her deceased husband, with a face that she had inwardly described as trollish in some of her more critical moments. And he was not massive like her father had been, who had so terrorized her from birth that she could almost understand why her mother had given up her life at such a young age. Only two months after Josiah had died, Arabella received word of her father's death.

Mr. Dawson, on the other hand, was the perfect height. She had only to tilt her head up a little to look into his face, and when she did, she found the gentlest hazel eyes she'd ever seen staring back at her. If there was any kindness to be found in life, she would be given a greater chance to know him. But life, she knew, was not kind.

Her heart was still smarting at Mr. Northwick's harsh treatment when he reached for her hand. "You must forgive me for my loss of temper. Your words drove me to it. But I am perfectly able to control my temper when I wish to."

She waited an instant before slipping her hand out of his. A number of replies flitted through Arabella's head. *Her* words had not driven him to it, she knew. If there was any desire to harm or to thwart, it came purely from the evils of his own heart. She desired to have peace with him for the sake of her son, but wished for as little intimacy as possible between them. The marriage he had once hinted at and was now demanding openly was out of the question—not with one who could only fill her with disgust.

He was looking at her expectantly, again awaiting her response. To say "you are forgiven" did not seem fitting when he would only repeat the offense. So she settled for something milder.

"It is of no consequence."

Upon their return, Arabella went to see David and had the pleasure of being able to hold him without Mrs. Billings admonishing her or trying to take him away. Perhaps she had had enough of her young charge for the day. She was happy to let Arabella play with him quietly in the nursery. And those two hours proved a great balm to Arabella's heart. She took dinner in her room, now that Mr. Northwick had settled in the manor house, and wondered when he would release her to return to London. He would not let her go with her son, so she was obliged to stay until he had decided they should return.

She loved living in Lincolnshire, but at least in London he would not attempt to live in her house.

THE NEXT DAY, Arabella decided to go into Horncastle with the excuse of looking for a new ribbon for her bonnet. It was not a big town, but the haberdasher's shop had a fair selection of goods. David was sleeping, and she could not bear to have Mr. Northwick prowling around her home, ready to invade her domain at any moment. A ride to town would be just the thing. She had the groom drop her on the main street while he took the carriage to the stables. The day was hot, and she was thankful for a full-rimmed poke bonnet which shielded her face from the sun. It was not too low in the back, and a slight breeze cooled the base of her neck.

Before she had gone many steps, a voice hailed her from the other side of the street.

"Mrs. Northwick, what a pleasure."

She recognized that voice and turned to greet Mr. Dawson, her smile already in place. If her rapid heartbeat gave any indication, she had harbored a secret hope to run into him. "Indeed, a pleasure. What are you doing in town?"

"I am to visit Christine and Gus, and I stopped in to see if I might purchase some sweets or tea to take to them as a small gift." He gestured forward before lifting his arm to hers. "May I accompany you to wherever you are going?"

"If I am not deterring you." She smiled up at him, and her heart fluttered so wildly when their eyes met, she had to look forward again. "I just thought to look at the ribbons in James & Smith. It is not a pressing errand."

Mr. Dawson paused in his steps and peered at her. "If you are not otherwise occupied, perhaps you might accompany me to the Greys'?"

The wild patter of her heart set off again, but this time in anxiety. "I should not like to impose. I have not been invited."

A second's reflection let her know that it was not Christine's reaction she feared. It was that Mr. Grey might read too much meaning into her visit. Then again, if she was visiting in Mr. Dawson's company, he could hardly think such a thing, could he? She feared he would. Before this thought was allowed time to fully form, she realized that the very fact of going anywhere in Mr. Dawson's company was a problem in itself. Her groomsman was loyal to Mr. Northwick, and he would surely report to him whom she had been visiting and in whose company.

"...so do say you will." Mr. Dawson was staring at her expectantly. She had missed all of his words but understood them to be sweeping aside any argument she might attempt.

Perhaps she would go. But she would have to be smart about how to carry such a thing off. "If you are certain I will not be an imposition, I will accompany you. However...although it is not far, perhaps I should take my carriage there so I might return directly home afterwards."

"In that case, I will ride with you and return to town to

collect my horse, if you have no objection." The way he smiled at Arabella made her want to throw aside all objections. It was as though nothing could happen to her when he regarded her so frankly.

"Very well." She tried to smile. "I will inform my groom. He has brought the carriage to the stables, but he can easily bring it around again."

"Let us visit the haberdasher's first." He moved forward again, pulling her close. "And then, after we have purchased the sweets, I will leave you in the shop and go speak to your groom for you. I should not like your boots to be soiled in any way by walking in the road near the stables."

Mr. Dawson's calm assurance provided a defense against her fears. She might pay for it later, but in this stolen joy of his attention, that possibility hardly seemed to matter. The haber-dasher's had nothing to interest her, and they then walked to the sweet shop situated next to the apothecary. Inside, they chose candied plums and had them wrapped in paper and tied with a green ribbon.

When Mr. Dawson had paid for them, he rested a hand on her arm. "Wait for me here, will you? I will see to your carriage."

"Very well." Arabella's breath quickened as she watched him leave. "Mr. Dawson!" He turned and looked at her inquiringly.

"Tell him...tell my groom that I sent you because I had forgotten that I needed to stop by Farlow Manor."

Mr. Dawson sent her a quizzical look before nodding and turning to go, but he did not ask her why. She had to find a way to make it seem as though Mr. Dawson had nothing to do with her visit to the Greys'.

When the groom pulled up, Mr. Dawson was sitting at his side speaking to him in the easiest manner possible. The groom actually smiled, something she had never before been witness to. Mr. Dawson seemed to have that way with everyone.

He jumped down from the box seat of the closed carriage and held out his hand to help her into it, bowing with a twinkle in his eye, as though he was playing at being her servant. It delighted her and touched her. He was kind—so good. His goodness never seemed to leave him.

Before entering the carriage, Arabella stopped and addressed the groom. "I have something I must give to Miss Grey. I shall not remain there long, and I will not need to return to town afterwards."

Such an odd statement—an outright falsehood—must have raised questions in Mr. Dawson's mind, but he did not voice them, further proof of his kindness. He merely looked at her intently as though he wished to ask, but then decided against it. He followed her into the carriage, and it pulled away.

The silence that settled over the *clip-clop* of the horses' hooves left Arabella anxious until Mr. Dawson smiled. "Would you like to wager that Gus will be the first to jump on the sugared plums, and that he will scarcely leave any for the rest of us?"

She laughed, some of her relief in being freed from constraint finding escape. "I would not dare. If you, who know him so well, declare he will do it, I can only believe it to be true."

He chuckled. "Poor Gus. I do pick on him rather mercilessly, but in my defense, I can only say that his skin is so thick he scarcely notices it."

"So unlike my own," Arabella said, smiling in an attempt to remove the pathetic nature of her statement. "I wish I might have thicker skin."

"I do not," Mr. Dawson retorted, ever in humor. He lifted her gloved hand and pointed to the space of bare skin between her glove and the sleeve of her gown, speaking quietly in the unlikely event that the groom might hear. "If you had thicker skin, one might not admire the alabaster appearance of it."

Her eyes darted up to his, surprised—her heart warming under his compliment. Their regard held for an instant before he dropped it and shifted forward, a slight flush coming to his cheeks.

"Ah, but how forward of me to say so. I beg you will disregard it, Mrs. Northwick. I do not mean to force intimacies."

"Oh, no... Of course, I..." Arabella let out a gust of air in a soft, troubled laugh. She had blossomed under his words, even if they were done in the spirit of flirtation and nothing more. But now he was saying he did not wish for intimacies, and her reaction had clearly revealed how open she was to receiving them. She was laid bare—vulnerable.

"We have arrived," Mr. Dawson observed as the carriage pulled into the Greys' residence. Before it came to a complete stop, his brows furrowed as he turned to her.

"Let me clarify my earlier statement. I do not wish to force intimacies or accost you with unwelcome flirtation, but I feel I would not be doing you justice if I did not tell you that your skin is the prettiest I have ever beheld, along with just about every other aspect of your fair form."

He then exited the carriage, leaving her with an explosion of happiness inside of her that brought tears to her eyes, even as she smiled. Outside, Mr. Dawson held the door for her and lifted his hand to assist her out of the carriage, his face reverting back to the generic kindness that the world saw, all signs of familiarity gone.

But she had seen another side to him that was only for her, and she knew as she followed him to the front entrance that she would remember it forever. She would store it up in her heart.

The door to Farlow Manor opened, and Mr. Grey greeted Mr. Dawson first before catching sight of Arabella, his voice notching up in surprise.

"Mrs. Northwick! I hardly expected to see you here, and in Theo's company no less. Lucky devil."

Arabella, conscious that her groom had not yet driven off to the stables, and that he seemed to be hanging on to every word, replied, "I believe Christine is expecting me, for I have something I've promised her."

Her cheeks burned in embarrassment when she realized she was carrying nothing but her small reticule which could hardly contain anything of value. But neither Mr. Grey nor Mr. Dawson asked, and her groom drove off. She could only thank the general lack of observation in the male species.

"Come in, then." Mr. Grey led the way, and Mr. Dawson stepped back for her to follow before he entered last and pulled the door shut. Christine came from the area of the kitchen, wiping her hands as her pug yapped excitedly at the visitors.

Arabella leaned down and allowed Guinea to lick her fingers. "Oh, you're a sweet thing. I wish I had brought you a treat."

She stood, just as Mr. Grey said, "Mrs. Northwick has brought something for you, Christine."

Arabella froze, swallowing. So much for the general lack of attention in the male species. She had not brought anything for Christine, and now she would have to confess the purpose of her ruse. But she did not like talking about such personal matters to others. She did not like confessing that she had to answer to a difficult brother-in-law. It was humiliating to reveal how problematic her life was.

Suddenly, she remembered her needle and thread that she always kept with her and the dainty scissors that had been the object of more than one set of admiring eyes. They were inlaid with mother-of-pearl. She reached into her reticule.

"It's a little gift, actually, to thank you for your warm welcome to the neighborhood, and because you are always bent on one domestic project or another. I thought these would give you pleasure." Arabella pulled out the scissors and handed them to her friend.

Christine's eyes widened. "They are very beautiful. Are you sure you wish to give them to me?" A crease formed in her brows. "I've hardly done anything out of the ordinary, and I shouldn't like to take anything so special from you."

Arabella gulped. She did love the dainty scissors, but if she were to give them to anyone, she'd like to offer them to someone as gentle as Christine or as welcoming as Honoria. She was sure there did not exist anyone as kind as either of them.

"I am quite sure," she insisted, then looked up and caught Mr. Dawson staring. His look held curiosity but not judgment, and she broke away under its intensity. "Please, take them. And I believe Mr. Dawson has brought you something as well."

"Except that Gus has already snatched it from my hands, and if I am not mistaken has already opened it," Theo laughed, looking at Mr. Grey who showed the box clutched in one of his hands.

"You said it was for us. I had to see what was inside." He grinned at his sister. "And sample it. You had better hurry and bring the tea so we still have enough left to eat."

"I told you so," Mr. Dawson said with a significant look at Arabella, and she had to laugh.

Christine brought the tea, and Arabella was supremely happy for that short hour while she drank, nibbled on one of the sugar plums, and then ate a shortbread biscuit that Christine had made. Guinea panted at her side, calming her with his warm presence as she rubbed the loose folds of skin around his neck. She had never had a domestic animal as neither her father, nor her husband or brother-in-law kept any. But there was something soothing about them. Maybe one day she could have one.

It was only when the wind shifted outside and brought dark clouds that seemed to draw the sun out of the room that her anxiety returned. She should not stay overly long. Her groom might be dissatisfied, and Mr. Northwick might be wondering where she was, deciding she had been away too long. She stood reluctantly.

"I should be returning to Penwood. It seems as though the weather won't hold. I daresay my groom will fuss about being out for too long in it." She attempted a laugh.

"All the more reason to stay and wait out the storm if there is one," Christine reasoned.

"You are perhaps right, Mrs. Northwick," Mr. Dawson said, unexpectedly coming to her rescue. "I should also return to town and fetch my horse. I will walk you to the stables."

When they bid farewell—with Mr. Grey mercifully refraining from inserting himself in their company—Mr. Dawson held out his arm to escort her to the stables, explaining that sometimes the stones could be difficult to walk on. It had not yet begun to rain, and although the sky was dark, Arabella's heart felt light at having just a little more time alone in his presence.

"I was thinking..." Mr. Dawson stopped his words short, and she lifted her head to look up at him and see what caused him to cease speaking.

He glanced at her a little shyly. "All of us are on a first-name basis, and I thought that perhaps you and I could be too. You could call me Theo, and I could call you Arabella. That is, if you did not dislike it."

They were nearly at the stables, and Arabella turned ahead, smiling. "That would be very nice." She paused, a sudden worry causing a crease in her brow. "But perhaps when it is just us." She glanced up at him, hoping he understood.

He met her gaze, the quizzical look back in his eyes, before his face relaxed into a smile. "Yes, when it is just us."

Arabella's happiness endured through the entire ride home, unmingled with the usual anxiety that followed her. When the groom dropped her off at the front entrance, she hurried indoors through the falling rain and removed her bonnet as soon as she was inside. The door to the study opened and Mr. Northwick exited, followed by Mr. Weald.

This was a man of ungenteel speech and manners, but who was often in Mr. Northwick's company. She could not imagine what they had in common and could only assume it was something of a business nature. However, she was a mere woman and he would never share his plans with her.

"Mrs. Northwick." Mr. Weald bowed deeply before her and she nodded her head in response. He turned toward the door.

"Send word when you have a suitable location," Mr. Northwick told him. "This new officer seems more astute than the last. No need to come yourself."

Mr. Weald agreed to it and took his leave, and Mr. Northwick turned to her.

"Running off again?"

"I went to town to buy a ribbon but did not find any that

would suit. Then I brought a gift to Christine Grey to thank her for the dinner she hosted." The words slipped easily off Arabella's tongue, as she'd had time to prepare what she wished to say.

"Well, if you have time to visit other people in the neighborhood, you certainly have time to dine with me this evening. I shall expect your presence at eight o'clock."

She knew it was not a request but an order, and she knew when to capitulate.

"Of course," she answered with a polite nod. Then she escaped to her room, where she could examine in private every moment of her time spent with Theo Dawson.

CHAPTER 4

Theo's unexpected encounter with Arabella had been nothing short of pure delight. He was more pleased than he could admit that she had accepted his proposal to address each other by their Christian names. When the rush abated, he could think of little else than how to contrive another encounter.

Still, that there was something unpleasant to disturb Arabella's peace he now knew for a fact. She seemed to fear what her groom might report back. Theo sensed that her hesitation in accepting his offer had more to do with whether others would hear of it than her own lack of inclination. What was more, he was quite certain she had not intended to give those lovely scissors to Christine. She had needed an excuse to show her groom she was visiting with a purpose, not for idle pleasure. That any woman should be so constrained in her own house goaded him.

As he rode back to Philip's stables, he hardly noticed the pouring rain. He was staying on alone in Boden for a couple of days until he must return to his life in Newark-on-Trent. He had intended to leave the day after the wedding, but his anticipation of seeing and spending time with Arabella caused him to delay his journey. Now, the time had come to return, but he could not bring himself to depart without arranging another meeting.

One idea after another for how to accomplish this paraded before his attention, but he dismissed them all. He could not visit her at Penwood Estate as he instinctively knew it would put her in a precarious position. He could not ask Christine to invite her, unless it was a very last resort, as he was not ready for Gus to have wind of his interest. Theo settled upon leaving a letter for her in Christine's keeping for the next time she should happen by. It would mean he must leave without seeing her, but she would have his direction, so she might correspond if she chose. Before he could carry out this plan, fate took a hand in the affair.

The day before he was to leave, Theo rode to Horncastle with the flimsiest of reasons, thinking if he stayed there long enough, he might have the pleasure of seeing her again. If not, he would stop by the Greys' on his way home—to bid them farewell and leave his letter, if he did not have better luck in person.

On his way into town, he passed a man astride a horse, standing stationary at a fork in the road. He turned in his saddle when he heard Theo's approach.

Theo lifted his hat as he rode by, but then upon reflection, pulled his horse to a stop. "You look like you might need some help."

You've got the right of it. Jenkins at your service. Jonas Jenkins."

"A pleasure," Theo replied.

"I'm the new preventive," Jenkins continued. "You might've heard Newell hung up his hat, so to speak, so I'm here to replace him."

"I had not heard, no." Not hailing from Lincolnshire, Theo could not possibly have known of it, but he did not say so.

"Newell was not keen to remain on duty after a set of rogues pushed his head down a rabbit hole, then drove a stake between his legs to fix him in place, while they carried the smuggled goods by, free as you please." The exciseman stared at Theo keenly, as though he'd had something to do with it.

Theo frowned. He could understand some who turned a blind eye to smuggling—though he couldn't agree—or even those who engaged in it themselves to feed their family, but he could not feel any mercy for someone who treated a man so harshly who was only doing his duty.

"I am sorry to hear of such a thing, but I am not from these parts. I've come from Newark-on-Trent."

"Ah." The excise man's look grew less wary at the news. "Then p'raps you can't direct me to Ashby after all. Thought I'd begin by having a look there first as I've got wind that some of the goods are stored in a house there."

"I'm afraid I cannot help. I can only tell you that Horncastle is in this direction, for it's where I am headed. Although"—Theo thought for a minute—"I believe Ashby might be north of Horncastle. My cousin is from here and has mentioned it as the place where he bought sheep."

"I'll accompany you a ways then," Jenkins said.

The officer turned his horse and rode alongside Theo, who wasn't entirely sure he wanted the company. As they rode, the excise man proved loquacious and didn't seem to have any misgivings that what he shared might fall into the wrong hands.

"I'm not to take over here as the preventive permanently. I'm more interested in breaking up the larger ring of tobaccer smugglers that string out from the coast all the way to Lincoln and down to Lunnen from there."

He went on to explain that he'd been given charge of a band of officers who would go after the land smugglers. They were to ensure that operations ceased—from the higher-ups who financed the operation to the lowest urchin sent through the fens to distract the excise men from their real quarry. He finished his soliloquy by mentioning an informer who'd had the misfortune to take snuff from a batch of smuggled tobacco and been poisoned by the same and finished by cocking up his toes.

Theo just listened. As they reached the entrance to the village, he was left to wonder if it was meant as a warning to him should he be involved in the ring or whether the man harbored hopes that he might be inspired to talk. Perhaps he was simply lonely. Customs officers did not, in general, have many friends.

They parted ways, and Theo quickly put the man out of his mind, except for the lingering distaste over the way the free traders had treated the unfortunate Newell. He hoped the man had been pensioned off well.

Once Theo had brought his horse to the stables, he turned to look down the street. The sight of a petite frame and springing blonde curls at the base of a woman's bonnet in front of him caused a surge of elation to spread through his veins. She was here! He would not have to rely on a letter after all.

"Mrs. Northwick."

He called out from behind her in a barely raised voice, but she'd heard him. She turned, a smile already on her face, the same way she'd greeted him the last time. Somehow, in the way men and women knew these things instinctively, he was certain she liked him the way he liked her. Knew there was something there worth pursuing, even if the circumstances in their lives did not render such a thing easy.

"Mr. Dawson," she said when he walked up.

He bowed and lifted his head before correcting her. "You mean 'Theo' I believe, and no, I won't shout out your name for others to hear, Arabella. But I am glad to see you. In fact, I had hoped to cross your path in town. Are you here on a particular errand? Might you have time to sit with me in the shade beside the river?" In his eagerness, his words spilled forth.

It was a shame there was nothing other than a pub in the way of restauration. He could not bring her there. But on the other side of the bridge, there were benches set along the stretch of the River Waring, and each one was underneath the leafy branches of a tree.

A slight lift of her eyebrows showed her surprise at his admitting to having come with the purpose of finding her, but her smile did not falter.

"With pleasure, Theo." As he took her arm, she laughed quietly. "I am not even certain if that counts as using your Christian name, so quietly did I say it. I am sure you did not even hear me."

"Oh, I heard," he assured her as he pulled the arm that was looped through his elbow closer to him. "And I am quite satisfied. What brings you to Horncastle?" It was too soon to tease and ask her if it was in hopes of seeing him that she had come into town, although he privately hoped it was.

"Oh, I had no specific reason for coming. I suppose I just need to leave the house at times. To see other faces."

Arabella did not meet his gaze when she said this, and he admired the slender set to her shoulders and the rim of her bonnet instead. It seemed to be her way—to keep what must be her true self hidden behind a beautiful façade. But he didn't think it was because she possessed no depth, and he suspected she wasn't even aware of her own beauty. He was determined to find out what caused her to stay so hidden. Such a thing was not easily done as she offered little in the way of facts about herself.

"How is David? Have you not attempted to bring him with you—along with his nurse, of course? It's just that the weather is so fine, and he might appreciate exploring new sights." Theo hoped he had not overstepped his bounds. After all, what did he know of babies? "Of course, that might not be a practical thing to do with one so young."

She turned to him then, a soft light in her eyes. "David is well, and he does delight in any carriage outing I bring him on, but I believe his nurse would not permit a trip to town. She has particular ideas about raising him. Besides, his uncle would likely forbid it. And...although I should like to have him with me always, I do suppose avoiding the dirt of town would not be easy with him still so little."

"Of course. You must be right, for he is scarcely able to walk," he replied lightly. "I clearly know very little about these things."

She had spoken more volubly about her son and revealed much in the process. As they crossed the bridge and he led her to one of the free benches, he made a note to himself to bring up David more often.

They sat in happy silence. People walked by behind their bench, paying them little regard. Neither of them were known to the villagers and fortunately did not seem to excite their curiosity. The Waring, which was little more than a creek at this stretch, rolled over the round stones below on the river bed and rushed forward underneath the bridge. It seemed they were in their own little world, and Theo wanted to make the most of it.

Arabella breathed in deeply and looked up at the sunlight that filtered through the trees above them. He could not so easily relax, though. What sort of hold could the boy's uncle—and even the boy's nurse—have over Arabella that she could not do what she liked with her own son? But if she was not ready to confide in him, he could not push her confidence. Seconds ticked by as he thought of what he might say next. It should be a commonplace gambit if indeed she was not ready to open up to him. But he wanted something deeper and more substantial than that.

A slight breeze tickled his brow and caused him to remove his hat. Even as he doubted its wisdom, he felt he had to try to coax her story from her. He would not get many chances like this.

"Was it very hard to lose your husband? I am sorry to speak in such an encroaching way, but I prefer real conversation over platitudes." Theo had the pleasure of seeing her turn to him again. He could get lost in the way her pale skin set off her blue eyes to advantage, or the way her nose crinkled when she smiled. She wasn't smiling now, however. In fact, she merely looked sad, and a little lost.

"I'm sorry—" he began.

"I have never told anyone this before," she said, "but Josiah was something of a tyrant when he noticed me. I was never more thankful than when he had got his heir, for after that he scarcely paid me any heed—although in the end, he left this world when David was not yet born and did not know he had an heir."

Arabella leaned down from the bench and plucked a wild daisy and twirled it between her gloved fingers.

Theo had never heard anything so bleak. Having won this confidence, he wanted to keep going, despite the unhappy nature of it. He kept his tone even, not wishing to scare her and bring the confidence to a close. It felt akin to trying to tame a wild cat in order to free it from a trap. "What brought about your betrothal to him? Had you been long acquainted?"

The rim of her bonnet shook back and forth. "When I was sixteen, my father wished to rid himself of my charge. I assure you, I had attempted to make his life more tolerable, looking after the house and seeing to it that his dinners were done the way he liked. I never spoke unless I was spoken to. And yet..."

She turned to him suddenly. "Forgive me. I shouldn't burden you with such things. It is not your concern, and you could not possibly care what became of a once sixteen-year-old girl."

Theo swallowed. In order to keep himself from grabbing her hands, he folded his own, then caught her regard and held it.

"Please believe me when I say that it interests me very much. And I care for no other reason than the fact that I think you are worth infinitely more than what your father and deceased husband appeared to esteem."

Arabella flushed straight to her roots, but the sight quickly vanished when she turned forward again, her bonnet hiding her face. Her voice trembled.

"Oh, Mr. Dawson. You are too kind." She put her fingers to her lips, and Theo did not correct her for reverting to a formal salutation.

He sought instead for ways to continue the conversation. He wished to ask about her current situation. Was her father still alive? Did her brother-in-law harm her in any way? Was she aware of how he longed to protect her from Mr. Northwick?

Could he court her?

The last thought flew into his brain with the others, complicating things further. But then, he reasoned upon brief reflection, what was courtship? It was not a declaration of marriage, but rather a chance to see if two people might suit. That they did not reside in the same town did not seem quite so complicated as all that. He wrestled his thoughts to the present, and at once, he knew just what to say.

"I would like to offer you my friendship, and my protection, if it pleases you to accept them." Theo waited to see what she would answer to this before he said more.

A brief turn of Arabella's head revealed that her eyes shone with unshed tears. "I don't know what to say."

"Perhaps you might tell me whether you would welcome my friendship." Theo was angled toward her, conscious that her answer meant a great deal.

Arabella tossed the daisy and placed her hands on the bench on either side of her. "I very much welcome your friendship, Theo. In fact, I would like nothing more than to come to know you better." She sighed. "I am only afraid I am not at liberty to give it."

Theo's thoughts centered on the sight of her hand on the bench. She welcomed his friendship, but something was holding her back. He placed his own hand beside Arabella's and allowed just the edge of his finger to make contact with hers.

"Tell me this, then. Do you feel you need protection? Are you in any danger?"

Arabella's eyes grew wide all of a sudden, and she gave a sharp intake of breath. Theo stared in concern at her reaction, but she wasn't looking at him. Her attention was directed across the river to the other side.

"It is Mr. Northwick. He must be looking for me. He cannot see me talking to you. Oh, I am done for."

Theo followed her stare. The man was searching the river's edge opposite to them and would soon turn their way.

A wave of anger rolled through Theo, made more powerful by his own helplessness. How dare Northwick terrorize Arabella in such a way? He got to his feet, prepared to shield her or do anything to keep her from being captive under her brother-in-law's authority. A lucky chance kept Theo from having to face the worst, because at that moment, one of Mr. Northwick's acquaintances spotted him and came up to shake his hand. The dark look disappeared from Mr. Northwick's brow and he became all smiles, transforming his features.

"Come." Theo grabbed Arabella's hand and helped her to her feet. He led them in the opposite direction, holding on to her as he marched ahead with purpose. "There is another bridge on the opposite side of town. We can go that way and get to the stables quite easily from there."

It was not until they had walked some distance, at as quick a pace as Arabella's gown would allow, that they came to a bend in the river that led to the bridge. A copse of trees on the opposite bank would hide them from view. As they crossed the bridge, Theo risked a look up river and found that Mr. Northwick was still engaged in conversation. He hadn't appeared to have remarked upon their presence or their flight.

"All is well, I believe. He is still talking."

On the other side of the bridge, Theo accompanied her into the outskirts of town, to the side of a brick house which was used for laundering purposes. The less-frequented alley was not quite suitable for genteel crowds, but it gave them the safety and privacy they needed. He stopped and faced her, and this time she lifted her eyes to his.

"You have guessed my secret," she said. "I am afraid of my brother-in-law. I am ashamed of it, but I hold little power where he is concerned." She dropped her focus to Theo's chin, tempting him to place his hands on her shoulders and pull her into him. He resisted the urge.

"But you have independent means, do you not? Why must you be in his power at all?"

"Because of David." Her words came out in a near whisper. "My husband assigned the sole guardianship of our unborn child to his brother. And Mr. Northwick has threatened me time and again that if I leave, I will never see my son again."

"What? The blackguard! Has he ever laid a hand on you?"

His breath held until she shook her head, then he let it out, limp with relief. The desire that had been growing inside of him cinched his resolve and sent a ray of determination along with it.

"I would like to court you, Arabella, if you would permit it. As a serious suitor, I will be able to offer you all the protection you might need. He cannot deny you a suitor, surely. He can't expect you to remain single forever."

Arabella shook her head again, and this time accompanied it with bleak laughter. "He wishes to marry me himself. He will never permit me to have a suitor."

Theo didn't speak for a minute, realization dawning. "And should you choose to seek out someone else, he will withhold your son from you, is that it?"

She looked at the ground and nodded.

He could never win out against her son. Nor would he make her choose. Disappointment rose in his throat, like a ball that was difficult to swallow. "Is there anything that will convince you to try anyway?" He knew the answer before she gave it.

"I cannot abandon my son," she said softly. "Even if I could be so selfish as to give him up so I might be free of Mr. Northwick, I cannot bear the idea of David being raised by such a man without my presence to protect him—in whatever way I might."

The strength of Theo's disappointment came as a surprise. It was as though a future he had not known he wished for was stolen from him before he'd had a chance to seize it.

"Well, we come back to my initial offer then—of friendship and protection." Theo attempted a light tone, despite his crushed hopes.

He reached into the pocket of his waistcoat and pulled out a folded paper. "If I cannot court you, I hope you will always think of me as a friend. This was the reason I came searching for you today. I must return to my mill in Nottinghamshire, but I wrote out my direction should you ever have need of me."

He handed her the folded paper. "I know you must have other friends closer than I. Honoria, for one. But let me be one more. I hope you will not hesitate to write should you need anything at all."

She took the paper and tucked it quickly into her reticule as though she feared someone would snatch it from her. "That is very kind, Theo. I will remember it, should I have need. And I will gladly think of you as a friend." She sent him a timid glance.

"Good." Theo reached down and took her hand, then bent down and pressed a kiss on the glove. He squeezed her hand and let it go. He had no wish to prolong the interview. The sooner he allowed her to leave, the easier it would be to bear the disappointment over the ending of all possibilities between them.

"I had best let you walk to the stables alone to throw off suspicion, should you encounter your brother-in-law. You can say you were visiting Mrs. Reid's establishment, where her maids are famous for making butter. It is well known in the town and many go to see the process."

He smiled sympathetically, adding, "Should Mr. Northwick ask where you went."

Arabella nodded and returned a wan smile. She raised a hand in farewell and turned to go, and Theo watched her until she turned the corner onto the main street.

CHAPTER 5

Fear quickened Arabella's steps as she made her way to the stables. Perhaps those few minutes spent talking to Theo had allowed Mr. Northwick to realize she wasn't to be found on the banks of the river, and he would start his search anew in the town. He would remain looking for her until he discovered her carriage was gone.

Penwood's groom was sitting in front of the stables with the other groomsmen. When he spotted her, he stood from the game of cards he had been playing on an overturned wooden bucket.

"I am ready to leave now, Paul," she said. "You may see to the horses."

He had been chewing on a stick, which he threw to the ground. "Ye've got no packages, ma'am. I thought ye was to purchase something."

Arabella stared at him for a moment. This sign of insolence was too much, even for her to bear. "What I do with my time in town is none of your affair. I will wait for you here."

"It's jes' that Mr. Northwick was looking for ye," he muttered before going into the stables.

Arabella was breathless, and she tried to recall what Theo had said about the creamery at the Reid residence. She would have to be ready to speak about that should Mr. Northwick come looking for her. Heaven forbid he had seen her with Theo as they made their escape to the bridge on the far side of the town. She would be in serious trouble then.

Slowly, she became aware of her surroundings as she gained control of her whirling, fearful thoughts. She now regretted telling her groom she would wait for him outside of the stables. The other groomsmen did not hesitate to stare at her as though she were available for purchase. She should have given him a specific location in the center of town where the population was more refined. Then again, she was at risk of encountering Mr. Northwick there. And as much as she could not avoid seeing him eventually, it would be best if she did not have to explain her whereabouts before she'd had time to calm her agitation.

It was not until she was safely in the carriage and on her way home that Arabella was able to reflect on the words she had exchanged with Theo. He had wanted to court her. She pulled her gloves off and put her hands to her cheeks. What must such a thing be like! To be courted by a man such as Theo Dawson. To marry a man such as he.

She could imagine it, though. They would walk hand in hand in the public parks, and even in the privacy of Penwood Estate. He would take David in his arms, and perhaps she would be carrying one of their own children. They would speak gentle words over breakfast, and he would round the table to place a kiss upon her lips.

It was possible that she had read his character wrongly, and that he had some hidden, menacing interior. But she did not think it was so. Even before he had sought to gain her approval, he was unfailingly kind to everyone around him. It was the type of man he was. And for her to be found worthy of such a man...

But such a lot in life was not hers. From as far back as she could remember, the world had taught her she was a woman of little significance. Dreams and happy marriages were not made for one such as she.

Arabella visited David in the nursery upon her return. She

did not stay long, however, as his nurse was in rare form and did not leave her alone with him for a second. She decided she would take tea in the smaller salon and wait for the inevitable meeting she must have with Mr. Northwick. It did not take her long to learn that if she did not make herself available for him each day, he would seek her out on his own terms, although he had not stooped so low as to visit her bedroom. She prayed he never would, but could not be reassured on that end.

She had finished one cup of tea when he walked into the salon, riding crop still in hand. He put his hat on the side table and glanced at her before coming farther into the room. It was as though he was deciding how to punish a recalcitrant child. Or at least it felt that way.

"You are here, Arabella. I have been searching high and low for you in Horncastle." He sat across from her. "I will take a cup of tea."

Arabella leaned forward to pour it for him, willing herself to be courageous and not tremble.

"You needn't have worried, George." The name stuck in her throat, but he noticed when she did not use it and would not accept the formal use of his name when they were alone. "I was merely visiting Mrs. Reid's creamery. Her butter is renowned in Horncastle."

He sipped his tea. "I see. I thought you had wandered off again for some other purpose. You have a tendency to do that."

She sat back and clasped her hands, her spine stiff. "I have already told you that I had something to give to Christine the last time, and that she was expecting me. There is really no reason for you to watch me so closely." Perhaps she could try to turn the tables on him. "I am wondering why I have so few visitors when I'm at Thimbleby. Did you not say you would pay calls on the gentlemen and that their wives would soon follow? The only visitor I've ever had in all the time we've been here was Honoria."

At that moment, a knock sounded on the door. He raised an eyebrow and downed his tea before standing and going to the far end of the doorway, where he would not immediately be visible, as the sounds of a servant hurrying to the door reached the drawing room. In short order, a footman came in with a card and announced that a Mr. Augustus Grey was here to visit her.

Arabella's heart sank. This was getting worse. She was not at all comfortable in Mr. Grey's presence. She did not fear him, but his interest in her was obvious—an interest she did not return. And now it would seem as though she were accustomed to receiving gentlemen callers. It was most unfair. She glanced at Mr. Northwick, who remained on the other end of the room. His face was inscrutable.

"Show him in," she said to the footman. What else could she say? She had time to glance nervously once more at her brother-in-law—who had not moved from his spot—when Mr. Grey was shown in.

"Mrs. Northwick, I hope my visit does not come as an imposition. I did not send word that I would be calling." He moved forward to greet her and bowed before her.

"No, not at all." Her words faltered. She did not dare offer Mr. Grey a seat, but she would be forced to do so should her brother-in-law not make his presence known. What was he thinking?

"You have a beautiful drawing room. Did you decorate it yourself or did it come into your hands this way?" Mr. Grey did not turn his head fully and still did not see Mr. Northwick at his back. "You certainly have exquisite taste."

"Please sit, Mr. Grey." She could not make him stand any longer.

He sat with all the ease of a man with no cares and one who was accustomed to getting what he wanted. It was the way of all men, it seemed.

"You must call me Gus. Are you not my sister's friend? And Honoria's? We are all on a Christian-name basis and you must be so with us, as well." He crossed one leg over the other. "You have tea, I see. I am partial to a cup of tea myself, especially when there are biscuits involved."

At last, Mr. Northwick stirred from his spot.

"Ah, Mr. Grey. So pleased you have honored us with a visit." His hearty voice coming from behind seemed to have been designed to make Mr. Grey jump. Deliberate or not, he did so, and got rapidly to his feet, spinning to see who had greeted him.

"Mr. Northwick. Pleasure. I hadn't realized you would be here. I hope I have not interrupted something." He looked back at Arabella as though a sudden suspicion occurred to him.

That sudden suspicion filled her with shame. It was just what she'd feared. Everyone would assume they were carrying on some sort of dalliance, when all she wished for was to be left alone.

"You need have no fears on that score. I had just finished having tea with Arabella. I *do* call her Arabella, you see, for we are on intimate terms. I mention it since you suggested using her Christian name."

Arabella cringed. She knew what that remark implied. He would assume she had encouraged it. That she had been too familiar with Mr. Grey to give him reason to think she wished for these intimacies. But she had not—*she had not*!

"Oh, well." Gus remained standing awkwardly as Mr. Northwick moved forward to reclaim his seat near the table that held the tea tray. "If, uh... if you have finished with your tea, I shall not disturb you with any requests for more."

Mr. Northwick gestured for Mr. Grey to resume his seat, acting as though it were his house to do so. "Do you come often to Penwood Estate? Of course, it is my first time meeting you here, so I cannot know."

"Ah, yes, that's right. You reside in the dower house while in Lincolnshire, is that not so?" Mr. Grey sat. "I believe my sister told me that. Or perhaps it was Honoria."

"You are correct." Mr. Northwick did not disabuse him of the notion, and Arabella was relieved. She did not much care what Mr. Grey thought of her, but she would not wish for him to tell his sister of her precarious situation. She could not bear for Christine to look at her askance and think she welcomed Mr. Northwick's continual presence in her home.

Then again...it wasn't really her home. It belonged to her son, and her son belonged to Mr. Northwick. She had nothing of value, except some money that had miraculously made it into a dower's fund that reached her, despite having neither a husband nor a father who cared about her enough to see that such a thing was done. She had to thank the attorney who had arranged it all. He must have stressed what was correct, and neither her husband nor father had wished to appear backwards in any attention before the marriage contract was signed.

With everyone seated, she lifted the teapot from the platter. "Really, Mr. Grey. There is quite enough for a cup of tea, and it is still hot. Shall I pour some for you?"

"Very well. I take two spoons of sugar and milk. I thank you." He reached out and accepted the cup.

"So what brought you to visit today?" Mr. Northwick asked, his eyes on her as though he enjoyed her discomfort.

Mr. Grey appeared to have overcome his initial surprise and he responded with his usual composure.

"I was passing by on the way to visit a nearby woods that we might use for a hunt come autumn. I felt I was on comfortable enough terms with Mrs. Northwick to pay her a visit." He looked at her. "I hope I am not wrong?"

"How is your sister?" Arabella asked, attempting a smile. She regretted not giving him the assurance he craved, but Mr. Northwick would take any admission from her as a reason to restrain her movements. Besides, she could hardly encourage Mr. Grey. He needed so little of it.

"Christine is well. She has adopted a stray cat, it appears. I don't know why she must open her home for anything on four legs that has a need, but I suppose she has always been like that. If I wasn't there to say no, we would have a menagerie."

Arabella did laugh at this. She could easily picture Christine running a home for abandoned animals. A forlorn thought quickly followed that she would have more of a home with Christine if she were an animal than she did here at Penwood as one made in God's own image. Her smile fell quickly after that.

Thankfully, Mr. Northwick's subtle antagonism seemed to fall off, and he engaged Mr. Grey in a conversation about hunting that left her gratefully silent. Perhaps her brother-in-law sensed it would do no good to cause people to talk by displaying an overt hold over her. She was so relieved to have the sounds of normal conversation around her, she used a pause to lift her voice.

"Shall I ring for more tea? And some cakes to go with it?" She glanced at Mr. Northwick instinctively to see how he liked the idea.

Instead, Mr. Grey stood. "That is very kind of you, but I really must not tarry. I've left my horse with your groom, and I should be heading back. Mr. Northwick."

He held out his hand, and they shook. Then he came and bowed before her. "Mrs. Northwick. It has been a pleasure. Don't hesitate to visit us again at Farlow. Christine is always happy to receive your visits."

"I will," she promised.

Mr. Northwick gestured forward and escorted Mr. Grey to the front entrance, and Arabella used his absence as a chance to ring for a servant to come and clear the dishes. It was the new maid, Rose, and Arabella gave her quick instructions before heading for the opposite end of the room, where a door led to the stairwell. She was on the point of leaving the room when she heard Mr. Northwick call to her from the other end of it.

"You must have given Mr. Grey quite the encouragement for him to think you would welcome his visit here, and just before evening. If I had still been in London, he would have made himself quite at home, I believe."

Arabella turned slowly, then remained frozen in place as he moved toward her, and the maid scurried out with the dishes. She strove to think of anything she might say that would convince him otherwise. "As much as you seem to think I have an interest in Mr. Grey, I assure you I have none."

"No? It must be because you are throwing your hat after Mr. Dawson then."

Her heart leapt to her throat. Had he seen them together after all? It seemed her brother-in-law *knew* things. As if he were everywhere and she would always be at his mercy. But she had to have more faith than that. Not even the devil could be everywhere at once. She lifted her head.

"I am interested in my son's wellbeing. That is all."

Mr. Northwick allowed a smile to touch his lips. "Touché. I must say I like that answer. I am also interested in what becomes of David. He is, after all, the heir to Penwood Estate and everything my brother left behind. In fact, you could not have given me a reply that pleased me more."

It seemed an odd thing to say, at least to Arabella. It offered her no reassurance. She gave him a feeble smile. "Well, I am glad to hear that we are agreed." She turned to go.

"Which is why you really must make up your mind to marry me, wouldn't you say? What better way for both of us to keep an eye on David than to be joined together as man and wife?"

He appeared to be waiting for a response, and Arabella knew she must give one. What would he do if she said no outright?

"You have brought up the idea of marriage before, but you must see that it will not do." The look of anger that crossed his features sent her next words on a more conciliatory path.

"You are aware, as am I, that such a marriage can be annulled. What would come of us then? Any child that was born under such a union would be illegitimate, and you cannot wish such a thing for your own child?"

He relaxed his stance, and a smile played upon his lips. "I am reassured to see that you have thought about children issuing from our union. I must own that I have contemplated that very thing myself."

A shiver that Arabella could not control passed through her, and she was certain he noticed it. She kept her features passive as though his words did not cause the sensation of horror they did.

He went on. "I do not think you need fear an annulment though. After all, who would contest it? Nobody that you know, for you have no family left. And there are no contestants clamoring for the estate, which is firmly in your son's hands and does not depend on our union."

"Since we are speaking frankly, brother"—Arabella put the emphasis on the word—"I cannot understand what you would have to gain from our union. Why is it you wish to marry me?" As far as she knew, he had his own house in Happisburgh, Norfolk and his own living associated with it. Josiah had always intimated as much.

Mr. Northwick took several steps forward until he was standing in front of her. "I would gain you, my dear."

He reached out and brushed a strand of hair that had fallen next to her face, tucking it behind her ear. "Ever since Josiah brought you home that first time, I have been jealous of him. He's always had all the luck, being born first and inheriting everything. Your father would not have stooped to negotiate with a second son, and I'm sure you would never have looked my way."

He stayed rooted in front of her, and Arabella didn't dare to breathe. The lack of air left her faint, and ill. Would she never wake from this nightmare? He seemed privy to every one of her thoughts as he studied her face.

"But now I find myself in a position of power as your son's guardian. You see, you cannot do anything without me. I am quite determined to have all of you, and not just your son."

"If you will excuse me," Arabella whispered and brushed past him.

She wished to avoid any contact with him, and he had all but blocked her way. She hurried to her room, where she closed the door and turned the key in the lock, then sat on the armchair. She breathed in and out, sending the blood back to her head. There was now a locked door between her and Mr. Northwick, but that meant a locked door stood between her and her son as well.

The image was apt. Her flesh crawled at the idea of being united with Mr. Northwick. He might be much younger and more handsome than her previous husband. But while Josiah had been displeasing to look at and unpleasant in temperament, he largely ignored her. The same could not be said for George Northwick. In fact, there was something sinister that lay beneath the surface, which terrified her.

But her fate had been sealed when David was born. She was alive solely to protect and love him and would do anything to keep him near her—even if that meant she must become a living sacrifice in the process.

CHAPTER 6

"I'm home!" Theo called when he walked through the door of his house on Tolney Lane. He placed his hat on the side table and his gentleman's cane beside it. He could hear the servants' activity from the back of the house and the sound of heavy footsteps on the stairs.

He had arrived in Newark without much difficulty, if one discounted the fact that his thoughts turned around Arabella without ceasing and left him with little tranquility. More than once he wondered if he had done well to let her go so easily. She returned his regard; there must be a way around the controlling Mr. Northwick, who seemed to hold her captive.

But it had been too early to push. His decision to court her had been of too recent a date. It was one thing to be sure enough of one's feelings to begin paying a woman particular attention. It was another to commit himself so irrevocably that he was ready to uproot her from a complicated situation and insist she leave her son behind. Of course, she couldn't do that. And at present, no ready solution sprang to his mind to circumvent it.

"G'day, Theo." His brother, Anthony, opened the door to the sitting room at the same time that the housekeeper reached the top of the stairs. He took one look at Theo, who was wearing one of his older coats and was covered with dust besides.

"I see you have not invested in a new coat in your time away. I'm almost ashamed to own the connection." Anthony was an aspiring dandy, who never dressed in anything but the latest fashion.

"Welcome home, sir," Mrs. Wilkins said, saving Theo from having to give a retort. The housekeeper was slightly out of breath from the climb, and she smoothed the front of her apron over her portly frame. "We thought you might have arrived yesterday, but Cook has been ready to serve your dinner these two days past."

"*My* presence does not merit setting out a full course," Anthony said with a grin.

"Mr. Anthony, you know that is not true. We have been putting out your dinner as well, but as you have not always been home when you said you would be..." Mrs. Wilkins stopped short.

Theo smiled at her. "You have been treated shabbily by Anthony here. As for me, I do not choose to dine out when I can have one of the meals you and Cook send up."

This brought a rosy tint to Mrs. Wilkins's cheeks. "Well, Mr. Dawson, I have known you since you were a lad, so I suppose that is where that partiality comes from, but I do thank you. I shall see to it that a tray of tea is brought up to you at once."

"I would appreciate it." Theo walked over to Anthony and gave him a friendly shove back into the sitting room. "In you go. Perhaps you might enlighten me as to what has been keeping you out late enough to miss so many of Cook's dinners."

Anthony laughed and threw himself down on the sofa in the middle of the room. "Earnie doesn't despise my company, though we're no longer in Cambridge. How can I turn it down when he proposes I visit him at the Hall or join him at the local pub?"

Earnie was a Mr. Earnest Fairgood, son of a baronet who owned Kelham Hall. The Fairgoods were Newark's cream of society, and some had once speculated whether Miss Bridget Fairgood might become Mrs. Dawson. When Theo had not been convinced enough of the suitability of the match to try for it, tongues wagged at this sign of folly. What were the Dawsons, after all? Nothing but miller merchants! But Theo had remained obstinate in his folly, Miss Fairgood had married, and Earnie and Anthony continued to frequent each other's society.

"I'm happy to hear you've kept yourself so splendidly occupied." Theo took a seat and pulled out a pocket watch to glance at it before tucking it back into his waistcoat pocket. "I don't suppose by 'local pub,' you are referring to the Fox and Feathers?"

Anthony's expression hardened ever so slightly as it did when someone challenged his good-natured existence.

"And why should it not? I am not too proud to go there for a mug of ale, and I shouldn't think you would object. After all, you sometimes go there yourself."

"Very true." Theo proceeded cautiously. It would do no good to set up his brother's back. "Although my objective is to share a drink with some of my workers, rather than to join in the raucous gambling sets at the back tables."

Anthony sighed loudly. "You are the perfect one to step into our father's shoes. You lecture so finely."

Theo dipped his chin and shook his head, a wistful smile on his lips. "I have no desire to lecture, I assure you. I don't suppose you have gone in to meet with Mr. Barrett at the mill?"

His brother had dropped all signs of showing offense at Theo's concession, but at this, his arms folded over his chest.

"You know I'm not keen on taking on the role of some underling manager at the mill. If I'm not to have any power to make decisions, why should I go and hang about there? It serves no purpose, I tell you."

The door opened, and Mrs. Wilkins brought in a copious tea tray that held a round of cheese and freshly baked bread from the smell of it. There was a chunk of dried ham, a bowl of strawberries, and along with that, various cakes, some with lemons, some with plums. There was even another plate with scones set beside a bowl of cream and a small crock of jam. The tray could barely contain the abundance.

"Mrs. Wilkins, you are a wonder," Theo said as he stood and took the tray from her hands.

"What a homecoming *you've* had," Anthony added, eyeing the feast.

When she had served them tea and left the room, they helped themselves liberally. They ate in silence until they were sated, then Theo put his plate on the table beside him and rested his hands on his waistcoat.

"It's not easy to be the second son," Theo said. "But it's not always a simple matter to be the firstborn either."

Anthony shot him a look of disbelief, and Theo argued his point.

"It's true. I would not have chosen to run a mill had my life been of my own choosing. That I am capable of it comes from Father's instruction, my time spent diligently at school, and from taking advice from Barrett. But I would not have chosen it."

Anthony leaned back in his chair and threw out his hand in a gesture of futility. "And what am I supposed to conclude from this? At least something is already in place for you. You don't have to start your fortune working from the ground up. All the opportunities proposed to me are things that take both luck and time, besides talent."

"You are right." Theo shrugged. "All I can do to even the playing field is to be a good brother to you and help you in whatever way I might. But I cannot do much if you have not found a vocation that pleases you. Is there not any field that interests you?"

"None, I'm afraid. You know I cannot stomach the idea of the church. I would be the biggest hypocrite to enter those hallowed doors. An attorney seems the most humdrum existence. I might like the idea of putting on a scarlet coat were it not for the fact that I would inevitably find myself at the wrong end of a cavalry charge. I suppose if I'd had my choice, I would be a man of independent means." Anthony laughed drily.

"How I understand you," Theo said with a quiet grin. He looked through the window, whose panes gave a view of the

River Trent. The water sparkled in the current that flowed by, and when set against the blue sky it was something to behold. Theo could not remain idle, however. He would have to visit the mill after such a long absence. That gave him an idea.

"Perhaps something might be done at the mill that's more than lower management. You once spoke of rivaling the cloth that comes out of Paris. With the war, there is little enough to be had except what one might get in contraband—"

"Much *you* think. There's enough contraband coming in to satisfy those who are hungry for such a thing."

Theo paused, staring at his brother with a sudden suspicion until Anthony looked up.

"What?"

"How do you know about contraband? When have you ever come into contact with smuggled goods?" Theo's brow creased as a more worrisome suspicion overtook him. "You're not working with the free traders, are you?" The memory of his chance meeting with the excise man came back to him—as did the disgraceful end to Newell's career.

"Have no fear on that score." Anthony swung one of his legs on the arm of the chair, but his careless gesture did not assuage Theo's fears. His brother seemed to be hiding something. "Go on. You were saying?"

Theo continued to study him but did not force the confidence. "Well, for all of the things you say you are not fit for, you've always had an impeccable eye for fashion."

"At last you have noticed, brother." Anthony laughed. "If you'd only let me handle the dressing of you..."

Theo ignored him. "I've placed an order for some of Cartwright's looms. They have arrived and have not yet been put to the test. Why not accompany me to the mill to see what sort of cloth we might achieve with them? After all, you may as well make yourself useful while you're figuring out what to do next."

A maid came in to clear the tea tray, which was now considerably lighter. The men remained silent while she made efficient work of cleaning up.

"I suppose I could," Anthony said, when the maid had gone. "Just don't ask me to come in, only to dismiss everything I say as being too far-fetched or not quite in the style of Dawson's Mill as Father used to do."

Dawson's Mill was built on three generations of men who valued good quality cloth as its staple, but only of the most traditional kind. When Anthony was on leave from school his first year, he had tried to talk to their father about expanding the line, but it had not gone well. Anthony was too young, their father had said at the time.

Then, Theo had been forced to take over the mill immediately upon receiving his degree. He had been hoping for a few years' play in London before he'd had to take over the family business, but it was not to be, and his father died not long afterwards, leaving everything in his hands. It was as though the elder Mr. Dawson had been waiting only for Theo to return from school in order to hand the mill over to his eldest son. And while Theo had proved faithful, it quickly became clear he was only good at running the business aspect of the mill. He had no particular skill in identifying fashion trends, much less leading them.

"I promise you I won't do that. Say you'll come with me. Let us go now." He stood. It had been a long afternoon, but he should not delay his visit to the mill, and it would be much more promising if Anthony came with him.

"Tomorrow," Anthony said as he got to his feet. "No, no. I'm not putting you off. I like the idea. But I did promise Earnie I would meet him for shooting practice, and I can't let him down."

"Very well," Theo said, swallowing his disappointment as he went to pick up his hat again.

IN THE DAYS THAT FOLLOWED, Mr. Northwick did not bring up the idea of marriage again in Arabella's hearing. She supposed he was satisfied with how firmly she was under his power and did not need to recall her to it. He would remind her again at an opportune moment—of that, she was sure. She spent as much time as she could with David, and when he was resting or when Nurse chased her away, she took the carriage into town. But that outing felt strangely empty, now that she was certain not to find Theo there.

Never before had she longed for something so much as she did a life with Theo Dawson. She had never dreamt of such a thing until he dangled the possibility before her. Her whole life, she'd assumed such happiness could not be for her. Now she was convinced of it. Her fate was completely under Mr. Northwick's control. If she had been fearful before, it was left only to add despondency to the fear. This was all she could hope for in life.

Honoria and Philip must have returned to Boden by now. She hesitated to disturb them when they had so recently returned from their honeymoon, except that she was desperate. Her brother-in-law's associate, Mr. Weald—whom she could not like —had come again and was closeted in the library with Mr. Northwick. She simply *had* to leave her house for a few hours, never mind what the groom might report to Mr. Northwick. After all, she didn't think her brother-in-law would care as much that she visited a married couple as he would if she visited Mr. Grey and Christine. It behooved her to be especially careful now that Mr. Grey had actually shown his interest by coming to her house. To the Townsends, she might go without repercussions.

She had only been once before to Boden House, and it was strange to think of Honoria being mistress of it. Arabella stood at the entrance, her heart hammering its usual fast pace at the fear of inconveniencing them. But as soon as the footman brought her card into the library, Honoria flew out of it and came to hug Arabella.

"You are still in Lincolnshire! I hardly dared to imagine you would be—I feared Mr. Northwick might have whisked you away to London. But I am glad you came."

Honoria pulled back to look at her, and Arabella felt a sudden urge to cry. It was rare that she was greeted with such an

65

open display of affection. Honoria's lips turned up at the corners as she studied her face. "*Hm.* You were afraid you might be disturbing us, weren't you?"

When Arabella nodded, she added, "I am beginning to know you. Do come in. You are not at all bothering us, and I am delighted you are here. You can visit the house with me and see the whole of it before I begin the transformation."

Philip came out of the library next and rounded the corner to the drawing room. "Arabella, you must always be welcome here," he said with a broad smile, setting her further at ease. He must have overheard Honoria.

He was coming to be something of a big brother to her. It was not that she could treat him as actual family. She could not burden him with her problems with Mr. Northwick, for instance. But she need not fear him. He had never been anything but kind and helpful in her regard, much like Theo.

"I believe your cousin has left Lincolnshire," she said. Theo was always on her mind, and now that she was with people who knew him, she had to speak of him.

"Yes, indeed. I had his note." Philip gestured to one of the chairs. "Honoria, you will wish to offer Arabella some tea, I know, before you drag her all over the house to look at renovation schemes."

"And I am sure you have been waiting for the same thing." His doting wife answered his playful words with a twinkle in her eye. "I will be back in an instant."

After Arabella had sat across from Philip, he continued. "Theo told me he would be staying only a day or two, so I knew I wouldn't find him here on our return. In the end, he stayed quite a bit longer than expected, for the date of his letter shows he was here over a week." He looked at her as though she might hold the answer to this mystery.

When Arabella remained too frozen with embarrassment to answer, he went on smoothly, "Theo deserves to spend time pursuing leisurely activities. I have never seen anyone more hard-working than he."

"Yes, he spoke about his family mill." Her voice came out timid, but she wanted to keep talking about Theo—to keep learning more about him.

"Indeed. He inherited the mill from his father when he was only twenty-one. We had intended to spend a few years in London together, but in the end, he could only come for quick visits."

"I see." Arabella mustered a smile, wondering what it might be like to be a miller's wife. She wouldn't mind at all if only she could be Theo's wife. With effort, she ripped her thoughts away from such an impossible fantasy.

There didn't seem to be any way to continue to talk about Theo without it becoming very obvious that she had a great partiality for him, so she was thankful when Honoria swept into the room with promises of the tea tray to follow. They began discussing the drawing room, which was set just inside of the front entrance. She would start by refurbishing the wall hangings, the chairs, and the sofas. The structure of the seats was good, Honoria assured her, but their upholstery sadly worn.

As they shared a pot of tea, Arabella relaxed and watched Philip and Honoria's harmonious marriage, and the way they included her. The few married women she had frequented in London had not seemed warm enough to confide in. And they were certainly not warm in affection toward their husbands. Honoria chatted on, describing the work that was being done in her husband's abandoned mine.

The previous year, they had discovered the mine to be filled naturally with mineral water, and they worked to create a healing spa there. Thus far, they had only reinforced its structure and begun to excavate the earth on top that would allow for a newly constructed roof, with windows set in to allow for light. They had not come far in the work, but Arabella had only had details from letters and was fully interested in the developments.

"Well, if you are finished with your tea?" Honoria stood and raised a brow, and Arabella stood as well.

"Yes, please show me what you plan to do in the rooms here. Perhaps I will gain some ideas from you."

"Dearest, you will not mind if we leave you, I am sure." Honoria went over and kissed Philip on the cheek, which he appeared to accept as though it were not a shocking display of affection. Then she led the way to the large dining room on the other side of the corridor.

Arabella followed numbly, and the longing to marry for love only grew stronger. Why? Why could she not have this? Honoria continued through the dining room, merely observing that there was not much to be done there, apart from the wall hangings, which would have to be replaced. She had already set the house-keeper to polishing the wood table and chairs and dusting the frames of the large paintings on the wall.

As she led her through the butler's pantry and up a set of stairs, she smiled at a passing servant before leading Arabella into an informal sitting room next to one of the bedrooms upstairs. There, she sat down promptly and indicated for Arabella to take a seat across from her.

"My friend. Will you please tell me what it is that is troubling you?"

When Honoria sat and waited, Arabella had no choice but to follow suit. But she was confused. "What gave you the idea something was amiss?"

"There is a heaviness to you." Honoria shook her head. "I noticed it right away. I believe your life has not led you to experience an excess of gaiety, but this current trouble appears to be burdensome, even for what you are accustomed to. It was not so at the wedding, so something must have occurred since then."

Arabella wanted to tell her. She wanted to pour out her heart and say she quite admired Theo, but that she had turned him away, knowing she would never be free to entertain his suit. It was impossible to open up about her own heart so easily. However, with Honoria looking at her so steadily, she took the risk of sharing a glimpse of her life, despite the fact that she had little hope of anything being done to remedy it. After all, having unburdened her heart to Theo and having him care had somehow lightened her spirit.

"My brother-in-law is the full guardian of my son, David. He has made it clear I cannot build my life anywhere else without his consent—or even travel—without there being consequences." She lifted her eyes to Honoria's. "He will take my son away if I do anything that displeases him."

Honoria waited for Arabella to offer more, and when she did not, asked, "Who knows of this? Do you have family who can help you?"

Arabella shook her head. "I have no family at all, apart from some distant relatives of my mother's, but they did not send a reply the one time I attempted to contact them. My father is dead, and my husband was the one who made the will, appointing his brother David's guardian. I am completely at his mercy."

Honoria clasped her hands together and exhaled through her lips. "That is indeed complicated. Would you give me permission to bring up the matter with Philip? Perhaps he will have some idea I have not thought of—some knowledge of the law."

Arabella nodded. "I do not hold out great hope. What has added to my difficulty is that Mr. Northwick has begun to pressure me to marry him. His persuasion has become more insistent of late. I suppose that is what has caused me to feel so oppressed."

"I imagine it has. Being married to a man such as he would not be easy." Honoria was silent for a bit before reaching over and clasping Arabella's hand. "I may be as powerless as you are to help, but you can count on me for my friendship. It is not much, I know."

Arabella smiled despite the lump in her throat as she squeezed Honoria's hand. "It is everything."

CHAPTER 7

I n the week that followed Theo's return, he managed to convince his brother to visit the mill with him once. The interest Anthony showed in the new power looms was all it took to convince Theo his brother did indeed have a passion for certain aspects of the business. He might not like ledgers and management, but he was intrigued by the production itself and had quite revolutionary ideas. Those ideas would likely pay off if Theo allowed him to run with them.

Afterward, Anthony had come carrying sketches with the notion to produce a lighter cloth for ladies and mentioned rivaling Bath's superfine for gentlemen's coats. He argued vociferously for the purchase of more spinning mules, despite the absence of ready capital. The spinning mules produced finer yarn, with over thirteen hundred spindles working at once, and having more of them was the only way to keep up with the new weaving looms, Anthony had insisted. If Theo was going to move ahead with the times, he really had no choice.

The fact that Theo could not coax his brother back to the mill following the one visit gave him pause, however. Could he allow Anthony to be responsible for a new venture before he had displayed a measure of responsibility? His brother would need to show himself industrious in more than just vision. He would have to negotiate additional contracts with the local sellers of cotton and wool to produce the types of cloth he had in mind. And he'd have to expand his negotiations with merchants in the cloth business, perhaps even going as far as London to get them. Apart from a few bright-eyed dreams, his brother had not yet stuck to anything he set his mind on, and it was indeed a risk to invest more on the hope that Anthony would do so now. Theo told him he would need a few weeks to think over his ideas.

At the close of one day, he returned home from the mill to find Anthony's note about having gone off to watch a fight with Earnie. As soon as he set the note on the side table, his sister Gertrude walked out of the sitting room.

"I had to hear of your return from Mrs. Gladding at church." She perched one hand on her hip and gave him a mock glare. Trudy was a managing sort of female, as she described herself, and was the only family he had left in Newark, apart from Anthony. As she was the married mother of two sons, she felt herself established enough to take him to task whenever the need arose.

He went over and kissed her on the cheek. "I've returned."

Trudy lifted her eyes to the ceiling. "I am thankful you saw fit to apprise me of the fact. I told Cook I would be joining you for dinner, if you don't mind?"

She waited until he shook his head before continuing. "Vincent is dining at Mr. Warner's to lift the gentleman's spirits after he lost his wife, so I am at my own disposal."

"In truth, I am glad to see you." Theo removed his hat and coat and rolled his sleeves up on his arms. "We will dine informally, if you have no objections. I do not plan to change."

"I've no objections." She sat on the sofa, while he poured a glass of sherry for her and one for himself, then sat across from her.

"How was Philip's wedding?" she asked, taking a sip and resting her glass on her palm.

"As nice as weddings can be." Theo drank, then set the sherry on the table at his side and closed his eyes.

"That doesn't sound very promising. I had hoped the wedding spirit would inspire you to contemplate taking a wife. I would love to have another sister."

He heard the clink of her glass on the table, and he opened one eye. "You have two other sisters. Is that not enough?"

"Not when I might have one more in the near future and yet a fourth in a few years, after Anthony has had enough of his wanderings. He has been setting the tongues ablaze since he came home, I will tell you. Even Vincent had to talk to him."

Theo's lips twitched at the thought. "I would like to have seen that."

"I will have you know that Vincent is the most noble, kind..." She pursed her lips when she saw Theo grinning at her. "Well, he means well," she finished somewhat lamely.

"That, I do not doubt at all. But you must own that he is not the best equipped to tame Anthony's wild ways. If anything, he will only stoke the fire."

"No, and you are right. Vincent made no headway with our dear brother at all." Trudy sighed. "That falls to you, I am afraid."

"I'm working on it." Theo finished the sherry and uncrossed his legs, his thoughts already diverted to the subject that had consumed him since his visit to Lincolnshire.

He trusted his sister, but never before had he asked her for advice. However, he was finding himself short of people he could confide in, and the need to unburden himself had only grown in the time he spent here.

"I met a woman, as a matter of fact." He kept his eyes steady on his sister as he said it, and she sat up.

"Did you?" Her voice was alight with curiosity. "Tell me everything. Who is she? Did you meet her at the wedding?"

"I met her before the wedding. We were first introduced when I went to Phil's last autumn," he said. "She has an estate in a neighboring town, and she sometimes resides there and sometimes in London."

Trudy crinkled her brow. "An estate? You mean her parents own the estate?"

"Arabella's a widow," he corrected. "She has a son who is not yet two years old."

Theo studied his sister's reaction, for it would be the barometer for what his entire family would think. It was worse than he'd feared. Her expression showed shock.

"A widow?" After a moment's reflection, she shook her head, frowning. "Theo, what are you thinking? You cannot be serious. You are *young*. You have your whole life ahead of you. You should be starting it with someone innocent and young as well. Not someone who has... has lost her innocence to someone else."

"It's not her fault that she was forced to marry."

His protest fell on deaf ears. "I am sorry, but in blunt terms, that is the truth of the matter. She has already had a husband. Who knows what sorts of habits she has learned from him?"

Theo got to his feet, agitated. "There might be some grain of truth in what you say, but you have not met her. And it is wrong to pass any sort of judgment on her until you have. And even then—" he muttered. He folded his arms and leaned against the mantelpiece. "I see I should not have spoken to you of this. I should have known better."

"Oh no. Don't say that." Trudy came over and laid a hand on his arm. "Forgive me, Theo. I would not have you withholding things from me. And...although I can't quite become enthusiastic about the idea, I pray you will tell me at least what it is you find appealing in her. Perhaps I might know of a more suitable candidate who shares the same attributes."

Theo looked at her in exasperation. "I know you mean well, Trudy, but you can't swap out a person you have feelings for with a similar model. It does not work that way."

"*Mmm*. I suppose not. Come. I hear Mrs. Wilkins laying out the table. Let us go eat." She linked her arm through his. "And I will beg you to tell me all about her anyway. I promise to be very good and not utter a single disparaging remark."

Theo followed her into the dining room, only partially mollified. He had not thought about his family's reaction to Arabella much, but if *Trudy* was so vocal about her hesitation, the rest of his family would be in open revolt. Trudy possessed the most easygoing temperament of all his sisters.

And why had he brought it up at all? With the way he'd left things with Arabella, she was not going to leave her son behind just to entertain his courtship. He could not ask it of her. It made no sense for him even to think of her, much less speak of his attachment as though it were a possibility.

As Trudy chattered away to Mrs. Wilkins, Theo took his seat, deciding the logical thing to do would be to force his thoughts from Arabella by sheer will. On his way home, he had thought it a simple matter. He would need only return to Newark and begin work on the mill for him to forget all about her. Instead, the opposite happened. If his mind had drifted toward her in the months before the wedding, now that he had seen her again and had her precarious situation confirmed, he could think of nothing but her.

"So," Trudy prompted as soon as the footman had seen to their dinner and left them to eat. "Tell me more about this widow of yours. What has captured your fancy about her? Is she forty with a large portion and warts?"

At a look from Theo, she choked back a laugh. "I shall not tease. Go on."

Theo speared a piece of meat and put it next to the potatoes on his plate. His sister's opening had not encouraged him to bare his soul, and he worked through his plate, methodically putting pieces in his mouth and chewing, while occasionally glaring at his sister in silence. She seemed to be in sympathy with his mood and grew more thoughtful as she ate her own meal in silence. This was why he liked her so well.

When at last he'd had his fill, he leaned back. "Arabella was forced into a marriage when she was only sixteen—and to a man much her senior."

"Good gracious!" Trudy stared at him. "By whom? Surely a loving parent could not do such a thing."

"No. Not a loving parent. A most *un*loving father. She had the misfortune to be wed to Mr. Northwick, who I understand was sixty if he was a day. According to Arabella, he was something of a tyrant who, fortunately, did not pay her any particular attention once he'd got her with child and was assured of his heir. Of course, he did not know it would be his heir because he died before his son was born."

Trudy's gaze was fixed on him. At this pause, she said, "And so now she is free to wed again, and you are contemplating filling the role of husband."

Theo lifted the silver bowl of fruit and offered it to his sister, then selected a peach for himself and began to peel it with his knife. He asked for only one course when he dined alone, and Trudy's arrival left no time to order otherwise.

"It is not quite so simple. Her deceased husband's brother has full guardianship of her son, and he has threatened to remove her access to him if she becomes betrothed to someone else. Of course, that is not something she could possibly consider, and that is how we left things." Theo focused carefully on his task of peeling, attempting to cut the skin off the peach without removing any of the flesh. It was easier than examining his own heart.

Trudy scrunched her brows as she sectioned her apricot. "There is something I don't understand. What has the brother-in-law to gain in keeping the widow nearby?"

"There is no easy answer, except that Mr. Northwick appears to be a man who likes control, and I believe he simply cannot accept that Arabella should remain outside of his rule. He can't be happy unless he holds her on a short leash."

"It makes no sense. He would willingly ruin the life of a woman for no other reason than to keep his hand on the bridle?" Trudy gave a frustrated sigh that let him know that in this, at least, she had entered fully into the problem. "His nephew will end up hating him by the time he reaches manhood."

"But even that will do Arabella no good," Theo said with dry irony. "She will have to give up her life all the same. And the boy will be under his uncle's mercy for the next two decades."

"It appears you are at *point non plus*, brother." Trudy wiped her fingers on her napkin, then folded her hands on her lap. "You have come back to us with your heart lost to a woman who cannot be yours. Have you hatched a scheme for leading the cavalry charge to rescue her?"

"Rescuing damsels in distress is for heroes, and both you and I know I am not one." Theo shook his head. "I have no plan. I fear I must respect her wishes. How can I ask her to give up her son? I cannot. And I have no legal authority to remove a man from guardianship, though he little merits it. No, I think in this case, I must attempt to forget about her and hope that she might somehow have a happy life, despite how little the circumstances promise such a thing."

"And yet you said you had met a woman, which is not a piece of vulnerability you have ever offered up before." Trudy shrugged with a sympathetic smile. "I am not sure your heart has caught up to your reason."

"Perhaps not." Theo speared a section of peach and placed it in his mouth. It was sweet and somehow comforting. "But I've learned that the heart is a mistrustful thing, and it almost never gets what it wants."

A WEEK LATER, Anthony surprised Theo by appearing at the mill without being coerced. He was dressed modishly in a coat of light blue wool and a waistcoat with purple flowers embroidered on white silk. Theo looked up from the ledgers he had been studying, trying to force them to balance.

"Now, here's a surprise. What brings you to the mill?"

Anthony threw himself down on the chair opposite from Theo's desk. "Father's office—well, now yours, I suppose—is favorably situated, do you know? You get more sun than any room in the mill."

"I must suppose it is why our grandfather chose it," Theo said. He got up from his desk and took a chair opposite from Anthony. If his brother wished to speak to him, he would not waste the opportunity by appearing distant. Perhaps he would be led by this conversation to know whether his brother was fit to take over a new venture in the mill. "I am very sure, however, that you did not come to talk about how well the office is situated."

Anthony maintained his blond curls in the style à la Brutus, and the fact that he rubbed his curls now, sending them into disarray, showed him ill at ease.

"You're always pushing to get to the point. Always in a rush. It's no small wonder I am in no hurry to grow up."

Theo bit back all the words he wished to utter—such as how Anthony would have to grow up before long if he did not wish to be cut off without a groat. But he was not irritated at Anthony, not really. Or at least, only a little. He was merely frustrated that, as the elder son, he seemed to be the only one who was forced into a role of responsibility. And not even his conscientiousness could win for him the wife he would choose if it were left to him. Duty was a hard taskmaster, and he could do nothing but submit to it.

When he didn't retort with a quick answer, Anthony looked sheepish. "I am not being fair. You certainly had no choice about taking on responsibilities when they were forced upon you."

"You are forgiven. But do tell me what's on your mind. The unfortunate chore of adulthood still awaits me with those ledgers, and I had hoped to finish this quarter's accounts before nightfall."

"I want to go to London," Anthony blurted out. "I will not hide from you that Earnie is asking me to go with him, and he will be a crack companion to have. He's got a house that's right in the center of things. I was planning to have a look around at the drapers and see what sorts of cloths are available—to see which way the wind blows in terms of fashion."

Theo studied him in silence. He had not yet made up his

mind if he was ready to allow Anthony to try his hand at the mill. His brother was still young. Could someone who had been sent home from school for participating in pranks be trusted to toe the line in London?

Theo bounced his fist on the armrest absently while he thought, but before he could respond, Anthony added, "Earnie's planning to leave in a fortnight."

Theo pressed his lips together, then came to a decision. A test of sorts. "I can let you go if you'll give me your word you won't frequent the clubs or participate in a single play for points."

"You must be joking." Anthony stood. He paced over to the other side of the room, where he leaned on a large wooden table used to examine and measure cloth. "You're asking me to refrain from doing what every gentleman does! What would I do with myself when Earnie and everyone else are at the clubs? It's the height of unfairness."

Theo stood, too, and faced him. "You may very well be right, but those are my terms. I cannot in good conscience allow you to go to London where the influence will be even harder to resist than here. I fear you're headed down the wrong path."

"I wouldn't be if you would let me go," Anthony argued back. "I will be there to study the latest modes, and that is as much done in the clubs as it's done on the streets. If you treat me as though I'm a boy—"

"Not five minutes ago you said you had no wish to grow up," Theo protested. "What am I to think of that?"

"I do not wish to grow if it means being staid and...boring. I want adventure. I want to see the world." Anthony paced again in the little space that allowed for it in the cramped office.

Something I was never given, Theo thought. But he didn't want to react from emotion or punish his brother simply because Anthony was freer to live the life he wished than Theo. However...

"I understand that, Anthony. It must be every young man's dream to have adventure. But you have not shown me that you're capable of refraining from the temptations such an adventure will provide. I will therefore have to say no. I am sorry."

Theo stood still as Anthony turned to look at him, his eyes brimming with reproach. A second later, the door shuddered in its frame as his brother left without a word.

CHAPTER 8

Arabella moved about the house with caution in her increasing isolation. Even Rose, who had shown herself to be kindly disposed toward her mistress, was being used almost exclusively as a kitchen maid, which meant Arabella had no ally in the house. She attempted to create a routine that did not put her in the way of her brother-in-law, but she had not counted on Mr. Northwick's daily determination to seek her out in an attempt to wear away her resolve. If she spent too long in the nursery, he would look for her there and sit closer than was proper as she attempted to engage David in play. Then he would leave, and Mrs. Billings would accuse her of being overly flirtatious, adding how wrong it was for an unmarried man and woman to live together in the same house. Arabella had lost the courage to reprimand the nurse for her insolence.

If she thought to immerse herself in the worthy endeavor of the upkeep of the house, Mr. Northwick would inevitably make some comment about what a fine mistress she was for Penwood that carried an unspoken expectation. And if she kept to her room, he would insinuate later at dinner that—desirous as she was of solitude—she was perhaps not a fit mother to look after David, since she appeared to suffer from melancholy. It was no longer an option to visit town with any sort of freedom. The groom had begun to inform his master of her every move, and if she went to see Christine, she was throwing herself at Mr. Grey. If she visited Honoria, she was encroaching on the newlyweds. Arabella was slowly losing her way.

One day, little more than two weeks after Theo Dawson had expressed his interest in her, and she had sent him away, Arabella stared through the window at the drizzle of rain that wept over the landscape and painted it in tones of mud and sadness. She saw a carriage drive into the pathway leading up to the stables, and her heart lifted at its approach. It appeared to be Honoria's carriage. Arabella hurried down the stairs, wondering if she should fetch David as well. It would do him good to see a friendly face since his nurse never smiled and his uncle was stern, besides being terrifying.

The footman opened the door at the sound of the knocker, and both Honoria and Philip came in, laughing over some private joke that somehow included Arabella in its warmth. Honoria's face, wreathed in smiles as it was, made Arabella want to shed tears at the sight of it. She managed to swallow the lump that had risen in her throat and paste on a smile instead. It would not do to openly show how miserable she was.

"Do come in," she said, standing behind the footman. "How lovely of you both to come. It is such terrible weather, and yet you made the journey."

"On the contrary, today is the perfect day for a visit." Honoria came forward with her hands outstretched to clasp Arabella's. "Philip cannot oversee his crops in weather like this. And the laborers are not working on the mine, since it's at a stage where they must drill from the top, and the inclement weather will only send mud and water pouring in. So here we are."

"Good day, Arabella." Philip bowed. "I hope you do not mind that I have tagged along."

"Not at all," she assured him earnestly. "It is good to see you both. I will have tea brought. It is just the thing to counter such damp."

She showed them into the drawing room with an invitation to sit where they liked, before going down to speak to the house-keeper. With that accomplished, she decided to go upstairs to the nursery and take David herself. Otherwise, Nurse might decide her presence was needed, and Arabella so longed to have time with just Philip and Honoria, and her son. She was not sure where Mr. Northwick was or when he might suddenly appear and spoil the serenity. With so little time with her friends, she must strive to make the best of it.

She was successful in retrieving David, although Mrs. Billings huffed when she took him. When Arabella returned into the drawing room with her son in her arms, Honoria and Philip were examining a framed decoration on the wall made of papier-mâché that had been painted gold.

"Is this your work?" Honoria asked, turning to her.

"Oh no." Arabella shook her head, smiling. "I have never learned to create anything apart from needlework. My father just had me learn to sew and keep things tidy."

Honoria leaned down to tickle under David's chin, saying, "Well, that is a useful trait. And you are a good mother. Nothing else is needed."

Arabella's heart glowed from the praise. "Please sit. The tea will be here soon. Have you seen Christine recently? And Mr. Grey?" she added as an afterthought.

Honoria and Philip exchanged a look, and Honoria spoke first. "They are both well. In fact, Philip and I came... Well, we came for the pleasure of your company, but I hoped to settle something once and for all by asking you about it directly, if you do not mind."

Arabella's nervousness expressed itself in a frown. "Oh! Why, of course you may." She could not imagine what it could be about, and the not knowing made her wary.

"We want to know—or rather, I should say, *I* want to know," Honoria began, "whether Gus has a chance of winning your regard."

Arabella stared at her for a moment, nonplussed. She had

expected anything but that. And what was more, she feared from the way Honoria phrased the question that it was their wish that she should like him, but she could not in the slightest imagine herself with Gus—Mr. Grey. After a moment's pause, she answered.

"I think very highly of Mr. Grey. And I should like to think of him as a friend, the way I think of all of you. But Mr. Grey has always shown such a strong interest in me that I can only hold him at arm's length. I fear I cannot give him any encouragement that I return his regard."

Honoria and Philip exchanged a glance, and when her friend returned her gaze to Arabella, it held a look of satisfaction.

"That is what I suspected. Philip did too, but sometimes Gus has portrayed things in such a way that almost had us believing there might be some encouragement on your end. We"—she glanced at her husband—"no, *I* wanted to find out. Philip would have left well enough alone."

"I hope I am not a disappointment to you," Arabella said.

"You could not be," Honoria was quick to reassure her. "And I hope you will forgive me for meddling in what is not my affair, as Philip has not been slow to remind me."

"Matters of the heart are better left between the parties involved," Philip said simply, and they all turned as the door opened, and the footman brought in the tea tray, followed by a maid.

Arabella feared Mr. Northwick would enter with the arrival of the tea, but he did not, and she was granted a little more of a reprieve to enjoy her friends' company. They waited as the servants set everything down, then Arabella measured out the tea leaves and offered everyone a cup once it was brewed. They each selected what they liked to eat as they waited for it to steep, and as the servants left the room, Honoria spooned cream over her scone.

"There is a girl in the village—the apothecary's sister—who might be a good fit for Gus if he would but open his eyes," Honoria mused, as though they had not been interrupted. "She does not have a large portion, but she has blunt enough to set up her own stables, and her brother is a gentleman. I think Gus views her as on the shelf, but she is as sporting-mad as he is, and I think they would deal famously." She picked up her cup and her eyes twinkled mischievously over the rim.

"I would try to stop my wife if I thought she would listen," Philip said, laughing. "But there is one element my love has *not* thought of. Who is going to bring Gus news of your disinterest, Arabella? For it certainly will not be I."

David grew tired of sitting on Arabella's lap and twisted around so she might set him down, which she did. She carefully removed his hands from the edge of the tray holding the teapot, admonishing him gently as she did so to avoid looking at either Philip or Honoria. As grateful as she was for their friendship, she was embarrassed by their direct speech and did not know where to look. She feared her face was still a fiery red when Mr. Northwick walked into the drawing room, putting an end to her peace.

"Ah, visitors," he said in what she detected was a falsely cheerful tone. "You did not alert me to the fact, or I would have come sooner." Arabella wondered if she would be required to pay for their visit in some way when it was once again just the two of them.

"I did not know where you were," she answered, then stood to follow David as he made a faltering circuit around the room.

"I was in my study, as I always am. You should know that." He sat, then addressed Philip and Honoria. "I hope you have been settling in nicely after your wedding. It was a very fine occasion."

"Thank you," Honoria replied, with what Arabella recognized as guarded warmth. Philip nodded and murmured his thanks.

"You should really have David's nurse here to help, Arabella. That is why I employ her." Mr. Northwick pivoted in his seat to look at her. "What will your guests think if you are forced to trail after a baby the entirety of their stay?"

"Oh, I shall think she is a fine mother," Honoria said without missing a beat. She smiled at him and bit into her scone.

In what seemed like an effort to ease the unspoken tension, Philip asked Mr. Northwick about whether he had acquired any sheep as he recalled him once mentioning the desire to do. Mr. Northwick replied he had not, because his business of supplying tobacco from the processing houses in Lincoln to the merchants in London kept him busy. From the ensuing discussion, Arabella learned that they were soon to leave for London, for he had some business to attend to there. A shipment of snuff and cigars were sitting, ready for him to bring to the London merchants.

Philip and Honoria stayed the expected half hour, although Arabella supposed they would have stayed longer had it been just the three of them. But Mr. Northwick's presence sent a gray cloud over the possibility for free speech. She, too, would want to leave if she were given the choice. When she saw them to the door, Honoria held Arabella's hands and kissed her on the cheek.

"You must write to me from London. More often than you did before my wedding, if you please."

Arabella could not tell her that even her correspondence was surveyed and limited, so she merely smiled and nodded. "I hope I will see you both soon."

When the Townsends left, her heart sank at the prospect of returning to her own drawing room. Mr. Northwick had promised to send for Nurse to fetch David while she showed them out and was presumably waiting for her there. Her pace was slow, for she did not wish to meet him, but when she arrived in the drawing room, it was empty.

A strange foreboding filled her, and her heart began to race. Surely her brother-in-law had accompanied Mrs. Billings and David up to the nursery—or gone back to his study. That was only logical. But there was something about the empty room that felt like a premonition that she was about to lose her only son. Arabella hurried forward to the opposite end of the drawing room and climbed the steps that led to the nursery.

When she reached the top of the stairwell, she spotted Mr.

Northwick standing on the far end of the corridor, unmoving. He stared through an open window with David in his arms. Then he lifted the boy and set him on the edge of the window. David shrieked from pleasure at the view and the breeze that ruffled his hair from this high up, heedless of the danger he was exposed to.

Alarmed, Arabella crept forward quietly, fearful that if she made a sound, Mr. Northwick would let him fall. Her brother-in-law's next movement caused her to halt as her strength left her. He lifted David and held him farther outside of the window, with a quiet laugh.

"Shall you go the way of your father?"

Terror jolted up Arabella's spine, leaving her limbs cold. She tried to call out, but before she could do so, Mr. Northwick pulled her son back inside.

"No, not today, I suppose. You would like to fly though, wouldn't you? Fly like a bird?"

"Bird," her son parroted. It was one of only a handful of words he spoke, and she had never before heard it.

Mr. Northwick turned around and saw her standing in the middle of the corridor, where fear had frozen her in place. He put on a duplicitous smile and walked toward her.

"You saw that, did you? I was just showing your son the view. Showing him he can be king of everything he sees as a North-wick." He stopped and peered at her more closely. "You weren't afraid for his safety, were you?"

Some instinct tugged at Arabella to deny it, and she forced a smile. "Not at all. Not when he is with his uncle. Shall I bring him to Nurse now?"

She held out her hands for her son, and he stared at her for a long moment until her arms trembled, before finally relinquishing David into her care.

"We leave for London tomorrow," he said. "Make sure you are ready."

"I will be," she replied, her words coming out so breathlessly she could not be sure he heard them.

ARABELLA ATE dinner with Mr. Northwick, taking great care to be neither quieter nor more distant than she was habitually. She had come to a conviction in the hours that followed the terrifying sight of Mr. Northwick dangling her son out of a window, where death was the only possibility if he should let him fall.

She had to leave Penwood in the dead of night and spirit David out of the house with her. Her success in this venture depended upon her convincing Mr. Northwick she was too timid to question him or thwart his authority.

The door to the main entrance would be heavily bolted, and the sounds of her opening it would wake a light sleeper. Her only hope lay in creeping out through the kitchen. There, the bolts were quieter and would not echo as in the main hall. In her favor was that, once Mrs. Billings fell asleep, she slept like the dead. From David's early life, this had caused many hours of lost sleep as Arabella feared something would happen to her son, and his nurse would not awaken to care for him. But now, Arabella would seize the advantage.

After dinner, she did not have the heart to pretend anymore and claimed needing to pack for tomorrow's trip to London as an excuse to retire early. Mr. Northwick did not object and only warned her that she would be riding with him at his side in the carriage, which made her even more eager to leave on her own terms. She went up to check on David, who had been put to sleep.

Mrs. Billings turned as she entered the nursery, and before Arabella had advanced into the room, said, "You had best not come in here. We are to leave tomorrow early and David needs his sleep."

Arabella bit back the retort that sprang to her lips. "I do not intend to wake him. I came merely to get some of his things for the journey."

"You'd best leave that to me, ma'am. I will be accompanying you, as befits my position, and I know best what the boy needs."

The nurse stared down Arabella, who did not have the courage to fight her. Instead, she went over to peer into the small bed and was comforted by the sight of her boy. She would have to leave with what she could grab when she came to get him and did not know how far she could go on foot, carrying him and a bundle of clothes. The one thing she did have was some money, as she had taken to the habit of hiding it should she ever need to escape. Mr. Northwick had always insisted on doing her banking for her.

The reality of her preparations struck home. Ever since she'd lost her husband and had been at the mercy of his brother—going from the kettle to the fire, so to speak—she had thought of escaping. It lacked only the flint to push her to take the step, and that spark had been today. Arabella went to her room and readied a small bundle of her own belongings that left room for some of David's and sat on a chair to wait. It would be many hours.

The candle flickered next to her, and her eyes roamed the room, falling on a square trunk that fit so neatly under the table she had forgotten it was there. It was filled with books and personal items she had had sent from the London house shortly after her husband's death. The servant who cleaned Josiah's room the day of his death had brought them to her, saying they were the only personal effects in his bedroom. She had glanced through them once, but as they were nothing but some books and a snuffbox, she had sent it to her house in Lincolnshire. It was placed in her spacious bedroom amid other items she had not found a home for, and she had promptly forgotten about it. Now, with nothing but time on her hands, she went and sat beside the trunk, bringing her candle with her.

She slid the trunk out from under the table and fitted the small key from her reticule into the lock. Once the trunk was opened, she lifted out a series of books whose titles intrigued her not at all. But after she had removed two layers of books, she came to one soft leatherbound volume with no title. She flipped it open and discovered her husband's handwriting. It appeared to be a ledger of his business dealings, along with some notes.

The sight of his handwriting made her ill. Reading the words was almost like sharing intimacies even after his death. She was curious, however, and skipped to the last page, which was written the day of his death.

STILL HAVEN'T RECOVERED the 10,000£ George lost in that tobacco failure. On this day, 16 November, 1809, I informed him he would be removed from my will and would not serve as guardian to my unborn child should I meet a precipitous end. He did not take it kindly.

LOCAL RUN: 100 half-ankers
  27 bales of tobacco
  525 bags of tea

ARABELLA SKIMMED the list of items, noting with some surprise that he seemed to trade provisions beyond tobacco. But what kept her attention was his personal entry. If her husband had removed his brother as guardian to David, why was Mr. Northwick still posing as such? Either no new will had been made, or Mr. Northwick had found it and destroyed it. Either occurrence would be of no help to her.

She tucked the slim journal into her bag. Perhaps something could be done with this information. In any case, she did not want to leave it behind for Mr. Northwick to take. The only item of any value was the jeweled snuffbox, and she decided to take that too. After all, Mr. Northwick would likely come into her room when she was gone and would surely confiscate it, despite the fact that it belonged to her son. After a cursory glance at the rest, she closed and locked the trunk, preparing to wait the final hours.

When the small clock on her mantel struck three, she crept out of her room and up the stairs to the nursery. There, she heard the loud snores of Nurse coming from the adjoining room as she tucked her arms under her sleeping baby and lifted him, cradling him to her chest. The warm weight of him gave her courage. After grabbing some of David's clothing, she turned to go and crept out of the nursery and down the stairs all the way to the ground floor.

She crossed the drawing room, easily finding her way in the dark, when the shadowed form of a man to her left caused her to stop short.

Mr. Northwick! Her heart beat violently until she could scarcely catch her breath.

"Ah, is that you?" he asked in a conversational tone.

She remained mute, staring at him in the dark. Mr. Northwick did not walk toward her but stayed in the shadows. Arabella, too, remained immobile. She could not have moved for her life. He had found her.

"They are waiting for the frigate to arrive with a full load." He paused as though hearing a voice. "I am quite sure they will kill me without a thought if I come back empty-handed, so don't think to fail me. Not if you know what's best for you."

Was he talking to her? Arabella could hear her own shuddered breathing in the silence.

"I will tell him," her brother-in-law went on. "In any event, you will need to move the goods on from here in the usual manner. Meanwhile, I will be transitioning to a more genteel profession. I have better plans than this living in the shadows." He turned his back, then went to sit on the sofa.

Arabella could not stand it anymore and inched forward, but Mr. Northwick did not speak again or come to her—he simply sat quietly on the sofa.

He must be walking in his sleep. Arabella had no idea he did such a thing.

Free from the constraints of her fear, she hurried forward and was able to cross the rest of the drawing room without any more startling words from him. But her heart hammered as she traversed the main hall and descended the stairs to the kitchen, where she quickly filled a bag with food and a flask of water, slid the bolt back and exited into the fresh night air.

Stars twinkled overhead giving her courage, and even the sound of a dog barking in the distance could not deter her from her purpose. It would be difficult to carry David for long, but she could reach the public road easily from here. It was not far. And she'd heard that farmers used it to cross from the coast to Lincoln, even in the middle of the night. One of them would surely allow her to slip onto the back of his cart in exchange for a small coin.

Her only hope was that goodness and mercy were on her side.

CHAPTER 9

Since the day Theo had shot down Anthony's request to travel to London, the atmosphere between them had remained chilly. Trudy had come to visit more often, now that her husband was traveling to London for a month to take up his duties on the Board of Customs. She had tried to soothe the brotherly relationship, but met with little success. Anthony allowed his offense to show.

"You want me to take on the drudgery of an adult, but you still treat me like a child. How do you expect me to want to settle on any path if you continually shut down my ideas?"

They were sitting at the table over port—an attempt on Theo's part to mollify his brother, but he couldn't help but respond to this unfair accusation.

"It's not your ideas I take objection to, but rather your side hobbies which risk ruining us all. If you fall into the River Tick, who is going to drag you out if not me? And the mill is not exactly pulling the profit I had hoped for."

"It's because you don't put your heart into it." Anthony folded his arms and leaned back in his chair. "You just put in your duty, and it shows."

The sight of Anthony's fine vestment on a gangly body barely grown caused a surge of affection to spring up in Theo. They were separated by a distance of seven years, and he was accustomed to seeing him as just a boy. But it was clear Anthony was becoming a man, for all that his boyhood was still in evidence.

"I have no choice but to carry out my duty where the mill is concerned. But I still have some say over what you do as your elder brother, and I'm not going to let you whistle away the family fortune at the gaming tables."

Anthony got up without a word and stormed out of the dining room.

Ah, I didn't handle that well. Theo felt older than his years—a father to a boy he did not sire. It was so wearisome.

He buried himself at the mill every day, while Anthony scarcely joined him for dinner anymore. His brother communicated this via a note in which his bitterness was evident. He would be joining Earnie every chance he got before his friend left for London, since Anthony was to stay behind.

Theo's thoughts grew more depressed as he considered his failing relationship with his brother and his lost chance with Arabella Northwick. He could not remove her from his mind, try what he would. Trudy's warning rang in his mind equally, galling him. She didn't know Arabella. She could not judge her without having met her, without having seen what a warm and gentle soul she was. Everything about Arabella was inoffensive, right down to her soft voice. Everything about her demanded protection. A protection he was willing to give, if only he were allowed.

HE WAS SITTING in his study at home, having left the mill early for once. It had been pointless to remain that day. Nothing was pressing enough to keep his attention, and he thought of nothing but her. After a long moment of staring at his hands, he separated a sheet from the stack in his desk and pulled it toward him. He sharpened the tip of his quill and dipped it into the inkwell, then paused before writing.

. . .

01 *AUGUST, 1811*

DEAR ARABELLA,

HE PAUSED AGAIN. What in heaven's name could he possibly say? Would her brother-in-law intercept her mail? Would she welcome his letter on such intimate terms when she had made it clear she could not contemplate a courtship with him?

Although paper was dear, he crumpled this first draft and began anew, dating the letter and addressing it more circumspectly to "Mrs. Northwick," should Mr. Northwick behave in a dastardly way and read what did not belong to him.

I hope life has treated you well since we last met, he began. He searched his mind for what could be a plausible reason to send a letter—a reason even her brother-in-law might accept.

Theo stared across the study, lost in thought. It was a large room and more comfortable than his office at the mill, with a window that looked out over the lane. His house was not located in the busiest part of Newark, but there was still some passage as people went by to access the river, or to bring goods in from the farmlands surrounding the city.

As he stared without seeing, a vision passed before his window that caused his eyes to sharpen into focus. It was a petite woman with blonde curls, carrying a boy who looked to be about David's age. Theo gasped and stood up partway. His obsession must have led him to conjure up Arabella's form in his own town, for it looked just like her.

He sat again, determined to be reasonable, but a timid knock echoing in the front hall had him leaping up from his chair and skirting the desk as he ran to the door. The rug slid under his feet and he almost lost his balance, but he righted himself against the side table close to the door and rushed out of the room. He swung open the front door before the footman could arrive. And when he had done so, he just...stared.

There, looking back at him, was Arabella Northwick, with her son in her arms. Her expression was one of worry, and her outfit was rumpled, her hair more wild than he had ever seen it. But her face was familiar and dear. She wavered on her feet, and in an instant, Theo swept David out of her arms into his own and placed the other hand around her waist. His heart was beating wildly, and when he pulled her up against him to support her, he thought it would leap out of his chest onto the floor.

"Come in," he managed to say. "You are not well. You must have journeyed very far. I will see that you have refreshment."

Theo turned and saw that the footman had arrived and was looking at him with something like astonishment. He snapped out orders, sharper than his usual tone.

"Have Mrs. Wilkins bring tea and food immediately. And some milk."

Arabella followed weakly at his side, and David started to fuss and attempt to go back into her arms. Theo shook his head at the boy with a smile.

"Not yet, little fellow. You shall have your mama in a moment, but right now she needs to sit."

David met his gaze unblinkingly and seemed to understand, for he allowed Theo to bring his mother all the way to the couch in the drawing room. For once, Theo was grateful he had not yet replaced the reclining sofa of his grandmother's, for that was precisely what Arabella needed in her current state. He helped her to lie down, then set David on the floor next to the couch. David reached over and put his hand over her nose then pulled her face toward him, causing Arabella to laugh weakly. This quickly turned to tears as she put her arm around her son.

"Forgive me," she told Theo, her voice faint.

Theo pulled an armchair close to the sofa where he could reach her and assist with David if needed. At her words, he leaned forward and took her hand in his, and when he felt the gloves, tugged at them until they came off. Her hand was as soft as he imagined it might be, though there were little blisters under her fingers, likely from her journey.

"There is no reason to apologize. I must tell you how very, *very* glad I am to see you."

This brought on a fresh onslaught of tears, and he let her relieve the strain of her emotions and simply held her hand. He knew what a difficult journey it must have been and could only imagine what sort of terror had caused her to undertake it. After a moment, he released her hand, fearing he had overstepped his bounds by removing her gloves.

Despite her obvious distress, they sat in a peaceful silence until Mrs. Wilkins came in carrying a tray. She made no mention of the unusual sight of a woman and child in her master's drawing room but merely took in the scene at a glance.

"Why, what a fine boy we have here. What is his name?" She set the tea tray down on the table near them but removed the actual teapot and placed it on the table next to Theo, out of reach of the boy.

He smiled at her gratefully. "This is little David, and this is Mrs. Northwick, a friend of mine and of Philip's from Lincolnshire. I know you will make her feel welcome."

"You may rely on me for that, Mr. Dawson." She took the cup of milk she had set on the tray and held it in front of David. "Are you thirsty? Well, if your mama says you may, I will give you milk."

"Thank you," Arabella whispered, her eyes filling again with tears.

Mrs. Wilkins offered the milk to David, who tried to wrestle it out of her hands but contented himself with drinking it when she held it firmly. This caused Mrs. Wilkins to laugh, and when he had gulped a few mouthfuls, she handed him a piece of cake, saying, "And I'm sure you would like this as well."

As Mrs. Wilkins fed David, Theo turned to the teapot. It was already steeping. As there was no mistress of the house, Mrs. Wilkins had taken to performing that task for him; he knew she guarded the tea leaves jealously and saw that no servant abused the trust by helping himself.

"Do you think you can sit up?" he asked Arabella.

"I think so," she said, but when she attempted to do so, she fell back down again.

Theo went over to two of the armchairs and gathered cushions that had been placed there and returned to help her sit up. Her shoulders were so frail they reminded him of a tiny bird as he put his arm underneath her back and tucked the cushions behind to give her support. He took his time.

She sent him a look full of gratitude that contained no tears. He smiled at her and went to fetch her a cup of tea.

"Milk? Sugar?"

She nodded and within minutes he watched her sip the hot tea, feeling consoled somehow that he was able to attend to her. So many questions sped through his mind as he watched Mrs. Wilkins engage David in quiet play. The boy clutched a piece of cake in one hand, heedless of the crumbs that fell over the floor. Arabella saw the mess and clucked her tongue weakly and reached for him.

"Leave it, ma'am. It's no bother. I'll tidy up afterwards." Mrs. Wilkins turned from where she knelt on the floor and cut another generous piece of cake. "You look like you need to eat something, you do."

Arabella had finished her cup of tea and exchanged it for the plate of cake, which she began to eat with generous bites. Theo had never seen her consume so much at once and realized she must have truly been ravenous. They carried on a sparse conversation until she and David had had their fill. Then Mrs. Wilkins whisked the tray away, promising to come as soon as Theo rang for her to see how she might be useful. He nodded, anxious to be alone with Arabella.

The door to the drawing room was shut, and he sat on a nearby chair, watching both of them. David wanted to be held, and Arabella lifted him so that he lay on top of her, where he promptly rested his head on her chest. Theo could not have asked for a better circumstance than this quiet rest on her son's part, because it would allow them to speak without interruption.

He scooted his chair even closer and leaned forward, his elbows on his knees. "Tell me what happened."

Arabella glanced down and caressed her son's head as the boy blinked in a slow rhythm, his eyes growing heavier.

"Mr. Northwick threatened David." She looked up at Theo. "He brought him up to the second floor, and I soon followed. He was dangling him out of the window of the corridor."

Theo clenched the muscles in his jaw, waiting for her to say more. She sighed. "I decided to appear as though the sight had not alarmed me—made it seem that I was prepared to follow him to London the next morning. But that night, I went to fetch David when the household was asleep. I took a few belongings and walked toward the public road."

He frowned. "But...but why did you not go to Boden? Philip and Honoria would have helped you willingly. I know they would have. And then you would not have traveled so far on your own."

"I couldn't carry David that far by myself. And I could not take a carriage," Arabella replied. Theo hadn't thought through how hard it must have been to be so isolated in Thimbleby.

"What did you do next?" He had balled his hands into fists, hating that she had been forced into such a vulnerable position, and that he had not been there to help her. "How did you travel from there?"

"I saw a sheep farmer rolling by with a cart of wool, despite it being still dark. His destination was Lincoln, and I asked if he might drop me near to Bardney. I feared that if I went to Lincoln, it would be the first place Mr. Northwick searched. I thought I might very well find a stagecoach office in Bardney, and I did indeed."

She paused to look at her son affectionately, then glanced up. "I took the stagecoach from Bardney to Waddington, and from there I alighted and negotiated fare with another farmer to take me to some other town. You will say it was overly cautious on my part, I suppose. But I was afraid that if I kept to the stagecoach, my trail would be too easy to trace, though I gave a different name."

"These farmers...did they treat you well?" Theo's throat was tight. "Were you unhurt on the stagecoach?"

She nodded. "The farmers were kind. They were glad enough for the coins I could offer them, and they saw that I had a young son. No honest man would hurt a woman who had a child with her."

She was much too pure, thinking such a thing, but Theo did not say it. Although how she could still believe in the goodness of people after what she had suffered was a mystery to him. The truth was, she had been supremely lucky on her journey here. She had indeed fallen into the hands of honest men. He shuddered to think what might have happened otherwise.

Arabella seemed to have regained some of her strength, and she attempted to pull herself into a seated position with David on top of her. Theo jumped up to help her. Now that the shock of her arrival had dissipated, his mind began to race as he sorted out what to do next. As much as the idea of having Arabella stay at his house thrilled him, he knew it would only damage her reputation should any of his neighbors hear of it. He must find another solution that would keep her close.

She watched him retake his seat. "I haven't asked you... I am quite sure my arrival is terribly inconvenient. I did not know where to go."

Theo scooted forward again. He could not help himself. His desire to reassure her in every way—to let her know what his feelings were—was too strong. "You did right to come here. You have my word on that."

He possessed himself again of her hand and held it. Her skin was warm in his, and her fingers felt right in his palm.

"To be honest, I haven't been able to stop thinking about you. I could not reconcile myself to the idea that you were destined for a life of bondage to that man. I meant what I said." He pressed her hand, not daring to reveal anything of his heart when she was so newly arrived. "I promise to be a friend to you."

She allowed him to hold her hand and even tucked her fingers into his, but the weight of her emotions was visible in the way she swallowed and blinked as she rested her eyes on her sleeping boy.

"I hardly dared come. It is only that I was so desperate." She looked up at him fully. "But what shall we do? I cannot remain here. I may no longer be an innocent, but a young widow's reputation is nearly as much in danger as a girl's."

With reluctance, Theo released her hand and sat back. It was too difficult to think when her hand was in his like that. And now he needed to apply his mind to the task. It was not enough that his brother still lived here. That merely meant two bachelors living with a young and very pretty widow. The way he saw it, he had two choices. He could either ask one of his sisters to serve as chaperone while they sorted out what to do next. Or... he could ask her to marry him.

Without allowing himself time for reflection, lest he lose his courage, he gripped his knees with his fingers.

"Marry me, Arabella."

"Oh no, I cannot." She tried to sit up straight, and David fussed as she shifted with him in her arms. "I am very sorry. I see that I have troubled you indeed if you feel compelled to save my reputation by offering your hand in marriage. It was most selfish of me."

"No, Arabella." Theo got down on his knees in front of her so his eyes would be level with hers. "It isn't like that."

The look of alarm she gave him shifted to the right as the door to the drawing room opened, and Anthony walked in. He stopped short on the threshold, and his eyebrows flew up. For a moment, he stood there in stupefaction, then his good breeding returned, and he whirled around.

"I beg your pardon," he mumbled, before leaving the room in haste.

Somehow Theo got back into his chair, his face very hot. He had always been of a phlegmatic nature and was not accustomed to feeling out of his element—and this in his own home and in front of his younger brother, no less. But Anthony's sudden arrival had thrown him off-kilter, if Arabella's look of dismay to his first-ever marriage proposal had not already done the trick. It hadn't seemed to be the look of alarm that came of one fearing to inconvenience another, as her words suggested. It had been a look that said, *please don't ask* that *of me.*

He sat for a moment before risking a glance at her face, which was as red as his own felt. She refused to meet his gaze.

"I wish to try this again," he said, with a deliberate calm. "The manner of my proposal—the rush of it—can be attributed to your particular case of needing to be protected, in which a betrothal would speedily solve the case. Although... I would still need to find a place for you to stay until the banns could be read."

With all the sincerity in his possession, he went on. "However, the nature of my proposal comes from no such altruism. I proposed to you because I wished to. I've wanted to in these long weeks since I last saw you, although I did not know it was what I desired until you arrived on my doorstep. You see, you have become something of an obsession with me."

Arabella was already shaking her head. "Do not say that word," she pleaded softly. "It reminds me of Mr. Northwick."

Chastised, Theo went silent. She was absolutely right. *What idiot uses the word obsession when proposing to the woman he loves? Would this proposal ever come out right?*

"I apologize most sincerely," he said, then went silent.

After a moment, she brought her eyes again to his. "I have thought of you, too. Many, many times over the past weeks. But Theo, I cannot marry you. We could not even post the banns. My brother-in-law would find me with the snap of his fingers that way, and he would be here before the week was out."

"We could marry by common license," Theo said. It was as though he was feeling his way through this conversation—as though he was groping for solutions and begging. It was not at all what he had envisioned when he would one day be brought to the point of declaring himself.

"Yes, but even were we to marry..." Arabella exhaled in a rush and looked down at David, who had settled back into sleep. She brushed his soft blond hair back from his forehead before lifting her gaze to meet Theo's.

"I don't believe I *can* marry. I have already broken the law by taking my son from his legal guardian. My life will be that of a fugitive."

"I can protect you—"

"But you can't protect my son. He will go to his uncle no matter what I do. Once Mr. Northwick finds me, you may be sure that he will punish me. I will never see my son again."

Her eyes held the weight of her sorrow. "I cannot take the risk to marry. I see no choice but to disappear somewhere and leave everything behind—my son's estate and his future, along with my hopes. My one objective is to see David safe until he comes of age, and to do that, I must go into hiding someplace that Mr. Northwick would not think to look for me." She leaned over and rested her hand on his arm. "Everything else must be forgotten."

CHAPTER 10

Theo excused himself not long after she had rejected his proposal, and Arabella could hardly blame him. Despite being left alone in the drawing room, she was not ill at ease. She should have been. Here she was, in a single gentleman's home—uninvited—and she had just rejected his offer of marriage. What did she expect him to do with her?

In truth, she had not formed any very clear plans when she fled to Newark. She merely went to the one place she was certain Mr. Northwick would not think to look for her. It was to be a starting base from which she might form new plans and perhaps permit herself to ask for help in renting out a lodging. It was a place she knew she would be safe from harm, and if there was the irresistible temptation of looking upon Theo's handsome face again, then there was nothing wrong with such a thing. But she hadn't counted on a proposal—hadn't hoped for it. She couldn't welcome it, though to refuse caused her entrails to twist and writhe, knowing she was throwing away her only chance at happiness.

Theo had been gone for a half hour, although he warned her he would not return right away. He had said it was to give her time to rest, and that she mustn't feel like she was imposing. He had even murmured at the end of that reassurance, "Though you've rejected my suit," with a wry smile that caused her stomach to hurt all over again.

If only he knew! If only he knew what it had cost her to say no. But there was one person who had a higher claim upon her heart, and that was her son. David had not asked to be brought into this world, and her every effort must be for him.

For the first ten minutes of her solitude, Arabella remained upright on the reclining sofa, but then she could not help but slide back down into a more comfortable position. The escape had been hard on her in a physical sense, and also on her nerves. It had been a journey of several days because of the way she needed to throw the scent off if she were trailed. And now, it was the first time she was in a place that felt secure. Oddly, considering she was all but a stranger to Theo Dawson, she did not fear being thrown out of his house, although she deserved as much.

There was a desk on one end facing the window and a marble framed fireplace next to it. The wall hangings were a faded yellow, and the porcelain vases and bibelots placed haphazardly about the room were not chosen for their harmony. It was a comfortable room.

Her father had possessed an austere drawing room that guests were shown into. It was the only place the guests saw, and he made sure it was tastefully decorated. Her deceased husband had a keener eye for decorating and seemed to do it out of pleasure. It had been a surprise to discover the talent upon arriving in their marital home. He had not seemed to her the kind of person who would care how a room was situated or furnished. After he died, she'd had no time to think about what sort of style she might like, even had she the inclination to improve a house that was not hers.

David woke and made movements to be released from her grasp and slide down to his feet, so she let him go free. He would need to be changed, but Arabella had begun to worry about the silence. Had she offended Theo by refusing him? Did he even now regret that she was still in his drawing room? Perhaps he was attempting to sort out how to let her know she was no longer welcome. Or—knowing how kind he was—perhaps he had sent someone to engage a room for her at some nearby inn, so she might make her way into the world from there. Why should he do more than that? She had told him in no uncertain terms that a future between them was impossible. He owed her nothing.

The sound of knocking on the front entrance followed by the din of voices in the corridor brought her to her feet. Arabella's heartbeat picked up until it was battering at her chest the way it always did when she was nervous. She was certain the female visitor had to do with her.

Upon listening further, it sounded as though the arrival had been planned, as there were no tones of surprise in the deep timbre of Theo's voice as he gave a soft greeting. Their voices disappeared into another room, and it was followed by the door closing.

Arabella waited, hardly able to think about what the arrival could signify as she mindlessly trailed David around the room to ensure he caused no trouble. Perhaps they were discussing her. Perhaps he had sent someone to fetch her.

She became aware of her surroundings when the door opened again in the corridor. She began to collect her belongings to prepare for her imminent departure, and in her confusion, wondered how and when she would change David. Before too long, her son would wet whatever furniture he sat upon, and she would become even more of a trial to Theo and his family. She looked around anxiously and saw that David was attempting to climb on a low chair that was upholstered in faded gold. She ran over to halt his progress just as the door opened and Theo stepped in, followed by another woman and the young man who had entered earlier. The man must be Theo's brother, but the woman did not strongly resemble Theo.

"Arabella, I wish to present you to my sister, Mrs. Gertrude Moore. Trudy, this is Mrs. Arabella Northwick."

In the commotion of their entrance, Arabella managed to peek at Theo to see what his mood might be. She had grown accustomed to doing that with her father, then with her husband, and afterwards with her brother-in-law. When the slightest shift in temper could mean degrading words or threats, she had learned to be ready for them.

His voice did not sound angry. In fact, if she had to guess, it seemed rather that he was anxious. She couldn't imagine at what might have provoked such a sentiment, however. Perhaps he was hoping they would all be at ease together? That was a nice thought. Or perhaps he was preparing to let her know he would be sending her off, since they had no further business to talk over. But then why would he bring his sister to meet her?

As these thoughts flashed through her mind, Mrs. Moore moved toward her with a polite smile that showed reserve. Arabella's heart sank. Of course Theo's sister wouldn't approve of her. She was a widow without a shred of character if she could simply show up on a bachelor's doorstep, seeking refuge. In the shame of this realization, she could hardly understand what Mrs. Moore was saying, much less look at her.

She managed to return the greeting and curtsy, then darted a glance upward. Mrs. Moore could not be much older than Theo. Despite her strong, almost mannish frame, she was a young bride and quite pretty. Upon closer inspection, Arabella did detect a family resemblance in the nose and mouth. Theo's sister turned her attention to David.

"What a sweet boy he is." Mrs. Moore bent down, then abandoned formality and dropped to her knees. "What is your name, little man?"

David looked at her seriously, then transferred his attention to the ribbon that gathered her puffed sleeve and began to tug at that. Arabella darted forward.

"No, David. You mustn't touch that."

But Mrs. Moore laughed. "I have two boys of my own, who are only a little older than David. Do not fret about me. I can defend my furbelows when the occasion calls for it."

She looked down at David and knit her brows. "If I am not

mistaken, your son needs to be changed. I will show you to a place where you might do so."

Arabella murmured her thanks, and Mrs. Moore stood and went over to the door where the other gentleman waited. Theo lifted his hand to gesture to him. "I nearly forgot, but this is my brother, Mr. Anthony Dawson. This is Mrs. Northwick."

His brother, who still carried the ruddy complexion of youth, came forward and bowed with more self-possession than she would expect at his age. He was very likely of the same age as herself, but women were always forced to mature more quickly. She curtsied, then gently retrieved David, along with her voice.

"I am very pleased to meet you, Mr. Dawson. Would you kindly excuse me while I take care of my son?"

"Of course," he replied, and she followed Mrs. Moore into the corridor and across the hall into another room that proved to be a library of an intimate size, with a great many books on shelves that reached up to the ceiling.

"I will be back in just a moment, after I fetch for you some things you might need."

Mrs. Moore left before Arabella could question her further. She knelt beside her son and began tugging his bottoms off underneath the white gown he wore. For the third time in her journey, she had come to the end of clean, dry cloths that might be used to swaddle his bottom. She'd washed the ones she had whenever she was fortunate enough to stay overnight in an inn. But they did not always dry immediately. If she were on her own, she would leave his bottom bare so that the wet cloths did not chafe his legs, but here she could not do so. She turned as Theo's sister reentered the room, carrying a bundle of linens which she handed to Arabella.

"Here you are. I suspect you might be in need of these, and I've always kept some in our family home in case I have need while visiting with one of my sons." She smiled at Arabella and it seemed to her that the smile was warmer now. Her rich brown hair was parted in the middle and pulled back in a simple style that suited her well.

"You are very kind," Arabella said, reaching for one.

She began to swaddle David, although not with a great deal of practice. She had grown more deft at changing him in the days since she'd fled, but she had never been allowed to change him before their journey. She was grateful that Mrs. Moore did not attempt to take over, although she probably had much to say about how Arabella's technique might improve.

Mrs. Moore watched her in silence, and when she had finished, said, "Theo has told me a bit about your situation and has asked me to do what I could to help."

Arabella could barely lift her eyes when she answered Mrs. Moore. "I beg you not to put yourself to any trouble on my account."

"Finding a solution in the short term, I assure you, will be no trouble." Mrs. Moore handed a wooden ring to David that she must have found with the linens. He waved it in his hand.

"My husband has gone to London for the month, and I was contemplating bringing my children to visit my sister and mother in Cornwall. However, given the developments, I have decided to remain in Newark for the time being. You will be no trouble at all."

"But surely your mother..." Arabella began.

"We will have a chance to go again in autumn. Have no fears on that end." Mrs. Moore paused, then met Arabella's gaze frankly.

"Considering you are already on familiar terms with my brother, I hope you will not mind if we dispense with the 'Mrs. Moore' and 'Mrs. Northwick' and simply call each other Trudy and Arabella."

"If you do not mind it, then I shall not," Arabella replied.

She gathered her things in a bundle, and Trudy held out her hands for the soiled linens. Arabella recoiled from giving them to her, but submitted when Trudy shook her head. "I am not at all of a squeamish nature. Let us go inform Theo, who I am sure is waiting impatiently to see if you have accepted our proposition. I am under the impression that he would not like it above half if you were to rush off again, where he could not find you."

"No, of course I shall not." Arabella's words trailed away into a whisper as she held David in her arms and followed Trudy out of the room. Theo did not wish her to rush off. Could he still have an interest in her? Surely not. Her cold refusal would have killed any lingering affection.

THEO HAD NOT BEEN GIVEN a chance to offer Anthony any sort of explanation, even when he entered the drawing room on the heels of Trudy's arrival. Therefore, Theo was unsurprised—when Trudy ushered Arabella into a different room to change David— that Anthony sat on a chair facing him, crossed his leg and folded his arms in expectation.

"Theo, you have been holding out on me. I am hurt." His tone sounded more gleeful than hurt.

Theo raised his eyes to his brother with a dry look and shook his head in silence. But he could not suppress the smile that came to his lips. Somehow, the fact that Arabella had refused his offer of marriage did not weigh on him as much as it probably should. After all, she was here. He had hardly expected such a gift. The fact that she came to him at all raised all sorts of possibilities. She must trust him—have feelings for him—or she would not have come. If he had possession of her heart, surely every other obstacle could be resolved, could it not?

Anthony was not to be put off, which Theo supposed was only fair.

"There is a widow named Arabella Northwick who has caught my interest," he said conversationally as he took his own seat. "I did not expect to have the pleasure of seeing her again so soon, considering her circumstances are rather complicated. But I am happy to have the pleasure of introducing you to her earlier than I had anticipated."

"Are you going to marry her?" Anthony asked bluntly.

111

Theo pressed his lips together, then sighed. "I asked her. She has refused me." He met his brother's gaze. "As I said, her situation is complicated."

"No thing is *too* complicated, however," Anthony said with the surety of a man untried in life's challenges. "It takes only a little determination."

"Spoken like a youth," Theo shot back mildly. "You have never been a slave to duty. Sometimes it takes more than determination to bring about a proper resolution. However, I shall argue no further on that count, because I do plan to see what a little focused persistence might accomplish. Now that she is here, I do not intend to let the matter lie so easily."

"Now, that is more like it." Anthony dropped his studied pose and became the younger brother Theo remembered well. Some of the tension between them had dissipated. "Tell me more about her complicated situation. Surely you can confide in me."

"I suppose I can." Theo looked up at the ceiling, noticing that the paint was cracking in various places, and that it would need to be redone. But who had time for such household matters when he had a mill to run? He brought his eyes back to Anthony.

"She was married off young, by a father who had little regard for her, and sent into the hands of an older husband who appears to have valued her only for the heir she might provide him. Mr. Northwick was a man of more than modest means, and a landowner besides. When he died, his brother was given full guardianship of her son and has not ceased to threaten her with removing the boy from her grasp should she not comply with his wishes."

Anthony scowled. "What an ugly customer. I detest a man who cannot choose an adversary worthy of him but must single out a defenseless woman." When Theo didn't respond, he asked, "What sorts of things does he coerce from her?"

Theo's thoughts went grim. "He threatens that if she should marry another man, she will not see her son again. And he proposes himself as a candidate."

"I begin to see why you say her situation is complicated." Anthony went silent, and they could hear the sounds of quiet conversation from the room nearby, along with a sudden belly laugh from the boy which made them both smile. "I am certain you will find a solution. She is lovely."

"Thank you." At this sign of his brother's unexpected support, Theo's voice almost cracked from emotion. He was already vulnerable as his mind raced to protect the woman who long since had entered his heart, and who had now come to his home for help. It had also been too long since he and Anthony had shared this sort of congeniality.

Arabella and Trudy entered the room again, this time with David in Trudy's arms.

"It is all settled," she said to the room at large. "Arabella and David will accompany me to my house, until we can sort out what is best to be done next."

Arabella flashed a shy smile in his sister's direction, then she raised her eyes to him. He couldn't help but hold her regard and smile to let her know he was glad. He was not sure what he would have done if his sister had not been ready to help him. He hadn't been entirely sure of it, considering her lukewarm reception to his announcement that he was courting a widow with a son—well, he could not say he was *courting* her, for she had refused that possibility along with his offer of marriage. But his marked interest called for a name, so he would be courting her without her realizing it. He could do nothing less.

At the end of their discussion in the drawing room, Trudy had promised she would accept the arrangement for a short while as a trial period. And she did not do it for his sake, for she was still of the same mind that the widow was not for him. But she would take in Arabella for her own sake, for no one deserved to be a prisoner to a man's whims the way her brother-in-law attempted to keep her. She would do it out of female solidarity.

Theo could not tell after Trudy reentered the drawing room whether she'd changed her mind about Arabella. How could anyone meet the widow and not be enchanted by her innocence and sweetness? Even Anthony had seen in her what Theo saw and seemed ready to champion her cause.

"I shall call for the carriage, then. Anthony?" Trudy's summons to her little brother were not a suggestion, and although Anthony would surely resent her high-handedness, he followed in a docile enough fashion, allowing Theo to have a precious moment with Arabella.

Trudy had handed David back into his mother's arms, but the boy wiggled to be set down, going over to the sofa and attempting to climb it. Theo faced Arabella.

"I am glad you will stay in Newark," he said. It was all he could think of to say. It was all that mattered at the moment.

"I should not accept. I shouldn't have come...." Arabella's fair complexion was heightened in color as she kept her attention fixed on Theo's neckcloth rather than lift it to meet his regard.

Theo didn't mind. He would not push her before she was ready. "I thank the heavens you did come," he said instead. "I promise to do all that is in my power to assist you."

CHAPTER 11

The Moore house was located a short carriage ride away, and although Arabella managed to respond to Trudy's occasional remarks as they rode over, she kept her gaze mostly fixed on David in an effort to contain her nerves. She wondered if she had made a mistake in agreeing to come here. How could she be anything but a burden to this woman to whom she had no connection? But what else could she do? She had no real connection to anyone in the world besides Mr. Northwick. Eventually, Theo's sister left off asking her questions and allowed silence to reign.

They stopped in front of a house set back a ways from a private road and more spacious than the one she had left. It appeared Trudy's husband had sufficient means to keep a large house in town, and as they entered it, the servants came to retrieve her bonnet and the bundle she carried. They showed no surprise at the sudden arrival of a visitor who came with a child and who planned to stay for an indeterminate length of time.

"I shall bring you up to your bedroom and will assign a maid to assist you. Felicity has shown herself capable of caring for babies, so I think you may trust her to meet all of your needs."

Trudy turned to the housekeeper, who stood waiting for orders. "Mrs. Stokes, see to it that Mrs. Northwick has a hot bath prepared in her room and make sure that Felicity is there to care for the child while she is occupied."

The housekeeper nodded and left to do her mistress's bidding. Arabella had always been timid, but words failed her completely as she followed Trudy up a wide, rounded stairwell, trailing her hand on the wooden banister that followed its curve. An oval tableau on the ceiling had been painted in the style of the Renaissance—an imitation, she thought, as the house did not appear to be very old. There were exquisite vases and paintings in every corner, and although Arabella had lived her entire married life in such luxury, it felt wrong somehow for her to be here now, for she was a fugitive and therefore an impoverished guest. She could barely breathe from the shame. She had not thought *this* implication through when she'd fled Penwood Estate.

Trudy showed her into the room where she'd be staying, and Arabella looked around. Her guilt made it difficult to appreciate just how peaceful the space was, with soft pink wall hangings stretching up from the white wooden baseboards. At one end, there was a large bed that was a vast improvement over the inns and farmers' carts she had slept in the last couple of days. There was plenty of room next to the fireplace to sit and read, and there was a desk on the side that allowed one to peer through the window. Below, a portion of the River Trent was visible from the trees. She turned to Trudy.

"This is very lovely. I do thank you." Arabella stopped short, not knowing what else to say.

Trudy nodded. "Enjoy your bath. I am sure you must be very tired, so I will not request you join me for dinner unless you would prefer it. I will have a tray sent to your room."

It was what Arabella longed for above all things. Total silence in a place that was safe from strangers—an evening with just her and her son. Still, she feared it would be wrong to accept.

When she hesitated, Trudy moved toward the door and added, "I will take that as a yes. Please feel free to sleep as long as you need tomorrow. As I said, Felicity will be more than capable of caring for David, and although he will sleep here with you, she will likely wish to bring him to meet my sons in the morning if you do not object."

"Thank you," Arabella stammered. Trudy flashed her an efficient smile and was gone in an instant.

The deep bath was heavenly, and Mrs. Stokes had provided Arabella with more clean linen cloths and some dressing gowns for David. She even brought one for her, explaining that Mrs. Moore thought it might be useful to her while her own clothes were being laundered. The garment was too long, but it was indeed the greatest of luxuries to slip on a clean and pressed nightshift after she had bathed. And it brought her deep gratification to be able to wash her boy and dress him in soft clothing, knowing there was nothing to disturb his comfort.

The servants brought a tray with a hot dinner as promised, and Felicity helped David to eat while Arabella partook of everything that was offered. She was hungry, but fatigue soon overcame her, and it seemed that even putting her hand to her mouth was a difficulty. Three maids had cleared the bath and were now removing the dinner, allowing Arabella to climb into bed with David, where they both fell asleep almost instantly.

The next morning, Arabella woke with a start from the sound of a young boy talking in the corridor as he passed outside of her room. She looked next to her and saw that David was no longer there. She had not even woken up when Felicity had taken him. Despite her belief that he was in good hands, she couldn't help but experience the usual fear that overcame her when it regarded her son. Before the dread had any time to take root, a maid brought in a tray with hot chocolate, bread that had been toasted in the fire, and a small dish containing both butter and jam side by side.

"Good morning, ma'am. Your son is with Mrs. Moore's boys and is eating in the nursery with Felicity and the nurse."

She moved briskly as she set the breakfast out on a tray, and when Arabella asked when she might see her son, the maid answered, "Just ring the bell pull or go straight up to the nursery, and you may see him as soon as you wish."

After ensuring that Arabella needed nothing more, the maid quit the room, and she was left to eat in peace. Her body ached from the exhaustion of the last several days, but the sensation of being clean, well rested, and *safe* was nearly overpowering. She poured the chocolate into a small cup and took a sip. Her eyes brightened immediately from the hot, sweet beverage and she tucked into the toast, spread liberally with butter and jam. Never in her entire life had she enjoyed a meal so much as this one.

When she had finished eating, her eyes fell on her traveling bag on the chair near the wall. She remembered Josiah's ledger that she had tucked impulsively in the bag and decided it might be good to see if there was more there about Mr. Northwick. She slid out of bed and reached for it, feeling the aches and pains of her efforts as she moved, then crawled back under the covers and opened it.

As she flipped through, she realized it was neither a pure business ledger, nor was it an intimate journal. It was a combination of the two, containing the dates and events of note, as well as various business dealings he'd had. Her father had told her before the marriage that Josiah Northwick was a self-made man, and that she should count herself lucky he was able to provide her with a newly acquired estate in Lincolnshire as well as a house in London, despite being of less genteel stock than she was.

The first entry was well after their wedding date, so she was not privy to his thoughts on their marriage. She read about his transactions with merchants and skimmed those entries until she came to 7 March, 1810.

ARABELLA ANNOUNCED that she thinks she is with child, and I have immediately brought the physician to confirm her suspicions. He did so, and if fortune is on my side, it will be a boy. I hope she can be useful in this, at least. She is pleasant enough to look at, but her head is rather

empty of ideas. I prefer it that way, of course, but an excess of it can
become a bore. If only she can be brought to bear a boy, her other faults
will be as nothing.

ARABELLA'S HEART froze as she read the words. Josiah had never
said such a thing outright, but he had hinted at her stupidity
often enough that this came as no surprise. Her father had never
praised her for her quick wit either, or acted as though such a
thing were possible. If he had, she would have striven to develop
one. If praise was bestowed, it had been merely for keeping the
house clean and staying out of the way.

The rest of the journal entry was spent speculating on how
best to ensure his heir would carry on the family name and his
decision to have his brother be made the sole guardian.

HIS MOTHER WILL NOT BE capable of making a sensible decision for his
future, of that I am convinced. No, it will have to be a man, and one I
can trust. I only hope I can trust George.

THIS LATTER STATEMENT reminded her of what she'd read from
the last day of Josiah's life that had caused her to snatch the
journal and take it with her. She had never felt the least curiosity
to open the journal while she was traveling. There was enough
upset and suspense as it was. But now, in the safety of her
temporary lodging, she had to see if anything from the journal
could help her in any way.

The ledger provided lists of shipments with dates and places,
and she began to notice a discrepancy in them. The amount
declared to the revenue services was not the same amount listed
for her husband's own gains. Each item recorded was linked to
the names of purchasing agents in London, and she soon
noticed a pattern of regular buyers. The tobacco was brought
through to Lincoln to be processed before making its way down

to London, and there were agents there as well who received a cut.

Her deceased husband had had his hand in all aspects of the trade, but it appeared he also had his hand in with the free traders, as well. Why would he keep such an incriminating account? Arabella squinted her eyes over the numbers and came to the conclusion that it would have been too many transactions to commit to memory, what with several ships coming from different ports in Lille, Le Havre, and Dunkirk. He probably thought no one would ever see it.

The sounds of a guest's arrival downstairs reached Arabella's ears not long after she had dressed herself. Perhaps Theo had come to see her! The thought caused her to hurry her movements as she pinned her hair back. She had always considered herself fortunate to have hair with natural curls and enough thickness that a simple knot held well. She had no need of a maid to ready her in the mornings, although such a luxury would be nice if ever she could find a maid she trusted.

Once finished, she smoothed her hands over the front of her dress and waited, her pulse beating in her throat. Should she go downstairs? What if she was not welcome there? After a moment's hesitation, she decided that if she could not go downstairs and encroach upon Trudy's presence, she had every right to go up to the nursery and see that David was well. One hour had been spent eating her breakfast and dressing, besides reading Josiah's journal, but it suddenly felt as though she couldn't go another minute without seeing her son.

She had not been in the nursery for long, where David played happily with a toy duck collection that included a mama and babies, before Trudy came to the nursery to find her.

"My brother is here and would like to see you, if you are at liberty."

Arabella's first flush of joy quickly fell into wariness. It seemed that Trudy's reserve had returned, and she wondered if she was the cause of it. She kissed David and murmured that she would return, but when she moved to go, he clung to her. So she picked him up and brought him, following Trudy to the stairwell. She should speak—say something to break the silence.

"I wish to thank you for the very comfortable room you provided me with last night, and for the care your maids gave to David." She rested one hand on the banister as she descended the stairs in Trudy's wake. "I am a stranger to you and am therefore all the more grateful to be the recipient of your kindness."

Trudy waited until they reached the bottom of the stairs to answer. "I will do anything for my brother. He rarely asks for something, so if he asked for this, it is because it's important to him. Besides wishing to help my brother—and although we are but strangers—I will add that I do not support the constraints your brother-in-law has imposed upon you."

She seemed to hesitate, and Arabella could hear Theo's voice coming from the drawing room, the sound of which lifted her spirits. She brought her attention back to Trudy as she waited for her next words, which did not seem to come easily.

"Do you not think it difficult, however... I am sorry, but I don't know quite how to say this. You realize that in having taken your son from his legal guardian, you are going against the law?"

The rise of her spirits rapidly descended at this reminder. "I know it."

Trudy held her gaze. "It is just that I don't wish for my brother to be hurt. He is a loyal and upright man and deserves a woman who will offer the same. From all that I understand, your situation renders it impossible to be anything more intimate to him than a near stranger. You have rejected his suit, knowing your brother-in-law will not permit it. And yet, you have chosen to come here with your son." Trudy shook her head as though baffled. "In short, what do you plan to do?"

Arabella lowered her eyes to the top of David's head which was a more comfortable sight than the direct reminder of her sins embodied in Trudy's expression.

"I do not know."

Neither seemed to know how to go on from there, and they

might have stood like that for longer if David had not bent forward suddenly in his attempt to be free, causing Trudy to dart forward to catch him as Arabella lifted an arm to his torso just in time. She set David down, chastened. Everything Theo's sister said was true. It had been most unfair of her to embroil Theo in such a way.

"Come." Trudy's voice had become gentle. "Theo is waiting for us." She led the way forward, walking with a longer stride to reach David before he darted past the doors to the drawing room where a servant was exiting. Arabella followed her numbly.

"Arabella." Theo's broad smile eased some of her pain, even as the truth of what his sister said caused her heart to ache still. She curtsied as Theo bowed in front of her, his eyes tender. Then he turned and went to pick up her son, tossing him up and catching him, causing David to shriek with joy. Arabella couldn't help but smile as she watched him. He would make the most excellent father one day.

"I am sure you both have things you wish to discuss, and as Arabella is not a maiden newly entering society, I will not play the duenna." Trudy reached over to take David from Theo's arms. "You, my little man, shall come with me and see if Cook has a cup of milk she can spare."

"*Ba ba ba*," David said in a happy babble, allowing her to walk off with him willingly enough.

Arabella was grateful for the many well-wishers her son had in this house. When Trudy and David left the room, she glanced at Theo, who was now regarding her with frank assessment. He gestured to the nearest sofa, and she took a seat at his side.

"You look well. I am very glad to see it." He smiled, watching her, waiting for her to confirm.

"Your sister is most generous. I slept deeply last night, and she assigned a maid to watch over David, who must have woken before I did. I cannot express my gratitude enough for your having acted on my behalf." Arabella paused guiltily as she remembered Trudy's admonition. She was not using him fairly.

"I would do nothing less for you. I hope you will believe that," Theo said.

Arabella wanted to tell him about her brief conversation with his sister but did not dare. Besides, what could she say in her own defense? She had decided to run away with her son and to run as long as she could, knowing that the consequences would be dire if and when she was caught. And she had decided that to marry would be impossible. If she *was* caught but had not married, she might be able to assuage Mr. Northwick's fury by promising to marry him. If she were already married to someone else, she would never see David again. Her boy would likely hate her for her abandonment by the time he reached his majority—*if* he reached his majority at all. After seeing Mr. Northwick's terrifying display as he held David out of the window, she could not even be sure he was not bent on some evil design to remove all trace of his nephew from the earth.

That reminded her. "I have a ledger—with a journal of sorts —penned by my deceased husband. I brought it to Lincolnshire with me."

"Did you?" Theo spoke cautiously, and a little furrow of confusion appeared between his brows. He was probably wondering what caused her to carry such an unpleasant memento with her.

"It was stashed with some of his things that the servant gave me after his death, and I had it sent to my home in Lincolnshire but never looked at it. The night I was waiting to leave Penwood, the trunk with his things came to my notice, and I picked up the journal and began to read it."

Arabella knew she was probably confusing him with her line of storytelling, and she hurried onward. "The last journal entry he wrote was the day of his death, and it said he was planning to remove his brother as David's guardian—or rather as the unborn child's guardian, for he did not yet know what it would be."

Theo's attention was arrested. "Is that so? What made him wish to do so?"

Arabella looked up and tried to recall the words. "He said he had been disappointed with the manner in which George handled certain business transactions. He lost the enormous sum of ten thousand pounds, according to the journal. I suppose that displeased Josiah enough for him to wish to remove him as guardian. In the journal, he mentioned having told him."

"And yet, you were there when the will was read. You are certain that Mr. Northwick was declared the full, legal guardian for David?" Theo frowned. "A journal entry is not enough to overturn a signed will."

She nodded. "I thought not. And there was another thing. Although I could be wrong, I believe he was heavily involved in smuggling, because his accounts list a certain amount to be declared to the revenue officers when the boats landed, and a larger sum to be sold to his agents in Lincoln and in London."

Theo widened his eyes at the revelation. "Your deceased husband had a hand in smuggling? What were the goods? Did he mention names?"

Arabella ran through the entries in her mind. She had read through many of them, and there were so many names mentioned, it was difficult to retain any of them. "I believe the best thing will be to hand the journal over to you and let you read it for yourself."

She then gave a gasp as the memory of a name returned to her in full force. "The journal mentions a Mr. Weald, and I know he has continued in the business dealings with Mr. Northwick after my husband died, for I have met him at Penwood."

She remembered the sleepwalking the night she left and wondered if his imaginary conversation had been with Mr. Weald. She would tell Theo about that another time.

He nodded, digesting this information, then lifted his regard to meet hers. "Yes, I think you might entrust me with the journal. Trudy's husband works for the Board of Customs in a senior capacity and might be able to find out something on these names."

A sense of lightness came over Arabella. She would not have

to deal with this all on her own. "I will fetch it for you before you leave."

The voices of Trudy talking to David in the corridor leading up from the kitchen let Arabella know their time alone had come to an end. It had gone so quickly. Theo reached over and took her bare hand in his. He lifted her fingers to his lips and kissed them. She darted her eyes to his—stunned, yet touched by the intimacy of this gesture.

"Forgive me," he said with a flushed grin. "I could not resist before I lost the opportunity."

The door opened, and he released her hand and leaned back. Trudy came in, still talking to David, and Arabella again remembered their earlier conversation. Trudy would not have been pleased to see her brother give his heart so openly. Arabella should regret it, she knew, but the conviction was difficult to hold on to amid the sensation of buoyancy.

CHAPTER 12

Seconds before his sister reentered the room, Theo released Arabella's hand. He had thought about her every waking minute since she reappeared in his life, and even his sleep was cut short by his thoughts of her. He could not but think that if she had come to him, it was because their future together held promise. He wanted to do so much more than kiss her fingers. He wanted to kiss *her*. But he would not do that until he could convince her to marry him. And that meant finding a solution to the problem Mr. Northwick presented.

Once the headiness of their interlacing fingers had passed, he began to think about the information she'd divulged. The journal might help him achieve his ends. If her deceased husband had determined that his brother must not be the boy's guardian, there had to have been a good reason for it. Theo would just have to follow the trail.

Trudy brought Arabella's son to her. "David has had his milk and is in rare form. We should take a turn in the garden and give the boys their fresh air. Theo, will you join us and let your nephews have a glimpse of your face?" she teased.

"It's a tempting proposal," Theo said, glancing at Arabella with regret. He would like to see her with her son outdoors as well, getting a bloom back to her cheeks. "However, I should have been at the mill already by this time. I beg you will excuse me. Arabella, I will wait for you to bring me what you promised."

She nodded and handed David to him as though it were the most natural thing in the world, then hurried off to fetch the journal.

Theo smiled at David and looked up at Trudy. "I might have need of your husband. Arabella's late husband appears to have been involved in smuggling, which leads one to suppose his brother might be as well. She has a journal with names and dates, and I can't think of anyone better than Vincent to entrust it to."

Trudy seemed to understand the entire significance at once. "This could prove hopeful—not only for Arabella, but for you. I'm sure Vincent will be only too happy to help with this as it's perfectly in line with his own mission."

Theo looked down at the boy in his arms. "David is such a charming little fellow. He takes entirely after his mother." He gave him a bounce or two as he heard Arabella descending the staircase. It had not taken any time for her to retrieve the journal.

"Allow me to have a glance at it first before I disturb your husband," he told Trudy. "I want to make sure it's solid enough evidence to be worth the effort."

Arabella came in and handed him the small green leather-bound book. He set David down and accepted the journal.

"I will return tomorrow after I'm finished at the mill. I am hoping you will invite me for dinner, along with Anthony, who will likely appreciate better company than I can give him at the moment." Theo also hoped that Anthony would agree to it and leave off his play for the night.

"Of course, you must come," Trudy said, rising to her feet. "I will see you to the door."

Theo bowed before Arabella. He had already kissed her hand, so this formal bow felt sadly flat. However, he would be seeing her again tomorrow evening, which was a great deal more than he'd had two days ago, when he feared he would never see her again.

"Until tomorrow," he said with a smile just for her.

"Until tomorrow," she repeated. He caught the medley of emotion in her response. There was what he hoped was affection for him, but there was something else—something darker. He could only guess it came from her many worries that left her with little peace. He would do everything he could to remove that burden from her.

That evening, Theo ate alone in silence. As he'd arrived at the mill late, he extended his time there and asked Mrs. Wilkins to have dinner set later than usual. While he ate, he took the time to read through the entirety of the journal Arabella had given him. Apart from his anger over the disparaging way the man had written of his wife, Theo was heartened by the discovery. He was convinced it contained evidence worth pursuing. Perhaps it could bring Northwick under scrutiny and possibly even arrest. They needed only to follow the leads, and he was eager to put the plan into motion.

By the time the dessert was brought, another idea had taken root. He was not sure if Anthony would return home at a reasonable hour, but he was anxious to speak to him and hoped he had not made plans with Earnie for any late-night outings. Although most of the smuggling entries were for tobacco and spirits, there were some listings of lace and silks coming from Lille. This was his brother's domain.

At eleven o'clock, Anthony entered the house, and Theo heard him toss his hat on the side table and lean his cane against the wall. He knew his brother's movements well. In moments, Anthony entered the study, likely having seen the light of the candle spilling out into the corridor.

"You're up, are you?" Anthony said, entering the room.

It was no secret that Theo preferred to read in his room until he was ready to sleep, and that he was an early riser as well. "I was waiting for you. I believe I will have need of you."

Anthony raised an eyebrow and sat in one of the two armchairs that were on the other side of the mahogany desk. Theo came to join his brother there.

"Arabella has discovered a journal from her late husband which hints at some smuggling activity. Or, more to the point, it looks from the dates and amounts like he was involved in a much larger operation. In the journal, he'd also mentioned he was going to remove his brother as guardian to his as-yet unborn child, which makes me think that as bad as Northwick was, his brother is far worse."

Theo had had all evening to plan how he wished to help Arabella and what role his brother might play. Anthony's expression was guarded, and it only caused the suspicion Theo harbored to grow.

"I need to ask you point-blank—as a brother for whom I hold deep affection—are you engaged in any sort of smuggling activity?"

At this, Anthony's face shuttered, and he folded his arms, but Theo refused to break the silence. He hoped his brother would be honest with him.

"You know Father didn't precisely turn away smuggled goods," Anthony replied crossly. "The brandy, the tea, tobacco... even our salt was got without paying taxes."

"I know it, although I cannot say I have ever agreed with him on the matter. However, even Father would have had something to say about the difference between benefiting from the free traders and aiding them in their activity. Smuggling is a hanging offense—or at the very least leads to deportation."

"I know that," his brother said defensively before sitting up straight. "However, if I may set your mind at ease, I am not engaged in their activities. I merely know some of the men who hide the cargo and where it's held. I can't tell you, though," he added quickly.

Theo clapped his hand to his head. "And your own brother-in-law the sub-Chairman of the Board of Customs."

Anthony shrugged it off. "Why should I care? You must own that Vincent is a great bore."

"He may not cut the most dashing figure, but he is on the right side of the law, Anthony."

Despite his reproach, Theo's tension had begun to ease. His brother was not in as deep as he had feared. "How did you meet them? Through Earnie?"

Anthony laughed. "Earnie would never soil his hands in such a way, although he's not amiss to taking casks from the free-traders. No, I met them in the local pub. The owner knows them. And although they deal with liquor, they are able to tell me about some of the French cloths that are being brought in if I buy them a drink or two. That is partly how I come up with my ideas for new patterns. And of course the rest is all from me," he added proudly.

"Do you suppose these men could give you any leads to the smugglers who ship goods into the London ports?" Theo asked after a minute. "Surely they must have some connections between them."

Anthony's eyes bulged. "Have you lost your mind? Not a minute ago you were lecturing me on rubbing elbows with smugglers, and now you want to trade with them?"

Theo chuckled and shook his head. He hadn't thought about how his words must seem. "No, I was thinking you could go to London with the information. Not to do business with them, of course, or even to have any hand in catching them, which would be entirely too dangerous and likely affront your sense of honor," Theo added in quiet irony.

Anthony fixed his focus on Theo. "London? Go on."

"Well, I know you've wished to go. I was thinking you could use the visit as an opportunity to look into what Northwick is up to. He does not know you, and if you have the names of those who work with the free traders, perhaps you will find a connection between them and the man himself. I am keen on finding out something on Northwick that I can use. I'm willing to go to any length—except for one that might bring harm your way."

Anthony's attention was arrested. "You would trust me with this? A fortnight ago, you said I was too irresponsible to hare off to London on a pleasure visit, for you feared I would gamble away our family fortune."

Theo hid a smile at the petulant tone. Anthony was still young. "Perhaps it is time for me to trust you. And I warn you that you will have to meet with Vincent, though he is not a great favorite of yours. I have something I need you to deliver directly into his hands."

He cast his gaze over the contents of his desk and settled it on the journal there. "Besides, there is too much at stake. I cannot afford to let Arabella suffer under that man. I must find a way to free her from him. I must find something on Northwick that will stop him from forcing his intentions on her."

Anthony nodded, then turned smiling eyes to Theo. "I think it will be great fun to dig up whatever I might find on this Northwick fellow. And I admit to being most keen to discover London and get fitted by a London tailor. You may count on me."

Theo stood and reached over to shake Anthony's hand. "Excellent. I'll send word to my banker there. You'd better be off to pack—and you can let Earnie know you're coming after all."

Anthony turned back at the door, his grin infectious. "If you give me your measurements, I might order you some new clothes as well. Goodness knows you need it."

"Off with you," Theo replied.

Arabella hesitated over what she should do during the day. Did she go down to the sitting room as though it were her own house? Did she stay in the nursery, or would she be a bother to the children's nurse there? Did she remain in her bedroom, which she had to own was spacious and comfortable enough?

She did go to fetch David and spent several hours with him in her bedroom until he grew bored. Those moments were the height of pleasure for her—to be in a safe and quiet place with her son, with no one coming to snatch him away or threaten them.

When David grew restless, she brought him back to Felicity

and at last went downstairs, where she cracked the door to the sitting room. It was less intimidating than the formal drawing room, and the bushes outside its window added a calming green. To her dismay, Trudy was already in the sitting room, and she almost darted back out again when Trudy called to her.

"There you are, Arabella. I was wondering where you were keeping yourself this long day, but I thought you might need rest and feared to disturb you. Nurse said you had taken David to your room for a time. She will be giving them supper soon."

At her welcoming gesture, Arabella came in and sat on a chair next to Trudy. "I rested very well. I did not wish to disturb you and thought you might have company or need some time alone."

"Good heavens, no," Trudy said with a laugh. "The whole point of having you here was so I would not have to spend all that time without any diversion. My boys are great fun, but eventually I need someone else to talk to. Besides, I should like to know you better. You seem to have captured my brother's heart."

"Oh, as to that..." Arabella's cheeks became heated, and she did not know what to say. Trudy did not break the silence but seemed to be honestly waiting for an answer. "I do not know why he should concern himself with me. He is too kind," she murmured at last.

"Do you have feelings for him?" Trudy asked, then smiled suddenly and stood. "Forgive me, I should have asked you if you wanted tea or something to eat before I began to pepper you with questions. Let me ring for refreshments."

"Please, do not trouble yourself," Arabella replied quickly. When Trudy turned back, she added, "I assure you I am in no need of anything at present, unless you wish to order some for yourself."

"No, I had tea not long ago." Trudy resumed her seat. "Perhaps it is not fair to interrogate you in such a way, especially when you are a visitor in my home. But, you see, Theo is...my brother is the heart of this family. He kept us together when my father died suddenly. He had to leave off his pleasures to come back to run a business he had no interest in inheriting and has attended to nothing but duty ever since. I cannot bear to have more weight or tragedy added to his life."

After a moment, Arabella replied in a quiet voice. "And I am weight and tragedy." She studied her hands. "Perhaps it is so. Why should he burden himself with a widow and child, when he has his whole future ahead of him?"

"Oh, there is nothing to stop Theo from burdening himself of a person if he has decided to do so." Trudy waved the notion away with her hand. "That is not what I wish to imply and not at all why I have brought the matter up. After all, is it your fault that you were forced to wed at such a young age? Or that you have not had the best luck in terms of family?"

She leaned back, and her face softened as she regarded Arabella. "What I truly want to know is whether you return Theo's regard. Because if you do not, fate has been most unkind to him. He will not recover easily from his disappointment."

With Trudy's gaze so steadily on her, Arabella was forced to look up, although she wanted to avoid the conversation. She did not give up confidences easily, but as she was in Trudy's home, felt she owed her the truth.

"I do return his regard." She rested her eyes on the bouquet of fat pink peonies that sat in a blue vase on the table in front of her. "It is not easy for me to speak about the state of my heart. It usually matters little what I desire anyway, since others are always dictating my life for me. But until I met Theo, I did not know there existed a man as...as noble, and good. I never imagined that such a man could notice a poor creature like myself."

"Nonsense. Wherever did you get the notion you were a poor creature?" Trudy smiled for the first time since they'd begun their conversation. "Well, I must own that I am vastly relieved, for if you do return my brother's regard, then all his efforts in your direction are not in vain."

"Not in vain, no." Arabella sighed and sat back, finding it difficult to continue to meet Trudy's forthright countenance. "I am uncertain if he has spoken to you of it, but I cannot promise myself to him despite what my heart might dictate. My son's future will not allow it."

"He has spoken of it, yes," Trudy murmured. After a moment's pause, she sat up straight as though coming to a decision. "However, I do believe you refine too much upon the point. Where one is determined, one always finds a way. Especially when love is the great motivator."

Theo, motivated by love? If only that were true. Arabella's sense of time stood still as she contemplated the idea. It became clear to her that, while Theo might not love her, she did indeed love him.

The clock on the mantelpiece chimed and Trudy looked at it, then stood. "Oh, good heavens. I have not at all paid attention to the time. Theo and Anthony will be here, and I promised I would confer with Cook on the matter of dinner. It's a good thing I did not ring for tea after all. I would have flustered her greatly, poor thing."

She walked to the door. "You will excuse me, I hope? If my brothers should arrive, I am sure they will be perfectly happy to wait here with you until we can sit down to dinner."

"By all means," Arabella said. "Although I will just nip upstairs and check on David. I am sure Felicity has everything well in hand, but he might be missing me."

The two women went out into the corridor at the exact moment a solid knock came on the door. Instead of turning to the kitchen, Trudy went to open it herself. Arabella paused to look at their visitor, hope taking flight in her breast. At the threshold stood Theo, with beads of rain dripping from his top hat. The sounds of the light shower had not reached them in the drawing room.

When he saw her, his smile brought dimpled creases to his cheeks. She remained frozen in place at the sight of him, realizing how wholly incapable she was of *not* loving him. It was physically impossible for her to stop her heart from beating for him.

He brushed the rain off his greatcoat, then entered and

removed it, handing it laughingly to the footman who had just arrived. He followed it with his hat, then greeted his sister, before turning to Arabella.

"I have been looking forward to this dinner since yesterday." He lifted her hand and bowed over it, and she was too struck by the recent discovery of the state of her heart to return a curtsy. Trudy turned to march toward the kitchen.

"If you are anticipating the dinner to that degree, I had best go downstairs and see what questions Cook has for me, and when the meal will be ready." Trudy paused in her steps. "But where is Anthony?"

"He had business in London and left today," Theo replied.

"Business? At his age?" Trudy's smile was accompanied by a look of confusion.

"Indeed. It has to do with that journal I mentioned. I thought it would be best if he delivered it directly into Vincent's hands. Although his other object is to take the town by storm from the sound of it. I sent him on his trip with my blessings and will expect him back in a month's time." Theo's smile was firm, as though he wished to close the subject.

Trudy's brow furrowed as she studied Theo, but she asked no further questions and left for the kitchen.

When his sister was gone, Arabella found her voice. "I had planned to go up to the nursery to visit David."

"Well, then I shall come with you." Theo held out his arm, and she slipped her hand into it, happy that he proposed to accompany her. Happy that he wanted to be with her, even if it meant visiting a nursery. What man would visit a nursery that held none of his own children? It was further proof of his goodness.

As they climbed the stairs, Arabella pushed herself to think of something to say, but everything she thought of seemed stupid, so she remained silent.

"How have you fared in my sister's house since I left you yesterday morning? Has she been treating you well?" Theo's arm was firm, allowing her to lean on it for support with each step.

"I feared to disturb her, so I kept largely to my bedroom. I went to visit David as well, and for a time brought him to my room so I might give Felicity a break from watching him. But he is ever active and was not content to stay there for long." They reached the top of the stairs and walked down the corridor.

"My sister would tell you that you must not stand upon ceremony in her home. She would not like for you to feel you could not move about freely."

"She did tell me, as a matter of fact, minutes before you arrived." Arabella paused outside of the nursery. "Your sister is kind. There is a strength to her I do not possess, and I fear that, timid as I am, I must be a burden to her."

Theo stopped to face her, his expression serious. "You cannot be burdensome. I beg you will not think so. You must feel yourself welcome in this house, and in my company—always."

Arabella nodded, looking down shyly. "I hear David. Shall we go in?"

Trudy's two sons were named Roger and Frank, and they called out when they spotted Theo. He swung them both shoulder height, causing them to shriek with laughter. He spun them around once as the nurse and maid watched with indulgence. Then he set his nephews down and went over to David, crouching at his feet. Arabella sat beside her son in a low chair.

"Good evening, young man," he said, smiling at David.

After a pause in which Theo allowed her son to grow accustomed to him, he held out his arms and David walked right into them. He lifted the boy up and brought him over to the window of the nursery. Arabella's breath hitched in sudden, irrational fear. But Theo only pointed to a sight outdoors through the closed windows, talking conversationally about the chestnut tree in the distance and mentioning something about a goat that he would introduce David to.

Her son soon found more interest in Theo's cravat, and although it must have taken him some time to achieve, for it was tied in a more formal manner than he usually wore during the day, Theo waited patiently as David tugged on it. Before it became too loose, he tossed him up in the air, causing David to laugh again and Arabella to smile despite the tears that filled her eyes.

She had not often given into tears before becoming a mother. It did not help a person to cry. But there was something so achingly happy about the picture Theo presented with her son. He would make a fine husband and father. She could not ask for one better.

And yet, he could never be that to her and David.

CHAPTER 13

Theo had not missed the tears pooling in Arabella's eyes, despite the smile she wore. Heavens, but she was beautiful. She seemed too frail a woman to care for such a strapping boy as David—to have carried him and brought him into the world. But despite her timidity, he was discovering a force in her that revealed itself in how she cared for her son. She would not allow anything to harm him. Delicate, and as fair as an angel, she would be a fierce warrior on her son's behalf.

He brought David back to his mother, allowing her to talk to him and cuddle him, which he sensed she needed. It was fortunate for her sake that it was the end of the day, and David was tired. He was more content to sit in her embrace than Theo imagined he must generally be. Only when he felt that David might be growing heavy in her arms did he suggest that perhaps they should go down to see if dinner was ready. Felicity leapt forward to take him at that moment with a deferential smile, and Theo held out his arm for Arabella. He was growing attached to the feeling of having her at his side.

They had no sooner entered the corridor than Trudy appeared at the top of the stairwell. "I was coming to get you, as we may now sit to dinner."

They went downstairs together, Trudy laughing over Roger

and Frank's antics that day and recounting the news she'd had from their mother in Cornwall.

At the bottom of the stairs, Trudy turned her head to Arabella. "Were you reassured at seeing David? Is he adapting well in the nursery, do you think?" Her voice was warmer than it had been the day before, and Theo hoped it was because they were becoming closer.

Arabella nodded, a genuine smile on her lips. "He seems much happier with your sons to play with. I have often worried about him being alone with no siblings, the way I have always been. To see him playing with others cannot but please."

"I have always been a proponent of large families—not that Vincent would have it otherwise," Trudy said, then, at a glance from Theo, added with a twinkle in her eyes, "No, I shall not continue in that shocking vein."

"Thank you," Theo murmured wryly. He was not particularly keen on hearing any details of his sister's marital intimacy.

They sat to dinner and ate, conversing as though they had known each other for years. He had to own that although his sister *was* forthright as Arabella had said, her natural kindness made her a good conversationalist, for she strove to bring Arabella out of her shell. He enjoyed listening to the details of Arabella's childhood his sister had coaxed out of her. Many of the descriptions were somber, though, and it made him long to go back to the young girl she had once been and whisper promises that all would turn out well—not that he could make such promises, even to the woman grown.

He learned that she liked to feed stray cats and would discover hidden areas where she could leave them food that her father would not likely find. She had feared that if her father discovered them, it would be a Hessian bag and a stone, then into the pond they would go. So she took great pains to bring food to places far in the garden her father never troubled to visit.

She had learned to embroider and was proficient at it, but as her father had hired an ill-qualified governess at a lower salary, she had never learned to play an instrument, nor had she learned

Italian or French. She could dance, she stated with pride, and Theo was able to say with perfect truth that he had never had a partner that brought him more pleasure than when he had danced with her before Philip's wedding.

The dinner passed altogether too quickly, and Theo was reluctant to leave. As they gathered in the hall, the footman brought his greatcoat and hat, and he put both on.

"I am thinking that if this weekend is fine, we might go on a picnic together. What do you think?" he inquired of his sister, knowing that she held the social calendar for the whole family. She had not been paying social calls as often as usual because of Arabella's stay, and because many of her friends and neighbors expected her to be away visiting her mother.

"We will be free this Saturday. Your nephews will be delighted by the prospect, of course. Perhaps you might teach Roger to fish. And Frank to pretend to fish," she added, laughing. Her youngest would not yet be ready to master that skill, but he liked to do anything his older brother did.

"I believe we still have some rods in a smaller size in the stables. I will bring them with me," he promised, smiling at Arabella as he bid them both farewell.

He walked into the night, and the rain began to fall promptly again, as if on cue. He could hardly have asked his sister for a minute alone with Arabella as he would have liked. As to that, he could hardly have *kissed* her as he would have liked. He needed to be satisfied with what she was able to give him—*and* what was proper for this stage of their courtship.

He simply had to find a way for her to be released from the hold Mr. Northwick had over her. Until then, he must content himself with the sight of her face, the sound of her soft voice, and the sweetness of her disposition. He sensed she felt as deeply for him as he did for her, but he must be the one to protect her reputation by behaving toward her with absolute propriety. Never before had such a thing required so much exertion on his behalf.

His days at the mill that week were busy, and he began

looking into the amount required to add more of Crompton's spinning mules, should his brother come back with a viable plan to add to their cloth production in a way that allowed him to recoup their losses. He didn't receive a letter from Anthony as he had hoped, but he did receive one from Vincent, thanking him for sending the journal. He wrote that it was a veritable coup, containing such specifics as names, amounts, hiding places, and trade routes. Theo was glad it had been helpful, but at the moment was concerned only with whether it could bring Northwick to his knees. He dashed a reply off to that effect.

Saturday dawned bright and clear, and with it, his mood. Mrs. Wilkins came to him as he gave orders to the footman to prepare his carriage. She was carrying a basket.

"I thought Miss Trudy would like a plate full of the lemon cakes she used to love so much," she said, handing him the tidy basket with a muslin cloth over it.

"She would, indeed," Theo said, smiling at the housekeeper's use of his sister's childhood name. He took this, then walked outside to where the groom was waiting with his carriage. He placed the items on it and climbed inside the coach, anticipating a pleasurable day spent in Arabella's presence.

When he arrived at the Moore residence, Trudy was marshaling the servants and children outside with the help of the nurse and another maid. As he had prearranged with his sister, Arabella and she would ride in his carriage with him and David, while the servants and his nephews would ride in the other. David did not yet know the servants quite like Trudy's children did, Arabella had reasoned. But Theo thought it was more that Arabella still needed to be reassured by her son's constant presence. He could not begrudge her such a simple wish.

Theo helped Arabella and her son into the carriage, insisting she take the forward-facing seat with David. He knew his sister would not mind sitting across on the rear-facing seat next to him. Arabella attempted to demur, but neither he nor his sister would hear of it. When he finally assisted Trudy into the carriage, he found himself sitting directly across from Arabella, with Trudy sitting across from David. His feet occasionally touched Arabella's as they rode, but he did not shy away or try to remove the accidental touches, and he noticed that neither did she. Still, she appeared excessively shy and focused her conversation on David, while he and Trudy entertained the boy with whatever they had on hand. In this way, the forty-five minutes were spent most deliciously, at least in Theo's mind.

They chose a spot near the Trent where a naturally occurring circle of trees off the path created a shady area of grass in its center.

"It appears I didn't need the tent I brought after all," Theo said, looking around at their green haven as he stepped down from the carriage. He turned to hand his sister out, and this was followed by Arabella handing him David, whom he swung to the ground, coaxing a peal of laughter from him. Last of all, he assisted Arabella to alight. "We shall benefit from the blanket, however."

"Oh, you must not think I come unprepared, brother," Trudy said, walking over to the other carriage and pulling the bundle from the back of it while the servants unloaded the rest. "I have everything we need."

"Everything except Mrs. Wilkins's lemon cakes," he said, holding the basket up for her to see.

"Oh, did she?" Trudy's voice softened. "I love those. Arabella, would you like to bring David to Felicity? She will be very careful to keep him from going near the water. Our maids have been trained very well on that head after a family lost—" She stopped short and looked stricken, before finishing. "I will just say that they have been very well trained."

Arabella had gone pale and glanced at Theo before reluctantly handing David to Felicity. He saw that her fear had momentarily overpowered her and at once intervened.

"Felicity, why don't you assist with my nephews for now? They are a handful. We will take charge of David."

He then scooped the boy up in his arms, and David rested

one chubby forearm on his shoulder as he looked around at the scenery. Theo's heart seemed to melt. There was such trust in the gesture. He scarcely knew David, but the boy had decided to place his confidence in Theo, it seemed. Children were so remarkable that way.

Theo couldn't help but wonder if he would be worthy of that trust. If he married Arabella, would he have enough influence to fight Northwick for the guardianship of her son? And if he lost, would Arabella ever be able to forgive him? He could not bear it if he lost his heart to David and Arabella, only to have them both cruelly snatched away. Full of sudden misgiving, Theo glanced at Arabella, whose smile had reached her eyes as she watched him carrying her son. He had to do whatever it took to be worthy of that trust—for David's sake, and for hers.

In silence they turned to follow the caravan of laughing children as Trudy directed the servants where to put everything. Arabella breathed what he thought was a sigh of contentment.

"Usually by this point, David is eager to leave my arms and go exploring. He must feel himself secure, indeed."

Her trusting words made Theo want to burst with pride. He covered up the emotion by pointing out to David one of the lower branches near to him. He tugged at it until he was able to retrieve two leaves stuck together, which he handed to the boy, whose attention was immediately ensnared. David pulled at it, then waved it as he looked around.

"Shall we see what Trudy's cook has prepared for our picnic?" Theo asked, when he trusted himself to speak. It was foreign to be completely helpless over his feelings—for this woman and her boy. It reduced a man somehow, to be prey to such vulnerability, but it made him want to be worthy of them. It was difficult to explain to himself, so he abandoned the attempt.

They walked over as the servants put the last of the dishes on the blankets. Theo set David down, and Arabella sank to her knees next to her son, tugging on his gown before he wriggled away to stick his hand into a bowl of stewed cherries.

"You must wait, David," she said gently.

144

Trudy stood in the center as she waited for the servants to file by with the last of the dishes before they went off to eat.

"Enjoy your meal. We shall not hurry over ours, but the children will be eager to begin exploring again, I think."

"Yes, ma'am," the footman said as he hurried to join Felicity and the nurse. Theo's groom also went with them.

Trudy sat at last. "We shall not stand upon ceremony, although"—she reached out and gently grasped Frank's hand who had already grabbed a piece of bread—"that does not mean we will become ruffians and jump upon a meal as though it were our last."

Her son looked up at her, waiting while she prepared a plate for him and his older brother. Arabella did the same for David, although the plate was really for her, and she would feed David from it. Theo loved watching her every move. He loved the way her slender hands chose the food for him, and how she kept one arm around him as she handed him small bites, one at a time. She did not think about herself at all when David was there, and he was more than tempted to feed her himself the way she was doing with David. When he looked up from these pleasing images, he found his sister's eyes on him.

He took a plate and filled it with all there was to offer, allowing himself to perform just one act of service for Arabella, which was to peel an egg for her. After murmuring her thanks, she promptly broke it in two and offered a piece to David.

After they had eaten their fill, their focus was wholly upon the children, who had nothing but play on their minds. Theo leaned back on one elbow, close enough to Arabella that he was not far from where she sat. David was in between them, and he began to play a game by stepping in one direction to lean on Arabella's lap, then turning and throwing himself over Theo's side as he lay on the blanket. Then, back again he went to his mother. This time, when David returned, Theo grabbed him with his free arm and rolled, causing the boy to laugh again.

"My son laughs when he is with you," Arabella said, her eyes soft. "I had thought him to be quite a serious boy, but you bring out the very best in him."

"Theo has always been a most indulgent uncle. I am not surprised that David has taken to him." Trudy cut a pear in sections, and after handing some to her boys, ate a piece. "He will make an excellent father."

Theo gave her a pointed look. He could only guess that for her to say such a thing, she had decided Arabella was an acceptable candidate for the position. But he could hardly give himself over to a studied pursuit while her situation was so precarious. There was much to be done to that end. *I truly hope Anthony is actually doing what I tasked him with in London and not just gambling away the family fortune!*

"The servants have finished," Trudy observed. "Let me watch David while my boys play." She met Arabella's gaze directly. "I give you my word that I will not let him out of my sight for a single instant. Nurse will watch my boys, and I will watch yours. I won't even let Felicity take him until you return."

"That is most kind of you," Arabella said, glancing at Theo. "But...I fear to trouble you."

"You need not. Theo will tell you I dote upon children." She smiled at David. "Will you come exploring with me?" She held out her hands, and after a moment's hesitation, he toddled over to her and allowed her to walk at his side with his hand in hers.

"It's true," Theo said as they stood. "She is excessively fond of children and will not allow her attention to wander."

He got to his feet and held out his hand for Arabella. "And I believe she is doing us a kindness, for she knew I wished to walk with you a ways. Will you?"

She set her hand in his, allowing him to pull her to her feet. "If we do not go very far. You will think me foolish, but I am so accustomed to worrying over David, I cannot allow myself to be far from him—although I *do* trust your sister with his safety."

"We shall not go far," Theo promised and led her onto the path along the river.

It was a path in name that stretched along the Trent, but it was wilder than the one closer to the town. They were not likely to meet anyone else on it, unless the person was there on a pleasure picnic like they were, or perhaps if a farmer strode by with the object of catching fish for dinner.

"I do not think you are foolish," he said after they began to walk. "You have only ever had David to worry about. I believe you would have worried about your father or husband had they allowed you to, but from the little you've said, I am to understand they always kept you at arm's length."

She nodded. "They did. I would have been happy to bestow my affection on them had they required it, but they did not need or want anything from me. Apart from, I suppose, the money and connections my father received for me and the child that my husband needed but never lived to see."

Theo cleared his throat, unsure of how to respond but longing to say the right thing. She did not appear to need a ready answer, for she went on.

"What a wonderful notion it is that most fathers will save up a dowry to give to a future husband in exchange for their daughters. They are showing the husband that she does not come empty-handed, but that the father has been caring for her, right up until her marriage. He wishes to let the husband know she is not unloved or unprotected."

She walked in silence while Theo waited, knowing there was more.

"I don't precisely know what arrangement my father made with Josiah, for he never spoke of it in direct terms. I only know there was no significant dowry made over, apart from my mother's portion that the attorney kept aside for me. And it was not because my father did not have the means. I understood that, on the contrary, Josiah provided my father with access to select circles—certain clubs, I suppose—that my father wished to be part of. So in a sense, they both had something to gain when I changed hands from one to the other. But neither of them did it for my protection, or for any love they had for me."

Theo was struck silent at Arabella's disclosure—the most he

had ever heard her speak at once. It was a signal moment, and one in which his words must be perfect, yet he still feared he would fail her. He wanted to be the first man to tell her she deserved to be loved and protected. She *was* loved and *would be* protected if he had any say in the matter. The magnitude of the moment made it difficult for him to have a ready reply.

"I have been talking too much again." Arabella put her hands up to her face, and when Theo spied her deep blush underneath her fingers, he stopped and gently pried her hands away, but she still refused to look at him.

"You have not been talking too much," he assured her quietly. "Arabella, do look at me, if you please."

He faced her, waiting until she lifted her eyes to his, *and oh* —how pretty, how fresh, how innocent she was! How could anyone treat her with so little regard? It made him burn to think of it.

"I will not attempt to press you into marriage, although my wishes have not changed. But I cannot allow you to speak this way without expressing how I feel in return. You must know that since you have come into my life, I have been able to think of little else but you. You inspire me to want to create a safe and happy world for you and your son. And although I cannot ask you to choose between your son and me, I must tell you that everything in me wants to be the one to protect you. And every-thing in me..."

He placed his hands on her sides, allowing his fingers to curl around to her back so he could gently tug her closer. She came willingly, placing her hands on his arms, her face tilting up to his in complete trust. He blinked as his heart thudded in a slow rhythm that seemed to resonate in the air, despite the rushing of the river at their side.

"And everything in me loves you," he finished before bending down, stopping just short of the touch of her lips.

He had drawn near enough to feel her breath on his chin, and he stayed there as his reason warred with his desire. He had promised himself he would not touch her until he could free her from the shackles of her brother-in-law. As this unpleasant thought inserted itself upon him, he held his muscles tense, unmoving, then drew back with a shaky breath.

"I should not—not until you are free to marry me."

Arabella had remained in a dreamy state with her eyes half closed and her lips parted. At his words, her eyes snapped open. Then she darted up on her toes and kissed him with a sweet gentleness that did nothing to cool his ardor. With every touch of her lips, he forced himself to behave rigidly as a gentleman, despite the intimacy of the kiss they shared. But then he abandoned the attempt and pulled her close as he kissed her as passionately as he desired. She lifted her hands up to his neck, and he wished she were not wearing gloves. He wished she were not...

Blast!

Theo pulled away again with a struggle. "Forgive me, Arabella." He stopped to master his breathing before continuing. "The temptation to kiss you was very great, but I do intend to honor your wishes. I just..." He looked down at her tenderly. "I wanted you to know that I have lost my heart to you."

Arabella, cheeks delightfully pink, blinked at his disclosure, then returned a smile full of bashful mischief. "If you will but remember, Theo, it was I who kissed you."

He looked at her, startled, before laughing. "Why, so you did!"

Wordlessly, he took her hand and tucked it under his elbow. It would be wise to rejoin his sister and the children if he did not wish to get them both into trouble.

"Shall we return?"

They walked a few paces when one of the farmers rounded the bend with a fishing rod in hand. A minute earlier, and the man would have stumbled upon them in an indiscreet embrace.

Goodness gracious!

He nodded to the farmer, then tugged Arabella forward as he felt her freeze at his side, likely having come to the same realization.

"Have you ever been fishing?" he asked in a conversational tone, attempting to set her at ease.

"Fishing?" she replied after a moment, darting a look at him in surprise. "Of course I have not."

"I shall have to teach you, then," he said. They followed the curve of the path that brought their party into view, with David and the boys running and shrieking in laughter, and Trudy chasing them from behind.

CHAPTER 14

Arabella floated next to Theo. She could hardly feel her legs or answer his questions—something nonsensical about fishing—or focus on where he was taking her, although she did register that David was alive and well. He had not fallen into the river but was playing with Trudy and her boys as the servants stood by, ready to catch one of them if they ran too far outside of the circle. Arabella had never seen a woman play with children before, and it warmed her heart to see it now. Theo's family was like something out of a fairy tale.

When she thought her cheeks had cooled enough to bear scrutiny, she glanced at Theo. He had been flustered as well by their kiss. The signs had been unmistakable—muscles tensed, a slight trembling, a bemused look in his eyes for just a moment before he recovered—except that he was then able to enter into ordinary conversation without any visible effort.

As for her, she would never be the same. Perhaps she shouldn't have kissed him when she could tell he had been using every ounce of his willpower to resist the temptation, but she could not regret her forwardness in this regard.

She might very well never marry, or might be forced into an unpleasant marriage at Mr. Northwick's insistence—he had that kind of power over her as David's guardian, should he ever find them. But she would know, even if only briefly, the bliss that came from being desired by a man she loved.

When David perceived her return, she held out her hands to him. He did not yet run with any sort of ease, but he did his best to follow the lead of Roger and Frank.

"Mama," he said as she picked him up and planted a kiss on his cheek. He began to suck on his fingers as he was wont to do when he was tired, and he tucked his head into her shoulder.

"It looks like it might be time to turn back?" Theo suggested when he saw David's sleepy posture.

"I think so," Arabella said, then glanced at Trudy. "That is, if you are ready."

"I believe my boys could go on for another hour, but I certainly could not," she replied.

She had not held back any energy in her play, as her red cheeks and breathlessness attested. She called to the servants to begin restoring their belongings to her carriage and encouraged Arabella to go sit inside Theo's coach since David was fast on his way to sleeping.

She did so, appreciating the comfort that came from holding her son. Theo did not leave his sister and the servants to tidy up alone, but after assisting her into the carriage, went over to help them. Arabella sank into the seat with David still on her lap and closed her eyes for a moment, listening to the sounds of voices and bustle coming from the outdoors as they readied for their return to the house.

She had never in her life been happier than she was at this moment. To have her son safe in her arms with no one to take him away. To have the regard of a man as worthy and handsome as Theo Dawson. What it would be like to be married to him and to receive that special regard every day of her life! To know that he was there to care for her and her son—and any other children God might see fit to bless her with. To have that kiss any time she might wish for it. He must have had practice, to kiss so well.

That last thought threatened to sour her mood, so she

brushed it off. Josiah had never kissed her. He did whatever business was necessary to ensure there would be an heir, but had not gone any further than that in cherishing her. Now that she had felt what it was to be cherished, she was not sure she could return to a loveless shell of a marriage. It would be better never to marry at all.

Before *that* thought could take hold and once again threaten her mood, the carriage door opened and Theo climbed in alone and took the seat across from her. He shut the door and tapped on the carriage roof for it to start forward.

When she looked at him in confusion, he explained, "My sister is traveling in the other carriage. She did not wish to leave her boys with the servants alone. Frank was showing signs of fatigue, and she was ready to coddle him for a bit. She may seem too robust to have space left for a heart, but I assure you she is quite sentimental."

"I believe it," Arabella said.

She glanced at him in the dim of the carriage, with the afternoon sun tilting below the line of tall trees on her right side. He was undeniably attractive. Even when she had first seen him in Lincolnshire, she had thought him so. But now, to have known him more intimately—even to see the hint of a beard on his face at the end of a long day... It was all so comfortable. She could easily spend every day with him for the rest of her life.

"Tell me honestly, how is your life with my sister?" he asked, settling himself more comfortably in his seat and allowing his leg to brush hers, though it was just the two of them and there was space enough. "Do you feel more at ease in her home, or do you still fear you are trespassing in some way?"

She rested her eyes on the dark green of his coat then lifted them to his face. "I don't suppose it is possible to feel I am anything but a trespasser no matter where I am. But your sister has been most assiduous in her efforts to make me feel at home."

He folded his arms on his chest and leaned back to peer at her more closely. He seemed more comfortable, more proprietary in her presence than he was before, as though their kiss had broken through any lingering formality.

"Why is it that you must always be a trespasser? Surely not in your own home! Not in your London home or at Penwood Estate? Those belong to you."

"Except that they are not mine, not really," she replied. "First, they were my husband's. I was allowed to have my own bedroom, where I spent much time in peace, except when... when he sought to visit me there."

Theo's jaw tightened at her words, and she hurried on. "Then he died, and immediately Mr. Northwick took over the management of my husband's property. He made it clear he'd allow my presence as a gift until my son came of age, because he was his guardian. He said I could remove to the London apartment permanently if I should wish it, but I would be doing so without David. My other choice was to follow him wherever he went and visit David whenever Nurse allowed me to."

Theo rubbed his face vigorously and exhaled. "I feel rage when I hear the way that coxcomb treated you. As though you are a servant in your own home. And the nurse as well! She sounds like a proper harridan."

It was the first time someone's anger warmed her rather than frightened her. She felt it as protection, and it was a novel experience. She wanted to give him something in return for the sensation of goodness and warmth that he constantly provided her and David.

"Tell me more about you, Theo. You say very little about yourself, you know, and I should like to be as good a friend to you as you are to me."

He regarded her, a smile crinkling his eyes. "What exactly would you like to know about me? I confess, I hardly think there is much of interest."

"You underestimate yourself." Arabella shook her head firmly, smiling. Then, after reflecting for a moment, asked, "You once told me you are not suited to mill work. Is there anything you do enjoy about it?"

"Ah. You've managed to ask the one question I find difficult to answer." He stared through the window, and she followed his gaze. The road had brought them back to the river, and before long they would be at his sister's house.

"I appreciate the history my family has in the textile business, and I even enjoy the idea of running the mill capably. But as I've mentioned, I am not perfectly suited to sitting behind a desk and do not lay claim to any sort of ingenuity in the cloth business. Truth be told, my younger brother is more adept than I am, although I fear he does not possess the business acumen to run the mill."

"Had you ever tried to talk to your father to see if there might be another role for you?" David was sleeping solidly in her arms, and the carriage was beginning to slow as it followed Trudy's carriage toward her house. They would not have much more time together.

"Convincing my father that I was not the right man to step into his shoes was simply not possible. I believe I would have had about as much success as you, had you tried to reason with your father."

"That is to say, none at all," she said dryly.

"I fear not." He wiggled his fingers at David, who opened his eyes as the carriage came to a halt. Theo did not move to alight. "I won't pretend it is exactly the same. My father was not neglectful or unkind. But his authority over me was complete. No one could have convinced him that the eldest son was not meant to take over the business he had started. And so I did what was required of me."

As the footman opened the door from the outside, she nodded in silence. *That* was a sentiment she could relate to.

Theo assisted her out of the carriage, then went over to say a few words to his nephews before turning to Trudy. "I will join you for dinner again tomorrow, if I may."

"As often as you'd like," she said. "Although I suppose Mrs. Wilkins might have something to say about the habit of you dining outside every night."

Arabella stood to the side, not wanting to intrude on this sibling exchange, or bid goodbye to Theo in such a public way. Of course there must be no more reference to that moment they had shared. Surely when he came to his senses, he would realize that such a kiss must not be repeated. He would never compromise her, she knew. If she told him she could not marry him, he would respect her wishes.

How tempted she was to throw off all reason and marry him anyway. Such a sweet life dangling just out of reach was almost impossible to resist. But she had David to think of. Her son bent forward suddenly to get down, and she gave him his freedom, even passing him to Felicity who was waiting to take his hand and lead him up the steps.

Theo bid goodbye to his sister, then turned and took Arabella's hands in his own as he had developed the habit of doing. He didn't speak but lifted them to his lips, smiled at her, then waited while she climbed the steps, not leaving until she had disappeared indoors.

To Arabella's disappointment, Theo did not come to visit them the next night, sending word that there had been a fight at the mill that almost amounted to a mutiny, and he had been obliged to stay behind with the manager to see to the root of it. A group of workers had protested that the new loom would soon replace the need for them, and they would be out of work. Others argued that they should be receiving higher wages since they were still performing the more manual bits of labor at the mill, such as carding and spinning. Trudy explained that as Theo knew he was already paying more than any of the other mills in the area—and that it was more than enough for the workers to feed their families—he had not given in to their requests. Now, a few from the two groups of protestors were stirring up unrest among the others, and Theo had to be on hand to quell it.

Despite his absence, Arabella had begun to relax in Trudy's

home. After she'd taken her breakfast in her room, she spent a happy hour or two in the nursery with David. She no longer hesitated to join the children and servants in the garden, where even Roger and Frank now called to her to show her something they'd found. It gave her a fair idea of what it would be like to have several children, all wanting her attention at once. It was loud and chaotic. It was lovely.

And she spent time in the snug sitting room, often in companionable silence with Trudy whenever she was there. The routine was just what Arabella needed to grow beyond her fears. It was so freeing not to have to constantly hide from Mr. Northwick, and to go anywhere she might like in the house.

She turned the page of a novel that had engrossed her the past two days, *almost* removing her thoughts from Theo. Trudy was sitting at the desk near the window reading her correspondence. She turned with one of the letters in hand.

"Vincent has written from London, saying he is very glad to hear you have found refuge here. He is a good man, Vincent, even if he is too staid to please Anthony, who—by the way—has indeed brought your late husband's journal to him. I should be astonished if such an extensive record of free trade activity came to nothing," Trudy said.

"I am glad to hear it. I hope...I should hope no stone will be unturned." Arabella did not wish ill on anyone, but this might be the one thing that saved her from the fate of life under her brother-in-law's thumb.

"It's very curious," Trudy continued, still perusing her letter, "but my husband says he knew Mr. Northwick. Not your brother-in-law, apparently, but your deceased husband. It's not someone with whom he would be likely to cross paths, for he tends to know the people in London who hail from Nottinghamshire or who are on the board. But he said he'd met him when he had just taken a bride, and they were discussing investing in some scheme together."

Arabella attempted a smile. "I am glad they did not conclude the investment, for it surely would have been something unsavory, and that would not do at all for your husband." As soon as she spoke, a sudden fear struck her. If Trudy's husband had met Josiah, perhaps he would also cross paths with Mr. Northwick.

Trudy seemed to read her anxiety. "I have told him that your stay here must be of the strictest confidence, for you are in danger from your brother-in-law. He has assured me he will not speak of it, so you need not fear."

"Thank you," Arabella said, and after a moment added, "But it does seem odd that they should have met. There are so many people in London, and they don't seem like two who could have much in common. Did he say anything else about him?"

Trudy scanned the letter. "No, nothing. Just that he had a fondness for snuff. That was something he remembered well."

"*Ugh.*" Arabella shuddered. "That he did. He could never do without his favorite blend. In the end, I fear it did not help him when he was ill, for I could hear him coughing much more than he had before. But he was much too addicted to be able to leave off, even when he was not quite comfortable."

"I suppose my husband remembers it because there is very little tobacco coming in through the proper tax-paying ports sanctioned by the government. Perhaps he suspected your husband had not gotten his through the proper means."

Trudy continued to examine the contents of the letter and gave a sudden, sharp intake of breath. "Oh, how horrid! He wrote that two people who promised to inform against the smugglers have had their tobacco tampered with in the last six months. The tobacco was poisoned, apparently, and they both died."

"That is terrible," Arabella agreed, frowning. She wondered whether Mr. Northwick might have had anything to do with it. She would have no way of knowing and supposed it did not do to heap sins upon a man based on mere conjecture. In any case, it could not have been her husband, since he had been gone for longer than six months.

Trudy finished reading her husband's letter, then turned to her sister, Sissi's. It was happy news, she announced to Arabella, as her sister was increasing, though she had her hands full with her husband's children from his first marriage.

This led to a discussion on when they might wish to leave for Cornwall and what sort of house Arabella might be able to rent there. She could not access her funds without alerting Mr. Northwick of her whereabouts, and that meant she must seek employment. But she would not worry about that just yet.

ARABELLA WAITED for Theo to appear. He did not come for several days, although he did send word to his sister with a sealed note enclosed for her. She had to be satisfied with its brief contents.

DEAR ARABELLA,

I am unable to get away from the mill just now, for tension has arisen that I must deal with. I find that when I am here, the conflict is resolved more readily, as the workers trust what I say over the manager. They need not—Mr. Barrett is instructed to act just as I would, but such as it is...

By the time I leave at the end of each day, your dinner will have been long over, and it is impossible for me to appear at your doorstep at such an hour. We have a meeting to settle labor differences Wednesday morning. I am hopeful that it will bring about a final, peaceful resolution—and that it will bring me to you.

Yours,
Theo

ARABELLA FOLDED the letter and rested her hand upon it. She knew why the workers trusted Theo. It was because he was trustworthy. One could simply tell. She didn't think he possessed a dishonest bone in his body.

It was a disappointment to learn he would not come again

for dinner that night, for she had been expecting him these past several days and almost feared she had merely imagined their last encounter. Despite that, there was much to keep her cheerful and occupied right where she was. Theo had written to her, which meant he still had feelings for her. That knowledge brought her comfort, even if she could not return a favorable reply to his request of marriage.

On Wednesday afternoon, she sat in the nursery alone with David, who had developed a slight cold. Trudy and Nurse had taken the boys out of doors for the afternoon to help them shake off some of the energy they had in abundance and give Arabella a bit of peace and quiet with her son.

"Knock, knock."

She heard the man's voice from the doorway, and her heart leapt. She knew right away who it belonged to, and she turned from her seated position. David sat in front of her playing with wooden blocks.

"Good afternoon," Arabella said, her face lighting in an instant smile. "I hope that your presence means you've been able to sort out the problems at the mill?"

Theo had paused to watch her from the doorway, but now he moved forward and sat next to her. David got to his feet and brought a wooden block over to Theo who took it from him and held out his arms. David sank into a hug as Theo kissed the top of his head. Arabella wondered again at such trust, and the longing for this man to be David's father became so great she almost promised him on the instant that she would marry him.

But then she came to her senses. She could not. For her son would never have Theo for a father. He would be taken from her, and she would no longer have a son. Mr. Northwick's threats on that matter had been clear. And she could not even be sure he would not dispose of her son in a terrible way when he found it convenient to do so. Her fear mounted and banished the brief moment of love and longing.

Theo turned David to sit on his lap, reaching over to pull the other blocks toward him. "I crossed Trudy in the garden before I came in. I heard the boys shouting and thought you must be there as well. She sent me up to you."

"No. I am sure she told you David is not well."

"She did. And to answer your question—yes, for the first time in a week, I do feel my mill will begin to run smoothly again. I promised that when we brought in the machines, we would not diminish the number of workers we've already hired. We would simply reduce their hours without reducing their pay."

Arabella could not help but laugh in admiration. "That will surely win you loyalty. Does your manager not agree?"

"No, and he is right in this instance. It is not a promise we can continue to make unless we are able to develop our capacity for production in several lines of new cloth, which I am hoping my brother will have some ideas for." He met her stare. "But I did not come to talk about the mill. I don't want to waste our precious time on *that* subject. How have you been since I saw you last?"

"I am feeling more comfortable," she replied honestly. "I know I cannot stay forever. Of course I cannot. But I finally feel settled enough to begin to plan where I might go next. Trudy has suggested I might try Cornwall. She said she can accompany me there and introduce me to your sister, Sissi, and your mother. At the very least I would have friends."

Theo picked up one of the blocks and handed it to David, who promptly threw it. He picked up another, and David pushed it out of the way, getting out of his lap and toddling over to a cloth doll with embroidered features, which he picked up and began to wave, causing the head to flop back and forth. He did not seem very sick at the moment, but she could discern some fussiness that was not usually there. Arabella darted glances at Theo while watching David's play, conscious that Theo had not immediately endorsed her plan.

"I...I want you to be safe," he said at last. "I cannot get behind the idea of you traveling hundreds of miles away from me, however."

When she looked at him, she saw his tone reflected in his

eyes. It was a balm to her heart to be loved. That's what she had seen there. But she could not give in to that heady emotion. She had to think about her son first—always.

"If I were to stay here, it would be intolerable for us, I fear." She looked down, realizing that David had left a smear of something on the skirt of her dress. She rubbed at it absently. "We would constantly be in each other's company, but we could not be together. I do not think it fair to you. I think you should be free to marry someone who is equally free to choose you. It is the least you deserve."

"I want only to marry the woman I love," Theo said with quiet conviction.

He held her gaze until she broke it. She had never known such temptation before—to stay and bask in that love. But she cared about him too much to act so selfishly. If she left, he would eventually forget about her and fall in love with someone else. It was the only thing to do if she truly loved him back, no matter how difficult it was.

David tripped on a block and toppled forward. He rolled to his knees and began to cry, pulling Arabella from her reverie. She went over to him and picked him up.

"Don't cry, sweetie. It is all going to be all right," she crooned, kissing him.

Theo got to his feet as well and came over to her, patting David's back. After a moment, her son decided he'd had enough of being constrained and made a movement to be released. Arabella set him down, and she was left standing in front of Theo.

He reached down to hold her hand. His was warm and solid, like him. Her heart beat in a steady rhythm, standing so near to him. It was becoming her favorite place to be—her safe place, her security.

"I don't want you to go," he whispered and leaned down, settling his lips briefly on hers. He pulled away again and glanced at David, who had rediscovered a crate containing other toys that were just out of reach, which did not hinder him from attempting to grasp them. Theo leaned in and kissed Arabella again, this time lingering.

Noises reached them of the children entering the house. Theo smiled and reluctantly stepped away.

Arabella's heart was in turmoil. She could be forever content to stand here in his arms, but responsibilities called. She went over to the crate and plucked out the toy David was trying to reach and handed it to him as the army of sound climbed the staircase and approached steadily.

"Arabella," Theo said, pulling her attention back to him. "I don't want you to go, but I will do—and be—whatever you need. I want to make sure you know that. You may count on me."

CHAPTER 15

When Theo had first arrived, leaving his sister and nephews in the garden to go stand on the threshold of the nursery, the sight of Arabella on the floor playing with David in perfect contentment settled something in his heart. He had to remember that there was life outside of mills, and management, and money. Hearth and home —and all that belonged to it—were what mattered most.

He had spent an exhausting week, attempting to pacify both his manager and his employees. He did not love being a man of business. It was not only because he preferred the country life to one in town, but also because he was apt to make decisions based purely on sentiment. He knew his father would never forgive him—though his father was now in his grave and beyond such mortal things—if Theo ran the business into the ground for lack of good management. But he could not turn away from his employees who depended on him for wages to feed their families, remaining deaf to their concerns. He would have demanded the same if he were in their shoes.

And now he was with Arabella at last, sharing her moment with David. Her gown was of the palest pink color. She always dressed as though she were a maiden entering into her first season. Had life been different for her, she could very well have been in her first season even now, attending all the balls London had to offer. If that had been the case, he would not have stood a chance. She was too beautiful, too good, too sweet. The demands for her hand would have been numerous. But here in Newark, in his own sister's house, he did stand a chance.

Here she was free of harm and under no threat—at her ease, watching over her son. That was what made him fall completely under her spell. *He* had been instrumental in bringing about that look of freedom in her eyes. Everything seemed to fall into place at that instant. He was meant to protect her on this earth—her and David, who had started to come willingly into his arms.

The idea that she would leave for Cornwall was wretched and wrong. But he could not frighten her away by presenting his case for her to stay just yet. He had to help her in whatever way she needed while he went after her villainous brother-in-law. *That* was true love, even if it meant he must suffer through their temporary separation. At least he would know how to find her if Trudy indeed brought her to Cornwall.

Trudy led the pack into the nursery but was quickly eclipsed by her sons, who came and threw their arms around Theo's legs.

"Oh good. You haven't run off yet," she teased. "Are you staying for dinner?"

"I plan to, if Cook will not be put out by setting another place." He glanced at Arabella and was rewarded with a smile.

Trudy's youngest protested Nurse's grasp as she removed a soiled article of clothing, and Theo said, "Frank, I will play with you if you allow Nurse to ready you for bed."

His nephew ceased his struggles, allowing Nurse to finish her task, and Arabella frowned in David's direction. "I suppose he should be readied for bed, too, although I hesitate to bathe him if he is ill."

"I will bring some hot water to your room, and we won't wash his hair, ma'am," Felicity said. "If his head's not wet, he'll be well enough."

His sister had not stopped praising the latest arrival to her servants downstairs. Felicity was ready to do anything she was bid and was quite capable besides. Trudy owned herself unsurprised if Felicity became head maid—or nurse—before long, despite her young age.

Arabella agreed and prepared to follow the maid to her bedchamber. "I won't be long. I've been dressing him in my room since he's fallen sick. It's warmer there with the sun coming in directly."

The nursery faced the northern side and even in summer it could be cool, which was beneficial for the seasonal heat, but less so for when the days were chillier. True to his promise, Theo sat down and played with his nephews while Trudy excused herself to warn Cook of the extra setting.

By the time Theo went down for dinner an hour later, he was already longing to see Arabella. How would he manage it when she eventually left Newark and settled far away? It was hard to bide his time and wait for his brother to finish his mission in London to bring Northwick to account. But Theo could hardly have gone himself. For one thing, Northwick knew who he was, and for another, he had the mill to think of.

The mill—his endless source of duty. And sometimes, just sometimes, his source of satisfaction when he knew it ran with efficiency.

He went to the dining room, where Trudy and Arabella soon joined him for dinner. After the servants had brought the dishes and retired, Trudy asked the question that was foremost in his thoughts.

"When is Anthony to return?" She handed the basket of bread to Arabella. The extra leaves had been removed from the table, and it was a cozy setting for three.

"I don't expect him for another fortnight," Theo said. He turned to Arabella. "As such, I hope you will not think of leaving us too soon. I should like to have more news than the brief letter I received from him, which was almost no news at all."

"Taking her to Cornwall was one of my better ideas, I think," Trudy said, with a half-apologetic look.

"I agree it will be the best place for her and David. However,

I am not so convinced of the need to rush off like that into a new situation," he said, speaking more to his sister than to her.

"No, except that it will be better if I accompany her there, and I am to go in September." Trudy turned to Arabella. "I fear it will not be comfortable for you to remain here when my husband returns, for you won't have the liberty you have now. Not that my husband would put up a fuss about your stay, for he would not. He is the gentlest of men. But it would be a different thing entirely to have a man around, do you not agree?"

Arabella nodded decisively. "I could not think of intruding upon your domestic arrangement, no matter how kind you all are. I would be pressed to leave at the earliest opportunity."

"Exactly. And I should not want for you to travel all that distance without accompaniment." Trudy met Theo's gaze. "You must see it's for the best. We will take care of her and help her to find a situation near Sissi. She will be well there."

He nodded, not at all convinced, but it was not the place to argue it. That was something he would need to do on his own with Arabella, just the two of them.

He could not push her to make a decision between David and him—that would be contemptible—but he could convince her to live nearby so he could see her whenever he wished while they worked on freeing her and her son from Northwick's grasp. After all, there was no way her brother-in-law could trace them to Newark.

Theo would not allow himself to think about how hard it would be to see her day after day and not permit himself to share a kiss with her again like they had shared near the river. To do so would be playing with fire.

The dinner was a moment of near bliss. His sister was there, which did not allow him to converse with Arabella on overly intimate terms, but Trudy was easy to be around. And she absented herself a couple of times, allowing him to brush Arabella's hand when he passed her a dish and speak as intimately as he desired. Arabella seemed to be warming up to him with each passing minute spent in his company, allowing her contemplation to rest on him for longer stretches of time. From everything she had shared with him, she had never felt for anyone the way she did for him. She had not been given the chance.

At the end of the evening, Theo kissed his sister on the cheek and thanked her for a lovely evening. She murmured something about needing the footman's help in the kitchen, and Theo sent a silent blessing after her. He turned to Arabella where she stood, petite and adorable, not shrinking in his presence. He stared at her for a moment, wanting to reach out for her, but refraining.

"Do not leave me too quickly, Arabella." He hadn't intended to speak of that just yet, and his voice was gruff.

"I do not wish to leave you at all. You must believe me." Her look showed all the sincerity and regret of one pushed to the edge. "I just cannot offer you hope of being one day able to accept your generous proposal. And I think that is unkind."

"I am yet hopeful that Anthony might bring me news of Northwick which will allow me to free you from his grasp. It's a slim hope, but faith has rested on much less," he replied.

"I, too, wish it. More than anything, I wish I could be freed from him. I do not even care for the estate at this point, although that would be unfair to my son, who deserves what is rightfully his. I care only for David's safety. And..." She gave a tremulous smile. "I do wish I were free."

"I will not torture us both by kissing you on the lips as I wish to," Theo murmured. "I will merely kiss you here"—he leaned down and placed a soft kiss on her cheek—"and bid you goodnight."

When he did so, she placed her hand on the back of his neck, causing him to grow still and linger, before straightening again.

"Good night, Theo."

"Good night, Arabella." He opened the door, breathed deeply of the fresh air, and stepped out into the night.

THEO SAT IN HIS OFFICE, attempting to go over the day's accounts and make the figures match despite paying the workers an equal amount for less production. He would not regret his decision, but he had to find a way to make the mill more profitable. Otherwise, they would all be living on charity.

The door to his office opened with such force it banged against the wall. Anthony stood on the threshold.

Theo looked up in surprise. "Anthony! I did not expect you for at least a fortnight." He stood with a smile and went over with his hand extended. If his brother had come back early it meant he had news.

"I have been traveling with very little rest, so I might reach you as fast as I could." Anthony looked it, now that Theo examined him more closely. The clothing he wore was dirt-stained, though he was in general meticulously attired. "And since I returned without Earnie, I am sorry to say it, but I had to withdraw money to hire a chaise-and-four, and then hire horses at the stopping inns."

Theo gulped at that expense but gestured to the chair in front of his desk and closed the door behind his brother.

"What was the rush? There was no need to return with such haste, although I appreciate the sentiment. I long to bring down Northwick even more than you do. However, I could have waited for another week to bring that about."

Anthony threw himself into a chair and rubbed his chin. "Do you have some ale? I am dying of thirst."

Theo had been about to sit opposite from him, but he went to the door and signaled for a servant there to bring some. "Of course. I should have thought of it."

When the servant returned with the ale, Theo handed it to Anthony and waited while he drained it before setting the empty tankard down on the desk.

"It is not good news," Anthony said without preamble. "In

fact, it's the worst." He buried his face in his hands and didn't lift it.

Theo froze, alert. He didn't believe him. What could be worse than being unable to free Arabella from her situation? "What happened?"

After a lengthy pause that Theo had to fight not to break, his brother lifted his gaze. "I'm afraid I told Northwick where Arabella is hiding."

Theo's eyes widened as he dropped into the chair. Fury mounted inside of him, but he kept it firmly in check. It would not do to jump to conclusions. Perhaps it was not as bad as it sounded. "You had better tell me all."

Anthony nodded. "I went to London with Earnie, and it was everything I could wish for. I barely remember my visit as a boy and was certainly not able to appreciate everything the town had to offer at the time. This time, I went to all the gentlemen's clubs that Earnie got me into. He's got passage everywhere. I cruised Bond Street and saw with my own eyes what passes for the latest fashion. I fancy that my style of dress is not too fair and far off."

Theo nodded his encouragement to go on, biting back the impatient words that he hadn't wanted Anthony to tell him *everything*, but rather to get to the point. There might be some detail that was important.

"As chance would have it, at one of the clubs, I heard a fellow address another as Northwick, and I turned to get a glimpse of the man. I hardly expected such a piece of luck, for London is teeming with people, and what are the chances I would meet the one I was searching for without any effort? He's younger than I expected, by the way, given what you told me of Arabella's dead husband."

When he paused, Theo said, "Yes, there is a great age discrepancy. What happened?"

"I believe my reaction to his name caused him to take notice of me. He smiled and nodded in my direction, and what could I do but do the same. Later on, he invited me to join him at the gaming table. Of course I could not refuse. Besides, I needed to find out more about him.

"When we sat over cards, he said, 'I noticed that you recognized my name. I was wondering if we had met.' He said it in that offhand way as though he didn't care in the slightest whether or not we had. It made me realize how green I am compared to him. I said—" Anthony scrunched up his face. "Well, I couldn't think of what to say, because he would never believe me that I had not heard of his name. So I told him I had some connections to a certain breed of gentlemen who had mentioned him. He was in the way of getting certain prime items for a song, if he caught my meaning."

Theo's heart sank, and his face must have shown it because Anthony answered. "I know. It's the stupidest thing to have betrayed my hand that way."

"But you didn't betray Arabella's—not with that disclosure. So there must be more." A shiver of anxiety shot through Theo.

"No. Not right away. I took the risk of bringing up one of the names in the journal you gave me. By the way, I left it with Vincent in London, and he said we did just right to hand it over to the proper authorities—in the prosiest way possible. Oh, *lud*, I could not bear it." Anthony clapped his hands over his eyes and leaned back.

He recovered quickly and angled forward again. "I told Northwick that my local contacts had mentioned him as someone I might possibly see in London regarding silks and laces. His look of surprise told me he is not dealing in textiles at all. But then he simply agreed and said I had heard correctly. He said perhaps he could lead me to the right people in London."

Anthony's brows furrowed as he appeared to think through the conversation. "I did one thing right. I made up some excuse to leave the table and managed to whisper a few words to Earnie before he could call out my name and tip Northwick off that we were related. I am sure he would have recognized the name Dawson, don't you think?"

"I am sure he would have," Theo said. "Nice work. So what happened next?"

"Nothing that evening. And I *was* able to develop some contacts with men involved in the cloth trade—not the lowest orders, mind you. Nothing dangerous. The middle men who are connected to the drapers and modistes who purchase the cloth. None of them knew Northwick, so I'm not sure my gamble paid off well."

Anthony folded his arms and leaned back. "But then why in the world would he agree to it?"

Theo shrugged. "Because he thought he might gain information is my guess. Although I'm sure he is connected to the smuggling trade somehow, even if it's not in textiles."

"True," Anthony said. "His other behavior has not shown him to be an exemplary man. I wouldn't be surprised if he added Captain Sharp to his list of talents." He paused for a moment as the idea struck him before continuing.

"So, over the course of the days that followed, I ran into him a surprising number of times. Each time we saw each other, he sought me out as though I were someone of significance. It would have been a flattering thing were it not for the fact that I was wary by then and expect he was leading me to disclose information rather than allowing me to gain anything from him."

"What sorts of things did you disclose?" Theo prompted.

"Well, I made up a name, but for the rest I told him only what was true. Said my father was a miller in Newark and that I had some sisters, only one of whom still lived in the city we grew up in."

Anthony glanced at him. "I know you will tell me I would have done better to keep my mouth shut, but you don't know what it is to be in a conversation with someone you need to gain something from but who is no greenhorn. My only two choices were to ignore him completely—but that would not allow me to find anything out about him—or to make things up so I might speak to him naturally as though we were friends or some such thing. But I didn't want to make everything up or I wouldn't keep track of it. And truly, I thought there was no harm..."

"I understand," Theo said quietly. His brother was young, and what could a boy like that do in the face of an experienced malefactor? "What happened then? Everything you have told me thus far would not lead him to us."

"I said my sister had two children and was married to a man named Moore. But I didn't tell him he worked for the Board of Customs, and he didn't seem to recognize the name. And there were plenty of times when I was just with Earnie and his cronies."

Anthony seemed to forget himself for an instant, showing boyish enthusiasm.

"London really is a crack place. While I was on my own during the day, I managed to see some of the latest patterns and gain some ideas for what we could produce here. I am sure we can match them for quality and style."

Theo nodded, once again reining in his impatience. He did not want to crush his brother, but he was beginning to wonder if Anthony had truly erred in his interactions with Northwick or only imagined he had.

"So what in the end had you rushing back to Newark? Why do you feel that Northwick knows Arabella is here?"

Anthony sighed, and any enthusiasm he had shown crumpled. "I hadn't spread about a false name anywhere else, and a couple of nights ago, we were at a club and someone called out, 'Dawson.' I responded without thinking, and only then did I look around and see Northwick watching me. It was detestable because he came over and started saying in that smooth voice of his as though he were a cat playing with a mouse, 'So you are Anthony Dawson after all, and not Wilkins as you'd said. I don't suppose you have any connection to Theodore Dawson?'"

Theo buried his face in his hands before forcing himself to look up. Anthony's look of guilt was plastered over his face.

"He then went on to say that his nephew had gone missing—being sure to clarify that he was his nephew's full guardian and adding that his brother's widow had run off as well—and did I happen to know where she was? I said of course I did not, but it did not look like he believed me. Theo, there is such an oily way about him! I am sure he will not let the matter lie but must come here to see if she has taken refuge with us."

Theo shot up from his chair and paced over to the window to stare blindly through it. "We had better prepare for the eventuality," he agreed.

Two stories down, the brown river raced by, bordered by a grassy bank that had been shored up to prevent spillover. With the green shrubs on either side, the river maintained a wild look.

Theo feared that Northwick would indeed come. But his question was what to do now? Should he tell Arabella and frighten her half to death with the threat of it, before sending her off precipitously without his sister's escort? Or should he say nothing and hope that he was wrong?

CHAPTER 16

Arabella left David in the nursery with Felicity and came into the sitting room for a quiet moment's reprieve before joining Trudy for dinner. She did not hear the knock at the front door until the footman came to announce Theo. She got to her feet, her ready smile faltering as soon as she saw the serious nature of his look. There was a crease to his brows, and his mouth was set in a straight line. Her stomach sank at once.

He must have come to announce he wished to end their familiarity. It would be very right of him, of course. She had plainly told him she could offer nothing beyond friendship. It had been wrong of her to hope for anything more, or to offer him hope in return. The sooner she allowed him to move on with his future, the better it would be for them both.

However, what she knew in her mind was not so easily reconciled in her heart. To think of not seeing him again. To imagine him smiling at another woman the way he smiled at her—or to kiss a woman the way he had kissed her. It hurt to breathe just thinking of it. Theo bowed over her hand, but his smiles and easy discourse were absent.

"Would you like some... Will you be staying for dinner?" She sought to turn the conversation to something light. Anything to distract him from uttering the dreaded words.

"Arabella, there is a matter of grave importance I must discuss with you." Theo gestured to the sofa and waited until she took her seat before taking his own across from her.

She did not so much sit as collapse onto the sofa, as the ever-present fear that shadowed her stole her strength. She remained silent, waiting, clutching her hands together.

He cleared his throat and shifted in his chair. "This is difficult for me to say. I hardly know how to get the words out."

Arabella could bear the suspense no longer. "Theo, you must say whatever it is you have in mind. I shall accept it. Indeed, you must not think I cannot manage it, for I assure you I can."

Though it broke her heart, she must allow him to go free. She would weep quietly in her own room, but Theo mustn't be forced to continue a friendship that no longer suited him. She would not tie him down in that way.

He let out a lungful of air, then glanced at her, and she saw the lines around his eyes that were not there before. "I wish I did not have to trouble you with such news. I had thought to say nothing of this, but I knew it would be very wrong of me, so..."

"I have no expectations of you, indeed I do not. You are perfectly free to think of me as...as a fond friend you once had."

Arabella's face felt hot from the embarrassment at speaking so frankly, and her hands trembled with an effort to keep her emotions in check. She was not accustomed to expressing such vulnerability with her words.

Theo's face registered surprise, then he got up and moved over to the sofa to sit next to her.

"You have it wrong, Arabella. The unpleasant news I have to disclose has nothing to do with my feelings for you, which have not changed—and indeed I think they could not." He exhaled as though readying himself to face an unpleasant reality. "Yesterday, my brother returned from London, and there he met Mr. Northwick."

Arabella had trouble following this new lead of information.

The knowledge and relief that Theo had remained unchanged in his regard for her almost succeeded in rendering her witless. Then the gist of what he was saying came upon her like a bucket of cold water. It shocked her, but must it necessarily be bad news?

"Was he unsuccessful then? In gaining information about my brother-in-law that might liberate us from his hold?" Her mind spun with the possibilities of what this could mean.

It all seemed so far off. And what was more, it was becoming nearly impossible to imagine ending things with Theo simply because Mr. Northwick would not allow it. The longer she stayed in Newark, the more remote that probability seemed. Her days spent in such agreeable and uncomplicated surroundings filled her with hope and made anything seem possible.

But Theo's face had closed up again. "Arabella, I fear Anthony has inadvertently hinted at where you are. I need not add that he did not mean to do it, of course. But we fear that Mr. Northwick has traced us to you, and that now he will come here."

She gasped, and the ensuing fear that overtook her was so great her head swooned. She opened her mouth to speak, but black spots appeared in her vision until she was falling in earnest as everything went black.

"Move the feathers out of the way. Those are not working. Here, I found some vinaigrette."

Trudy's voice pierced Arabella's consciousness, and the unpleasant aroma of burning that was waved before her nose was replaced with a truly pungent odor that wrenched her eyes open with a start. She began to cough. Theo put one arm behind her and assisted her.

"I have you," Theo murmured. "Do not fret. All is well."

Their earlier discussion rushed back to her, and she knew all was not well. She was lying on the sofa with his arms under her, and she looked up at him, then Trudy. "Mr. Northwick is coming here."

He shook his head and glanced at his sister. "Do not trouble yourself about this at present. I don't wish for you to swoon again. It is not a sure thing that he will come. I should not have mentioned it and brought you such distress."

Trudy took a seat beside Arabella on the other side of the sofa. "Theo has told me what happened and what he fears. Now we must make plans for how to proceed. I have proposed to him that we leave early for Cornwall. It will not be a difficult thing to do. I have only to write to my husband to inform him of the fact and then write to my mother and sisters to apprise them of our early arrival."

She rested a hand on Arabella's arm. "The only difficulty will be packing in haste. I cannot be ready to depart for two more days."

Arabella nodded, attempting to fortify herself. "Yes, I think that is best. I must leave here." She glanced at Theo. "Do you think Mr. Northwick will arrive in Newark before we are to leave?"

His gaze was tender, but she could see the pain of separation in it. It was her own pain.

"First, we must remember that even if he recognized Anthony's name and connected it to me, there is no reason that he will believe you are here as well. It is a great chance and might not warrant the trouble of journeying so many miles. And then, even if he does come, I don't think he will travel at the breakneck speed that Anthony did. He will likely take his time and travel in easy stages to reach here. Again, that is only if he decides to come."

His arm was still under her, and he seemed to hug her closer. She was fully conscious of the impropriety of their embrace, especially as they would soon be parted. But she could not pull away from the fortifying sensation. She had never felt anything like it before him. She had never known what it was to be cherished in such a way. To bask in such love. It stole her words. It almost stole her breath.

When she remained silent, Theo leaned down, his lips close to her head. "I agree that for your safety and David's, you must go. But I think it highly unlikely that—if he comes—he will arrive before you leave. I think you may be easy on that head, but by all means let us prepare for your departure, little though I wish it."

She nodded. It was her only option.

TRUDY MADE good on her word and spurred the household into action. She did not tell her servants about Arabella's risk of being discovered. Although she trusted them, it made little sense to offer an excess of information for no reason. She merely explained that she had put her visit off long enough, and now that Mrs. Northwick had agreed to accompany her to Cornwall, there was no reason to put it off any longer.

However, she explained to Arabella, she had taken the precaution of telling her servants not to admit any strangers to the household. If they were to ask where she had gone—not that she expected anyone to be impertinent enough to do so—the servants were to say that they had not received leave from their mistress to discuss her whereabouts.

"That ought to silence anyone who dares to try," Trudy said with a mischievous smile. But when she saw Arabella's troubled expression she added, "Not that I think he will truly come, dear. You must remember we are all taking what we think is an excess of precaution."

Arabella let out a quiet sigh. Despite her heavy heart, she met Trudy's gaze. "I do wish to thank you for taking me in. And for taking me to safety on the coast of Cornwall. I cannot express my gratitude enough for all you've done."

Trudy moved over on the sofa and put her arm around her. "We will find a way to turn everything out for the best."

She stopped and smiled at Arabella. "And what is more, I have seen enough to be convinced that you and Theo do indeed belong together. This makes me even more motivated to find a way to make you my sister."

Arabella could not reply in words, but she returned her embrace.

She had already packed her meager belongings, along with the few items she had bought to extend her wardrobe since she'd arrived in Newark. She had spent too much time in her room alone, and the solitude now became oppressive. She decided to go upstairs and hug David. It always set her heart at rest to spend time with him—to bask in all that was innocent and pure. It made it seem like anything was possible.

The nursery was empty, and she went downstairs to look outdoors. It was a walled garden and perfectly safe, and although there were many little corners made up of bushes and leafy branches, it was fairly easy to see at a glance where people were. It was even easier to hear them. When she went outside, however, there was a perfect silence, save for the buzzing of insects and the songs of birds. She furrowed her brows, telling herself she would not fear for her son or mistrust the servants who watched him. They had always treated David as though he were one of Trudy's. Still, something seemed off, and it left an unsettled feeling.

The kitchen! Of course. Felicity loved to take David down to see Cook, as he had become a favorite of hers. She hurried down the stairs leading to the kitchen, not crossing any other servant's path on her way down. Cook was there kneading a loaf of bread.

"Have you seen my son?" Arabella asked, her voice coming out breathless.

"No, ma'am. I haven't seen him since this morning. He must be out with Nurse." The cook paused in kneading, but when Arabella asked nothing further went back to her work.

Fear began to take root despite her attempts to quash it. Arabella ran upstairs to find Trudy, now out of breath in earnest.

"Trudy, I have not been able to find our boys anywhere—or

Nurse. They are not in the garden. Where do you think they have gone?"

Trudy paused in the packing of her trunk to think. "It is odd. I suppose Nurse and the maid took them to the stables. She sometimes does that, for they love to look at the horses, and it's a fine outing for when the boys get restless."

She regarded Arabella with concern. "I see why you are worried, but in this instance, you may be easy. The stables are only a short distance from here and are off the public road. You have nothing to fear, whether it be carriages rolling past at a dangerous speed or a certain troublesome man you would rather not meet."

She gave a reassuring smile, leaving the latter part vague. Arabella tried to look confident. "I will attempt to meet them. I haven't been out for a walk, and I believe the fresh air will do me some good."

"I agree. We dine in two hours, so you have plenty of time. Are you ready to leave tomorrow?" Trudy asked. Arabella nodded and lifted her hand in a wave.

At the bottom of the stairs, she tied on her bonnet and took a few minutes to slow her breathing. She would not go rushing out of the house as though wild dogs were at her feet. It was time she took herself well in hand and learned to be more courageous.

When she felt calmer, she opened the door and stepped out. The weather was warm but not overly hot. It would not be long before the cooler wind of fall chased the heat of summer away.

The house was farther from the center of town, and Arabella began to relax as she walked on the quiet road toward the stables. She passed no one on the way there, except for one carriage that went in the opposite direction. A quick glance told her it was no one she knew.

She entered the dark of the stables, blinking to clear her vision and relaxing when she spotted David, firmly in the arms of Felicity.

"Oh, you've come, ma'am." The maid sent her a troubled look. "I hope you do not mind that we took the boys here."

Arabella smiled and shook her head, pausing with her hand on the stall to counter the weakness that overcame her from the relief she felt. David saw her and shrieked his excitement.

"Hosses!"

She walked over to him and held out her arms, and he went into them willingly. She hugged him, keeping her smile in place. She would soon leave this town and go where she was never to be found. The only matter of importance was David.

"Yes, horses. He is a fine one, isn't he? The black one?" She looked at David, whose eyes were fixed on the horse's every movement.

"Back," repeated David. "Back one."

The nurse pulled Robert and Frank from the far end of the stables and greeted Arabella before asking, "Shall we return, ma'am? The boys will be wantin' their supper."

"Let's do that." Arabella shook her head at Felicity's offer to take David. "I'll hold him."

They were nearing the house when a carriage pulled up with a familiar face at the reins. *Theo*. Her heart lifted at the sight of him, then plunged again when she remembered he was coming to say goodbye. She would have to steel herself and tell him firmly to forget all about her when she left. He deserved better than to waste his life on someone who could not return a yes to his most worthy of offers.

Theo handed his reins to the footman and, after a few words, allowed him to drive off with the carriage to the stables. He came over and bowed to Arabella, then greeted David in her arms.

"How are you, little man? Have you been going for a walk with your mother?"

David just stared at him, and it was left to Arabella to answer. "Nurse and the boys were visiting the stables. I came to find them, and we are now on our way home. David must have a bath and..."

Her words trailed away. There, strolling along the side of the road in approach was the terrifying form of the person she feared most. Surely not. Surely he could not be *here* in the place she had come to regard as a safe haven? He could not have come all this way, and so quickly?

In her abrupt silence, Theo turned in the direction of her focus. She felt his muscles go tense next to her. They were reduced to frozen silence until Mr. Northwick closed the distance and stood in front of them.

David turned and tucked his head in her neck, and she squeezed him more tightly. Mr. Northwick missed nothing and greeted her with a cold smile.

"Arabella, what a surprise to find you in Newark-on-Trent. I had not thought to look for you here as you have no connections to this town. Or so I had thought, although"—he turned his speculating, unfriendly countenance to Theo—"I should have known better. I could have saved myself a great deal of trouble had I thought to follow you to Mr. Dawson."

He turned and gave a mocking bow to Theo, who moved to stand in front of her and David.

"Oh yes, you must certainly feel entitled to Arabella, as you've had these few weeks to form something of an attachment. And, of course she may throw her lot in with yours. *I* certainly have no say over what she does."

Mr. Northwick paused, and Arabella felt the cold dread steal over her as his scrutiny went to David in her arms. "However, I have a legal right to my nephew as his full guardian. So you may hand him over, if you please."

"No, George—please don't," Arabella said, unable to resist the tears that filled her eyes. At the panicked tone in her voice, David burrowed in more deeply.

"Have you no common decency?" Theo asked, the anger in his voice kept barely in check. She had never heard him sound so hard, so unyielding. "A boy needs his mother."

Mr. Northwick raised an eyebrow. "And he shall have her... unless she prefers to remain here with you. I have always told her that she would be welcome to live with David under my protection. If she chooses not to do so, I can hardly be blamed for it."

"It is because the caveat is that I must be married to you," Arabella could not help but retort.

"That is despicable," Theo said, standing even closer to her. "Such a union is not even legal and will not stand up in court."

"But who is to dispute it?" Mr. Northwick asked without passion. He was all cold logic. "Surely not you. Do you have the means for a protracted case? Do you want your precious Arabella's name dragged through the mud? And then reduce whatever child she carries to illegitimacy?" He shook his head. "I think not."

There was no one on the road to hear their discussion, but Arabella felt the shame of it as though there were a great cloud of witnesses. She was ashamed that Theo was there to hear it, as though she were a mere bargaining piece. Just when she felt all was lost and there was nothing more to be said, Theo stepped in front of Mr. Northwick.

"I know all about your smuggling venture. Do you think I need to bring up a case about your illegal marriage to one who is all but your sister? No—I can bring charges against you for the smuggling. Your name is linked to the free traders, and I have proof of it."

Mr. Northwick laughed then. "Because your boy of a brother has some names he thinks me to be associated with? Even if I were, not one of the customs agents on the coast is beyond a bribe. I do wish you well in your endeavor. But I believe I will be taking my nephew now, as is my legal right."

He moved deftly around Theo and plucked David from Arabella easily, though she tried to cling to him. David began to wail, and Arabella could take it no longer as the tears began to fall.

"Wait! Wait," she cried. Mr. Northwick had turned away, and she ran the few steps to catch up to him. "I will go with you. Just let me stay with David. I'll do anything you say."

Mr. Northwick stopped then and turned. He flicked a glance

at Theo then looked at her. "I believe I've made it clear that the condition for you to remain with your son is to marry me. Had you not fled with my charge, I might not have forced a choice that appears unpalatable to you. But since you have, I cannot take any chances, and those are my terms."

David leaned forward, stretching his arms out to her, and she tried to take him, but Mr. Northwick swiveled away with her son in his arms. She stopped to consider. "I..."

"No, Arabella," Theo protested.

She whipped around to face him with pleading eyes. "Please let me handle this."

She turned back around but could not go on. She couldn't say the words.

"Let us just say that marriage to me will be a sign of your gratitude that I did not bring charges against you for kidnapping my nephew. That transgression will be enough to throw you in Newgate—*if* the courts have mercy and don't do worse."

"Arabella, don't listen to him." Theo stood behind her, but she knew he was just as powerless as she was. There was nothing he could do to relieve her situation. No one could save her. And no one could save her son—except her.

She lifted her chin and met Mr. Northwick's gaze squarely. "I will marry you."

CHAPTER 17

As Arabella's hope extinguished, Mr. Northwick's face took on a look of satisfaction.

"Ah, I am infinitely glad to hear you say it. In that case, you shall find me quite generous. If you do indeed hold to your word, the courts shall hear nothing of your lapse. However, I shall expect the banns to be read as soon as it can be arranged. We will not wait around for some missish notion you might still have. Do we have an understanding?"

Arabella nodded miserably. "Let me take David and wash him. I will need to pack our belongings." She reached out her hands for her son, but Mr. Northwick was already shaking his head.

"I don't think so. I shall keep my nephew with me while you pack his things and your own. I have my directions written down so you might find me at the inn." He handed her a card with a name, but she didn't know the town well enough to recognize it.

"You may spend one more night in Mr. Dawson's sister's house if you wish—oh, yes, I do indeed know everything—and join me tomorrow before eight o'clock when I am set to leave. Or you may come and stay in the room I have hired for you and sleep there with your son while you wait for our departure. Just know that if you stay here, you will not be sleeping with David tonight."

"I will come to the inn. I will come as quickly as I can. I will perhaps need an hour."

Arabella rested her eyes on her son, who had stopped crying and looked at her dully. He had recognized his uncle and seemed to shut down in the presence of his authority. Gone was his inquisitiveness and joy; he had surrendered to his uncle's grasp. It made her want to pack as quickly as she could so she might run to him and reassure him. Oh, if only she could hold him tonight, she would protect him from everything. Never would she let anything happen to him. Her life meant nothing, if she could only spare his.

Mr. Northwick nodded. "We are agreed then. I shall order a dinner and wait for you there." He turned and walked down the street, and David looked at her over his shoulder and reached his arms out to her, his wail piercing her heart.

With a sob, Arabella ran to the stairwell that led to the house. Theo called out from behind her, but she could scarcely hear him.

He caught up to her and stopped her with a hand on her arm. "Arabella, what can I do? There are no legal grounds to stop him from taking David. How else can I help?"

"Take me to the inn after I pack our belongings. I don't know how to find it." Arabella knocked on the door to be admitted as there was nothing to open it from the outside. The servants and children had already gone inside.

Theo stood beside her, his fist on the door jamb. "I can do that. But is that all I can do? Surely you cannot marry him."

He pulled her gently to look at him. Even now, even when she knew all was lost, just to stare directly into his eyes that were at once so warm and familiar sent tremors through her core.

"Theo, I must," she said. "It is not my wish, but I will do anything for David. I would give up my own life for him. Please understand this."

She saw him swallow and he dropped his head, putting one hand to his eyes as the footman opened the door.

Arabella did not delay any longer but went directly for the stairs, ignoring Trudy's startled voice asking Theo what was wrong. She did not stay for his answer, but rushed upstairs where she gathered her belongings and bundled them into the thin blanket that had served to carry her things when she'd fled from Penwood Estate. She had acquired enough new clothing and accessories that they no longer fit, so she left some behind. She needed to leave room for David's things.

When she had finished gathering her belongings, she hurried up to the nursery, filled with fearful trepidation that her brother-in-law had lied and was already making off with David to some place where she could not find him.

Upstairs, Nurse was directing Felicity, who gathered all of the items belonging to David and was stuffing them into a traveling bag that was nicer than Arabella's blanket. Trudy must have been upstairs to let them know.

Felicity sent her a worried look. "Ma'am, I have everything here, but I just must fetch his gown we washed, though it be still wet."

"It is of no consequence," Arabella replied. "It may be of use to someone here. Thank you for packing these," she added as Felicity came to the door with the bag.

Arabella reached for it, but Felicity shook her head and gathered both bundles in her arms. "If you please, ma'am. Allow me to carry both these for you." She headed toward the stairs at a brisk pace, and Arabella hurried behind her, slightly comforted by the maid's assistance.

At the bottom of the stairs, Theo and his sister were waiting for her. Arabella paused before Trudy. No matter how much of a hurry she was in, she must properly thank Theo's sister for her kindness in keeping her and David safe these past couple of weeks. Trudy reached out her hands and took Arabella's.

"I do not know how to thank you," Arabella said with difficulty.

"Please write to us." Trudy glanced at her brother. "That is, if you can."

"I will." Arabella went to take the items from Felicity, but Theo had already retrieved them and was holding them in his hands. There was much more she wanted to say but couldn't. "I have left some clothing behind that I hope you will find good use for."

Trudy reached out and pulled her into an embrace that caused Arabella to gulp back tears. When they stepped outdoors, a dry breeze swept some of the leaves from the trees and hurled them down the road. Theo's carriage stood in front, with the footman at the bridle. It was an open tilbury, so there would be no private conversation as they drove to the hotel, but perhaps that was for the best.

Theo helped Arabella into the sprung seat, then took the reins from his footman and climbed in on his side. "I'll swing back around for you," he called out to the footman before driving away. Perhaps they would have some privacy after all, but what was there left to say?

"If you can, ask your brother-in-law to bring you to Lincolnshire," Theo said as they drove forward, his horse pulling the carriage steadily toward her fate. "The Townsends and the Greys are there, and they might be able to help you."

"I will try," Arabella answered. In truth, she little cared where she went with the mantle of despondency that had settled around her.

Theo wove along the streets that became narrower and more congested as they neared the center of town. He kept his eyes fixed on the road, and she did the same. From a distance, she saw the name of the inn on a swinging sign and knew that her brief respite was over. It also meant she would be reunited with David, if Mr. Northwick had spoken true.

"We are nearly there, although I must tell you something before we arrive." Theo still didn't look at her, and his voice had gone a notch deeper. He maneuvered a difficult passage, then glanced at her.

"I love you. I will always love you. And I want you to remember that—especially when life proves difficult."

He turned his eyes back to the road and she looked up at his profile. "I love you too, Theo. I wish..." Her voice failed her. She swallowed hard. "But then, it has never mattered what I wished."

They were at the front entrance to the inn, and from where Arabella sat, she could see through the small panes of glass into the tap room of the inn. Mr. Northwick was there holding David, looking around the room and drinking a glass of ale, likely confident of her arrival. Her disgust that he would bring her boy into such a place warred with her relief at being reunited with her son.

Theo indicated for a boy standing nearby to come and hold the horse's head while he stepped down and went around the carriage. He lifted his hand to her and his eyes went up with it. The lines around his mouth were pronounced as he helped her down and led her over to the door of the inn. A servant opened it for them, and he tugged her to a stop.

"I shall not go in," he said.

She met his gaze, then dropped hers, shaking her head. "No. No, I suppose there is no point in doing so. Goodbye, Theo."

Arabella didn't look at his face or wait for a response but stepped forward into the dark tap room, blinking her eyes to accustom them to the darkness. When she could see, she hurried over to where Mr. Northwick held her son, who now turned at the movement and saw her.

"Mama," he called out and stretched his arms out suddenly so that she could retrieve him.

She hugged him tight and began to sob quietly into his neck in spite of the crowds. She no longer cared what anyone thought. The single hour that she was away from her son had ripped her apart, and the thought that she might never see him again—the thought that he might have feared she had abandoned him... Any pain she felt in parting from Theo was swallowed up in the sensation of relief at holding David again. She had made the right choice.

"Let us not make a scene," Mr. Northwick said dryly, taking her elbow in a firm grip and leading her out of the tap room and into a private parlor. "Do not think I intended for us to eat in the common room like someone of vulgar birth. I was merely waiting for you there, and I would have appreciated more restraint on your part."

Arabella did not reply, but stemmed the flow of her tears, focusing on cooing soft words into David's ear, who was content to be held by her. She sat at the place her brother-in-law indicated, mainly because she could not remain on her feet any longer. The emotion and exhaustion of the day had been too great for her. She waited while Mr. Northwick went to the door and called for the servant to bring their dinner. Arabella decided she would eat and also encourage David to eat. She must keep up her strength.

When the food was brought in, Mr. Northwick kept up a stream of commonplaces while Arabella focused on feeding David and eating something herself. She answered only when required.

As she had already chosen her lot and had accepted becoming his wife, it was time to be as wise as a serpent and innocent as a dove. Her chief objective was to bring David up to manhood, when he might inherit what was properly his. She cared for nothing else and therefore must not show how great an aversion she had to her brother-in-law. But then, she'd already had practice doing that with Josiah.

"I will show you to your room. You will see how generous I can be despite the way you have treated me. I've had a cot brought there, so you might keep David with you all night." Mr. Northwick gestured up the stairs, and she began to climb them, treasuring each moment for what it was. She would have a private room with David.

Perhaps she could slip out in the dead of night... Could she? How would she gain access to the finances she needed? She would not be able to return to Theo for help. It would be the first place her brother-in-law searched.

When he opened the door to her room, she remembered what Theo had asked of her and met Mr. Northwick's gaze fully for the first time that day, forcing herself not to reveal her inner terror.

"Where will we be going from here? Do we return to Lincolnshire or to London?" She held her breath while waiting for him to respond. She began to think of any reason that might appeal to him to choose Thimbleby and was prepared to beg. Theo was right—having friends nearby could only help.

He stared at her for a long moment before answering. "I have decided to return to Lincolnshire. After all, my business there was not yet concluded before I was forced to leave it in search of you."

And yet you went to London, she thought. The second thought came hard upon the first. *He had probably hoped to find me there.*

There was no point in saying more, since that was precisely where she wished to go. She nodded and went into the room, careful to hide any signs of relief in his choice of destinations. It would not be beyond him to change it just to spite her.

Mr. Northwick remained at the threshold and did not follow her into the room, much to her relief. But he reached his arm around the door and pulled the key out of the hole. "I will be keeping this. I would not wish for you to be tempted again in a way that would result in an unhappy outcome for either of us."

He raised the key and gave her a look of significance before closing the door. She heard the lock turn on the other side.

Arabella sat on the bed with a long exhale and looked at David on her lap. He climbed up and stood on her knees, looking around at the room. She would remember the small mercies. Tonight, it was just her and David, and that was a very great mercy.

She smiled at him and brushed his hair from his forehead. He was sucking on his fingers again, which he had almost ceased to do since arriving in Trudy's household.

"Ah, my sweet David," she said with a smile as she brought him back to a seated position. She kissed the spot just below his cheek on his neck, making a sound that tickled him. He began to laugh, and she felt her heart ease.

Tonight she had absolutely everything she needed, and that was enough.

THE JOURNEY back to Lincolnshire took three days, and Mr. Northwick behaved as much like a gentleman as a man such as he was capable. He explained that now that she'd agreed to marry him, she would see just how much life with him would suit her. She needn't worry about decisions that were too complicated for her but must leave it all in his hands. And in what was only a thinly veiled threat, he added that as long as she was a docile and submissive wife, she would have as much time as she wished with David and with any future children they might have.

This reassurance was offset when she met his insistence that she eat something with the words, "I told you I am not hungry," and he responded by gripping her arm hard and telling her that as she did not know when their next stop might be, she had best heed him.

When they finally pulled up in front of Penwood Estate, Arabella's arms and legs were tense from the strain of appearing perfectly docile while preparing herself for an unfriendly move on the part of her brother-in-law. She also worked hard to keep David happy on the voyage, for any threat of tears caused Mr. Northwick to show exasperation.

She followed him out of the carriage and looked up at the manor and the dependencies that were attached to one side— letting her attention roam to the arch cut through the stone wall leading to the stables. The sight sustained her and gave her strength. This was the only place she had ever in her life felt at home, and it was because she had made friends here. True, it had not happened in her first visit while Josiah was still alive, but since she had been widowed, she met Honoria and Philip, and

Christine. Even Gus had been something of a friend, when he was not pressing his interest.

And she had met Theo here. She suspected—no, she *knew*—that she would never love another man again. He would move on with his life. He needed an heir, and there was nothing holding him back from marrying someone else. He had probably been ready to move on the moment he saw that all of his interest had come to nothing, despite his love for her. After all, he had escorted her to the inn as she had asked him to, but had not come inside. They both knew there was no point in his doing so. He would love again, but not she.

She turned to her brother-in-law, who had paused in his steps, then followed his gaze to the front entrance. There was a carriage there, and coming out of the front door were two women she recognized immediately. Her heart gave a great leap —an impossible ray of happiness amid the gloom.

"Honoria," she said, moving forward. She could not help herself though Mr. Northwick was watching. "Christine. This is the most delightful surprise. We have only just arrived from—" She caught herself. "From London. The visit lasted longer than expected. Will you come in for tea?"

She did not look behind her to witness Mr. Northwick's reaction to that. He might punish her later, but she would have her friends *now*.

Honoria met her, smiling. "We would be delighted, although —are you sure? Perhaps you will need time to freshen up or rest after your travel?"

"Not at all," Arabella assured her. She accepted Honoria's hug and Christine's hand on her arm.

"Welcome home, David," Honoria greeted her son, smiling at him and holding out her hands. In that decisive way her son had, he seemed to remember that Honoria was a welcome set of arms. He leaned forward and allowed her to take him.

At once, Arabella was pounds lighter and not just in the very literal sense. She had not stopped carrying David, or holding his hand, or sleeping with him in the inns where they stopped. She would not let him out of her sight. But to know that he was being loved by someone she trusted, and that she could just care for herself for a moment, was a relief so immense she felt her smile broaden despite all that was at stake.

"Do come in. I will speak to the housekeeper." She went inside, not daring to look at what her brother-in-law made of this show of spirit. He had accepted it early on in her widowhood, but as time marched forward, the noose around her liberty cinched tight.

"I will go find Nurse," Mr. Northwick said from behind her. "She will be anxious to have David in her care again."

She ignored him and ushered the women into the drawing room. She refused to let her heart sink at the idea that Mrs. Billings would take over the complete care of her son as she had done in the past. Arabella had grown too comfortable and happy at having David with her at all times. It would be heartbreaking to give that up.

When they went into the spacious drawing room, she turned to her friends. "If you will care for David, I will go see about having a tray of tea brought. It will be faster if I go to the kitchen myself."

"Wait," Honoria said. "Don't go just yet, for I am not sure if we will have time with only the three of us again."

At a subtle gesture from Christine, Honoria moved farther into the drawing room, away from the door. She gave her finger to David to play with and he began to tug at it.

"We received a letter from Theo just this morning," she said in a hushed voice. "He told us all that has happened and paid dear to have it expedited so we might receive it straight away. It is providential that we arrived even before you did, so we could be here to welcome you."

Against her will—for Arabella was trying to keep her emotions entirely in check—her eyes filled with tears at this sign of grace and hope. At this, Christine came and put her arm around Arabella's shoulder. She had friends here. And she would think about Theo's noble gesture later in the privacy of her room.

"I don't know when you left Lincolnshire," Honoria continued, "But we saw Mr. Northwick in town two days after you were supposed to have left for London, and he blamed the delay on you being unwell. I gave him a note to pass on to you."

"That was very likely opened," Arabella added.

"It contained nothing to cause you alarm," Honoria assured her. "It was just to let you know that we hoped to see you once you were recovered. But now, Theo has told us everything in his letter. We are determined to do all we can to be a friend to you, though *all* does not appear to include freedom, if not even Theo was able to do that."

There was a sound coming from the corridor, and Arabella spoke clearly in a credibly emotionless voice. "I am sorry not to have let you know about the change in our travel plans. I appreciate your forbearance in coming to visit again."

"Well, it is partially my fault," Honoria replied in a tone that matched Arabella's. "If I had paid another visit sooner, I would have seen you before you left. But you see, we were particularly taken up with the renovations for the spa. They succeeded in putting in the new roof and are even now whitewashing the walls. You must come and see it."

The door opened, and the nurse entered. When Mrs. Billings spied Arabella's guests and David in Honoria's arms, she paused and curtsied in front of them.

"Good afternoon, Miss Bassett. Miss Grey. I'll see to little David now, ma'am," she said, her tone showing that she expected no opposition. Mr. Northwick entered the room behind her.

"It is Mrs. Townsend now." Honoria looked pointedly at Arabella and—despite a sweet smile—said in a voice that held an edge of steel, "Do you wish for your son to go with his nurse?"

This show of solidarity breathed hope into Arabella. She had dreaded the return to Penwood, where no one would be on hand to lend her support. Instead, thanks to Theo, her welcome was unmistakably threaded with goodness.

She glanced at Mr. Northwick, knowing some battles were not worth the strength to fight. "Yes, David will need a bath after his journey."

Arabella reached out and took him from Honoria, but when she attempted to give him to Mrs. Billings, David clung to her and began to howl in protest. The delightful sensation of being wanted was accompanied by pain as she listened to David's tears. She needed to avoid trouble, and the easiest way to do so was to force him into Mrs. Billings's arms.

"I will come to see you after you've had your bath and supper," she murmured into his ear, then handed him to Mrs. Billings, attempting to shield her heart from his cry that was audible from the echoing corridor and all the way up the stairwell.

"Have you called for tea?" Mr. Northwick asked.

"I've had no time, but I shall do so now." Arabella went over to the bell pull, abandoning the idea of going to the kitchen. She would not leave her friends alone with Mr. Northwick, nor did she wish to waste any minute of her time with them. There was no way of knowing if she would be allowed to resume her visits again.

Tea was brought, and Christine and Honoria shared the local gossip that included two new babies being born, Philip's abundant spring harvest due to the irrigation canal he had dug, the Mercer's son who had come home from the war and married a local girl, and other news of that nature.

Mr. Northwick was at pains to show himself to be agreeable company, so much so that Arabella was convinced no one could believe him capable of forcing her to choose between an unwanted marriage or her son. Both Christine and Honoria were exceedingly polite to him, which Arabella noticed had the effect of making him more affable. He took it as tribute due, and she at last understood that far from believing in his innocence, they were doing it for her sake, to protect her from his ill humor.

When at last Arabella walked her friends to the front door, with Mr. Northwick accompanying her every step, Christine smiled and kissed her cheek. And when Honoria turned to go, she gave her hand a significant squeeze that seemed to Arabella to promise continued support and friendship, in whatever form it might be allowed.

CHAPTER 18

For the first two days upon arriving in Lincolnshire, Arabella hid in her room or in the nursery, but it began to appear as though she would not need to hide. Mr. Northwick was surprisingly forbearing about the fact that she did not choose to meet him for dinner, nor did he question when she remained least in sight. He even stayed silent about Honoria and Christine's visit, stating only that, while she might receive visits, he did not wish her to pay any until they were safely married. Surely, she would understand that she had not precisely won his trust.

She had not expected such restraint from *him*. The only thing that could explain his behavior was that he seemed more and more distracted by some problem that weighed upon him. Mr. Weald arrived the day after they returned, and Arabella caught a glimpse of his back as he followed Mr. Northwick into the study, where they closeted themselves for two hours.

She did not dare to listen in an overt manner, but her brother-in-law's sleepwalking that she'd overheard before fleeing Penwood, combined with the details she'd read in the journal, caused her to slow her steps as she went by the study in case a chance word spoken might shed more light on his activities. The conversation inside sounded anything but genial, but she could not make anything out without risking being caught eavesdropping.

It was fortunate for her that she had not remained outside of the study, because seconds after she'd passed the room and disappeared into the library, she heard the door slam open and Mr. Weald's voice raised in anger.

"I told you I didn't want any part of that. That's a hanging offense, and I have my limits."

"Keep your voice down. All that's required is a bit of courage," Mr. Northwick replied. "Listen, this is not a conversation for now. Let us focus on what's coming in tonight."

Arabella heard no more, because Mr. Northwick accompanied Mr. Weald outdoors, where he presumably saw him off on whatever mission they had agreed upon. She paused, catching her breath at having nearly collided with the men. She did not want them to associate her in any way with their activities, despite wondering if it would help her to have proof of wrongdoing. But no—such a thing was too dangerous. It was better that she discover what she could by chance.

David did not seem to be overly traumatized by the transition to his old home. He now accepted Nurse's ministrations without fussing. And although he showed an inclination to favor his mother when she was in the room, he no longer cried if Nurse whisked him away for some imagined need. So Arabella began to relax incrementally. She did not send a note to Honoria and Christine for fear of her mail being intercepted, but she was rewarded with another visit within a week. This time it was Christine on her own, and as fortune favored her, it coincided with Mr. Northwick's departure on some errand. She ushered Christine into the drawing room, finding her more loquacious than usual.

"Honoria was unable to accompany me at the last minute for she has been taken unwell, but I did not wish to put off my visit." Christine smiled at Arabella, who realized that it was the first time she was meeting her alone. She had always felt closer to Honoria, but perhaps that was for lack of opportunity.

"It was most kind of you to come. I cannot tell you how much I rely on your visits," she replied as soon as they were alone in the drawing room, and she had rung for tea to be brought. It had never been her habit to show any vulnerability or need, but Arabella had begun to realize the value of female friendships, and she longed to nurture hers.

"Do you?" Christine exclaimed. "Well then, I am doubly glad I decided to come on my own. Are you able to ride into Horn-castle to pay us a visit as well?"

Arabella shook her head, replying in a low voice in case any servants were spying on her. "Mr. Northwick has forbidden me to leave the house until we are married." She refrained from shuddering over the thought of a match that was so distasteful to her.

"Is there nothing you can do to avoid this marriage?" Christine's brow furrowed. "I know my brother expressed interest once. This is most forward of me, but is it lack of an alternative suitor?"

"Oh no." Thinking of Theo's proposal, Arabella's voice came out more forcefully than she had meant, and she blushed.

"To own the truth, I...I had another offer. But I was obliged to give up the idea, for it would mean losing all access to my son, and I cannot do that no matter how much I long to marry—" She clamped her lips shut. She had said too much.

"Theo," Christine guessed with a gentle smile. "He is a most worthy gentleman."

When she said no more, a surge of jealousy rose up in Arabella that was so strong it stole her breath. Christine loved Theo, too. And what was more, *she* was free to marry him. Arabella was certain it would end up happening in just that way, since her best friend was married to Theo's cousin. How unfair life was.

She turned away, knowing her face was still warm from exposed emotion, and suddenly the idea of taking tea together seemed too much. If only Christine would leave right away. Why did she have to come and torment her with her freedom?

Christine cleared her throat and waited until Arabella met her regard. Then she smiled in a way that was so unlike what Arabella knew of her—so full of mischief and determination. "Well then, I am even more determined to find a way—any way —for you to be free of this burden so you might marry your love. Tell me what you know of your brother-in-law."

Arabella was so stunned at the swift transformation of the Christine she thought she knew into the true Christine, she had to laugh. Rose came in through the open door at that moment, carrying the tea tray, and Arabella was unable to warn her friend that they were not alone before Christine added, "Is there anything Mr. Northwick might want more than the guardianship of your son?"

At the sound of the plates rattling on the tray, Christine shot her a look of alarm. Arabella was uneasy, but the truth was if any of the servants were to hear such an indiscreet comment, she would choose Rose. However, they must pretend as though nothing had been said and hope the maid would forget it.

The tray consisted of a generous selection of cakes and fruits, along with fragrantly brewed tea. She was grateful she had never had to fight to convince the cook to show proper hospitality when there were guests. It was something her husband had expected, and it had outlasted his death. When all had been laid out, Rose stood to the side and folded her hands, and Arabella bit her lip, wondering if she should send her away—wondering if she had misjudged the maid's trustworthiness.

She steeped the tea and handed a cup to Christine. "Please help yourself to anything you like. Honoria is always praising your abilities in the kitchen, so I hope my offering will not disappoint."

"As long as it is sweet, I shall most likely appreciate it," Christine said, heaping her plate.

Attempting a natural pose, Arabella turned to Rose. "Thank you. That will be all."

Rose turned to go but then slowed her steps. "Excuse me, ma'am. I did not mean to overhear, but the door was open." She glanced at Christine, who then turned to Arabella with a guilty look.

The maid walked back until she was very near to them and could speak in a low voice. "The other day, Mr. Northwick was escorting his guest to the stables, and he passed by the window in the kitchen, where I was heating the water for tea. He was telling his guest—that Mr. Weald, who's not a gentleman for all he says he is—how to dye the hemlock leaves so they look like tobacco."

Arabella turned an amazed stare from the maid to Christine. In truth, she did not doubt Rose for a minute, but why should she tell her this now?

As though she had read her mind, Rose added, "I'm allus being accused of stepping above my station, and perhaps that's so. But I think he's mixed up in ought he shouldn't be, and I think it wrong of the master to keep ye here like this, so there— I've said it."

Having done so, she glanced one more time at Arabella, who gave her a reassuring look. "Thank you for this information, Rose."

The maid left, taking care to close the door firmly behind her. Arabella sent a significant look to Christine. "As you have just seen, I must be very discreet with what I am telling you, for there might be other listening ears who are less friendly."

Christine nodded, her tea momentarily forgotten. "I had not thought I was speaking so loudly. But it seems like she answered my question, in a manner of speaking. Your brother-in-law appears to stop at nothing, no matter what he's after."

"From what I've witnessed, I can only believe that to be true. I certainly cannot trust him with my son. In fact, the event that caused me to flee—and everything I tell you, you are free to share with Honoria and Philip, and...even Gus, for I consider you all true friends." She paused, holding her breath, as she remembered the event in question.

"Mr. Northwick held my son outside of a window, and I was terrified he was going to drop him."

Christine turned pale. "What happened next?"

"I was behind him, and I didn't make a sound. I was so afraid that if he was startled he would lose his grip. He said something about not doing it that day, which led me to believe he could easily take my son's life. He saw me then, and somehow I knew I must pretend I was not frightened. I'm not sure why I thought that." Arabella set down her cup when her hands started to tremble.

"I understand," Christine said slowly. "When someone is evil like that, their behavior becomes unpredictable, especially if they have been caught out at a moment when their true nature shows."

She thought some more. "This alone cannot be used to prove him unfit for guardianship, but if what your maid says is true... there must be a reason he asked his associate for such a thing. No one dyes hemlock for innocent purposes."

Their conversation had been quiet, but Arabella dropped her voice even lower. "I might have the answer to that. Theo's brother-in-law works for the Board of Customs, and while I was in Newark, he wrote to Theo's sister recounting the case of two informers who'd both died from having their tobacco poisoned in London."

Christine's eyes widened. "Do you think Mr. Northwick had his hand in this? It is too bad that such a thing would be difficult to prove. Even if we could convince Rose to testify about what she heard, no one is likely to believe a maid over a gentleman."

Arabella needed no time to reflect further, for she had come to a decision. "When Josiah died, he left behind a journal that intimated—on the day of his death—that he had told his brother he would not be serving as guardian to my unborn child. There had been tension, I believe, over a money matter. I don't know when he told him, but there is a chance that his tobacco might have been tampered with, too—if Mr. Northwick is indeed the culprit. And I still have my husband's snuffbox."

Christine emitted a soft gasp. "It appears there is *much* here that could be used to prove him unfit as guardian to your son.

Smuggling, poisoning, reckless treatment of a child—we just need the proof." She clasped her hands. "You never told me how your husband died. *Could* he have been poisoned, do you think?"

"The doctor did not hint at any such thing. My husband was old, and he wasn't in the best of health. At the time, the doctor concluded it was an attack of the heart." Arabella thought back to his last day. He'd coughed a lot, but was he worse than usual? She could not say.

"What about the snuff?" Christine asked. "You said you kept his snuffbox. If we can prove the contents are poisoned, could you link it to your brother-in-law?"

Arabella thought about it. "I do not know. Josiah always liked his laced with a heavy perfume, and perhaps it hid the scent of poison. I'm not sure we can trace it to his brother, though. Could a doctor determine if poison was used based on the contents of the snuffbox?"

Christine thought for a minute. "Perhaps not a doctor, but surely an apothecary. I have one in Horncastle I can ask—his sister is a friend of ours. And he will remain discreet. Shall I do so? Do you have the box?"

"I do." Arabella got to her feet, just as the front door opened and the sounds of Mr. Northwick's voice reached them. She sat back down again, the blood draining from her face. "He is always here. I shall never escape him."

"Do not think that way," Christine urged. She spoke quickly as the sound of his voice approached the drawing room. "If you can go for a walk at some point today, leave it hidden in the grass near the front gate—on the right-hand side when you're facing the gates. Your property is on a public road, so no one will suspect anything if our carriage should pass by. I will simply have my footman get down as though to examine the horse's hooves, and I will retrieve the box. Just hide it close to the stone gate so I can find it."

The door to the drawing room opened, and Arabella had only time to nod quickly. Christine picked up her cup of cold tea with a steady hand, and after taking a sip, turned to see Mr. Northwick.

"Good day," she said. "I have just been enjoying a visit with your betrothed. May I offer you my felicitations?"

Arabella almost betrayed her surprise at Christine's words. She'd said what would most likely please Mr. Northwick and cause him the least amount of suspicion about the nature of their discussion.

His brows lifted, and he smiled. "She has told you about our upcoming nuptials, has she?"

"Indeed, she has," Christine said. "I hope you will permit us to assist in the celebrations in some way. Honoria and I might lend a hand in making the dress, for instance." Arabella could only wonder at Christine's hidden wealth of talents—in sewing, baking, and in duplicity when needed.

"Oh, that will not be necessary. I will hire the finest dressmaker Lincolnshire has to offer," Mr. Northwick replied. He added magnanimously, "However, you are free to come and assist in preparing for the wedding breakfast, which of course you will all be invited to. Even Mr. Grey, although I believe your brother was once smitten with my Arabella."

Christine smiled sweetly. "You have found him out, but as you see, he did not win her hand."

She stood. "Well, I believe I have overstayed my welcome, and I must be going. Arabella, you will see both of us much in the next fortnight. I hope you will not wish us away."

Arabella was able to laugh naturally, if only for how little she truly knew Christine, and how much she was coming to appreciate her. "I shall never wish for that."

Mr. Northwick held out his arm for Christine to take. "Arabella, there is no need for you to walk your friend to the door. I am already up, and I will see her out."

"Oh, then do let me say goodbye first." Christine came over and pulled Arabella into an embrace. She looked into her eyes and said, "You know you may rely on us for assistance over the coming weeks."

Arabella nodded, not trusting herself to speak. She wanted to believe in miracles—wanted to hope for good outcomes—but hope had been in vain in the past, and there was no guarantee she would have her happy ending.

And yet...her heart filled with something she'd never had before. It was the fullness of friendship and love. That alone made almost any prospect bearable.

CHAPTER 19

Theo stood at the window of his office and stared at the same dreary sight that had met his eyes for the last week. He had never realized how ugly the dirt roads and buildings and the muddy river banked by scraggly bushes could look. Then again, he had not thought those things ugly when he had been walking beside Arabella. When he had been kissing her on the path by the river. What a risk that had been— to kiss in broad daylight like that. A woman to whom he was not even betrothed. But he couldn't bring himself to regret the lapse. It was one of the precious memories he turned over in his mind when he particularly wanted to torture himself.

His last sight of her had been of her walking into that inn alone. He couldn't bear to accompany her inside and watch it all unfold. She was disappearing from his life, but he didn't want to see the man whose hand had brought it about. Northwick had already won everything else—everything of importance. He had guardianship of David and had found a way to bind Arabella into marriage. The man did not play fair, so of course he would win.

The night before leaving for Cornwall, Trudy came to eat dinner with him. Anthony had stayed at home too, as he had been in the habit of doing lately. It revealed a normally hidden vein of affection for his older brother that Theo appreciated. The dinner was copious, but he did not feel like eating any of it.

"When do you think she will marry?" Trudy asked gently when it was clear she could not expect conversation about more mundane matters.

"He said he wanted the banns to be read as soon as possible, so surely before the month is out," Theo said. "They would have to be read in London at her parish, but I'm not sure where his parish is. Lincolnshire? Or somewhere in Norfolk?"

He rested his arm on the table, too weary to pick up his fork. He didn't know that utter despair could sap the will of a person to eat—could sap the will to live.

"I'm sorry I was not able to find out more about the smuggling," Anthony said, not for the first time. "Despite my being certain he was part of some major operation in London, none of the other men I met knew who he was."

"Well, did you at least get inspiration for textiles?" Trudy asked.

Anthony's eyes brightened. "Indeed, I did." He turned to his brother. "The new weaving machines are something else. I've been playing around with them to try to create some new patterns. I've produced a few samples and shall have more soon. We will see how well it can sell."

Theo nodded but offered no comment. At this point, he did not care. He saw Trudy exchange a glance with Anthony as though urging him to say something.

"As a matter of fact," Anthony said after a studied moment, "I had a look at the accounting books."

The surprise of this statement brought Theo out of his misery. Anthony was not one to pour over financial ledgers. "You must have noticed how tight we are right now, then."

Anthony nodded. "But I project that we will be able to justify the expenditure of these new machines—and maybe some of those spinning mules—with my new patterns. I made contacts in London and have written to one of them who is eager to see what I have produced. He promised me an order if I could get him some good quality cloth that rivaled the stuff people are smuggling in from the Continent. He simply can't risk any more trouble with the law should the preventives catch him with more smuggled goods."

"You looked at the accounting?" Theo said. He was still stuck on this piece of novelty.

"It's impossible to see if a cloth venture is truly going to work without looking at all its components. One must have the idea for the design and access to the raw materials. But one must also know how much it costs to make and what it will sell for to know if it's worth it. The two go hand in hand," he explained, as though Theo were a novice to the mill. Trudy shot Theo an amused glance. "So I've sent off a sample to Mr. Bainesworth and am waiting to hear back. I expect to have a reply in three days."

"That is good work," Theo said. It was hard to lift his eyes— difficult to show interest in what his brother was doing when his own life seemed to be spiraling downwards. But he couldn't waste this opportunity to encourage his brother. Not when he was trying so hard. He glanced at Trudy, and she smiled at him approvingly.

The next couple of days were spent seeing Trudy and her children depart for their journey to Cornwall, then resolving another workers' dispute at the mill. Anthony intervened and met with each of the men responsible for different aspects of production until they were working together harmoniously. He was stepping up in a way that Theo would have been delighted to see if only he could find any reason to be delighted about anything.

Meaningless. Everything is meaningless.

Theo frowned and trod the familiar path back to the window to stare out at the bleak view. Except that today, the sun was shining, and it made the river sparkle enticingly. The weather refused to align itself with his mood. *It's all meaningless*, he thought again. The morose phrase went on and on in a loop in his mind. There was no reason to find anything delightful, now that the woman he loved was beyond his reach with no hope of remedy.

EMBOLDENED by Christine's artless duplicity regarding the nuptials, Arabella allowed herself to thaw slightly toward Mr. Northwick. She still did not dine with him or invite him to believe there was a softening of her heart toward him. *That* would have been beyond her power. But she did want him to be lulled into thinking she had entirely surrendered to her fate.

In a sense, she had. She'd faced the facts that there was very likely little that could be done—especially not in time—before she was forced to take the repulsive step of uniting herself with such a man. But she would not give up hope until she was sure there was no longer hope to be had. And even then, she would not give up—not even on a life that had little to recommend it. Her son deserved more.

In this spirit of confidence, she dared to follow Christine's instructions to leave the snuffbox with its contents near the gate, where her friend could find it and have it examined. And she went back two days later, her heart in her throat, and discovered that it was gone. She could only hope it had gone into the hands for which it was intended.

She recalled Mr. Northwick's efforts after her husband's death to retrieve whatever were Josiah's private effects. She had thought nothing of those efforts at the time and had replied that everything of note must be in his study. It hadn't occurred to her that a snuffbox or a pile of books could be worth mentioning. And since her brother-in-law had let the servant go who had sent the trunk to Lincolnshire under her orders—as he'd decided to trust no one he hadn't hired himself—he did not learn of its existence. The fact that he did not insist on finding the missing items could only be attributed to the fact that he didn't wish to raise suspicion by being overly insistent—or that he was not ready to show his true colors so early in her widowhood.

She went up to the nursery, where she was greeted by the happy sight of her son calling out, "Mama!" in the most gleeful voice. His chubby little legs carried him forward, and she picked him up. Her caresses were cut far too short by Mrs. Billings, who frowned at the display.

"Mrs. Northwick, Mr. Northwick has told me his nephew must not be pampered if he is to grow into the role for which he is designed. You must not give in to his childish whims."

"But he is a child," Arabella protested. She allowed Mrs. Billings to take him out of her arms and set him on the floor, once again feeling helpless. She tried to play with David in a more subdued manner than she had done but soon gave it up when his nurse called him to come and have some cake. Even a mother could not compete with sweets. She wandered downstairs after that, and when she caught sight of Mr. Northwick wearing a pronounced scowl, attempted to escape back to her room.

"Arabella," he commanded.

She stopped and turned to face him, her heart heavy. What was it now?

"I've just discovered a trunk full of Josiah's books in your room. After his death, you said you had nothing of his."

Arabella stared at him without blinking before saying the first thing that came into her mind. "What were you doing in my room? You have no right to be there."

He took no steps to move closer to her, but his menacing voice felt just as threatening.

"You will soon learn that it is my right to go anywhere I desire in this house. But lest you think to turn me from the matter at hand, there are some items missing. I never found them in his study, and now that I know you've been secreting his belongings in your room, I can only assume you know of their whereabouts."

Arabella was weary of being afraid. The only items she had taken from there were now in the possession of Theo and Christine. What would he do when he found out? She lifted her chin and spoke with deliberate calm.

"George, you are right in that as my future husband, everything in my room is yours. I invite you to look for the items there if you think I am keeping things from you. It is true I had a trunk placed there with Josiah's things, but it was so long ago I had forgotten its existence."

She looked down, amazed at her ability to mask her true feelings. "I think you must have suspected that Josiah and I did not share a tender attachment. I thought there was nothing in there but books on topics that held no interest for me and were too generic to hold any for you."

Mr. Northwick studied her, but she could tell that he had softened under her admission. He seemed to have believed her. Perhaps it was her calling him George and reminding him of their upcoming marriage—heaven forbid that it should take place. He smiled and came and put his fingers under her chin.

"I will have a more thorough look in your room, then, if you are inviting me to it. You can have no notion of what is important and what is not. A shame you did not remember the trunk when I first asked you of it, though."

"I am sorry." She shook her head, appearing to be regretful. "It was a bewildering time for me when Josiah died—and I, carrying his child. I was not able to remember things clearly."

"All the more reason you will benefit from my guidance, my dear." Mr. Northwick turned in the direction of the stairs. "I shall go look now. Do not fret if I cannot find what I am looking for. I shall not take it out on you. I suppose it hardly matters after all this time."

Thankfully, he did not expect an answer. Arabella went into the drawing room and sat on the sofa, staring straight ahead yet seeing nothing. She had to do whatever she could to escape marriage to him. Trudy's husband was following up on one trail, and Christine's apothecary friend on another.

And what about Theo? Had he already given her up as lost? This last question occupied her mind the longest.

CHAPTER 20

Two weeks had gone by, and Theo had even stopped shaving every day, or eating much of whatever was set before him on the tea tray. He stared at the numbers columns without comprehension and had stopped making any attempt to show an interest in the mill, especially when—even at his best—he had never felt all that strongly about it.

Mr. Barrett brought papers for him to look at, specifying that another copy had been given to his brother, since Mr. Anthony had begun to show an interest. Theo riffled through them, but the purchase orders listed held no meaning. He could not focus his mind on the names or amounts. To his right was a half-drunk cup of tea that had begun to stain the porcelain. He wondered how many days old it was. There was a plate of half-eaten cake as well, and he was surprised it was not crawling with insects. He touched it and found it dry as a bone. Did not the servants come in here and clean?

Oh, right. He had yelled at the one who had attempted to do so a few days ago. Theo sighed and dropped his head on his arms, hitting his nose on the desk in the bargain. The pain shot him upright as his eyes filled with tears. He got up from his desk and pinched his nose, expecting the flow of blood to follow. It felt like being on the losing end of a fight at the boxing saloon.

After a minute, he cautiously released his nose and found that it was not bleeding. A rush of good sensation followed the pain and then began to fade away slowly. He blinked.

What am I doing here?

Theo looked around his office as the thought took him hostage. What *was* he doing here? How could he have let Arabella walk out of his life without fighting for her? He had already done that once, when he'd proposed a courtship in Horncastle, and she replied that she was not free to contemplate it. He had been intrigued by her, but not invested enough to insist. Only then she had showed up at his house and stayed with his sister, and he had kissed her, and *by George,* he was invested!

He was the worst sort of lazy coward, leaving her to fend for herself against a villain such as Mr. Northwick. Even if nothing could be done to stop this marriage—even if Arabella herself told him he was standing in the way of a marriage she desired because it meant keeping her son—he would be there to be rejected by her a third time. He would watch her walk into the church on the day she married, though he had not been invited and would be the last person welcome. He would disregard the desires of his own heart and act as a helpless spectator to the very thing that caused him the most pain in the world.

But he would go.

In sudden determination, Theo marched forward and took hold of the latch to the door of his office that had stayed firmly shut these past weeks. He had vaguely remembered appearing at the mill each morning and remaining closeted in the office, until he eventually left it to go toss and turn each night in his bed.

Before he could open the door, it swung inward with such a force, Theo fell backwards. It was Anthony.

"Here you are. Theo, you look a mess, if you don't mind my saying it. You need a bath." His brother grabbed him by the elbow and led him to the two chairs that were placed next to the desk and sat him down. "But before you go, you need to hear this. Trudy sent me with news."

Theo stood and moved toward the door. "I don't have time

for this. I have to go to Arabella. I need to find a way to see her before it's too late."

"Vincent heard from some preventive up north. A man by the name of Jenkins. Our esteemed brother-in-law apparently sent you a letter about this as well, but wrote to Trudy just in case yours was delayed."

He didn't remember the last time he had looked through his mail. Then, as the familiar name registered, Theo stopped in his tracks.

"Jenkins? I've met him. What's this about?" He returned to his seat.

"Jenkins sent word to someone on the Board about one of Northwick's associates. The man has *turned* on him." There was an eager light in Anthony's eyes. "We'll get what we need from him to stop Northwick, but Vincent said he doesn't have it yet. Jenkins first has to convince this Weald fellow he won't be tried for his association with the free traders, and apparently that's not an easy feat, because he's in deep. In fact, he's going to need to run away to the Americas or something like that, and they need to persuade him not to do so until he's testified. If one of the smugglers finds him, he won't live to see nightfall."

"Weald! Arabella mentioned his name." Theo was up from his chair again. "So this is the proof we need to go after North-wick. Did Vincent say when they'd have more?"

"No. It's all on Jenkins. But at least you know where to find Northwick when it comes out. If you're set on going to Lincolnshire, I'll send word to Philip's estate the minute I hear more from Vincent."

"Then I must not waste any more time here." Theo started toward the door, but paused before leaving the room. "Anthony, can I rely upon you to run the mill in my absence? That is, you've been doing it lately anyway, so not much will change."

"Of course," Anthony replied. "I'm your brother. I'll do what-ever you need."

Theo went back and held out his hand, giving Anthony's a firm shake. Then he left before he could do something so unmanly as hug his brother, or cry from an excess of emotion—or both.

It was too late in the afternoon for Theo to start out and he chafed at the delay. He used the time to pack and to dash off a letter to Trudy, and one to Vincent in London, before settling down for a sleepless night which he broke before dawn. His carriage was hitched and he left by five o'clock in the morning, unable to stay another minute.

It took him two days to reach Boden, and if he had been able to demand it of his horses, he would have accomplished it in one. When at last he pulled up in front of the house, it was early afternoon, and he expected to see Honoria or Philip come out to greet him. But the footman who answered the door said they had gone out to the mine, so he continued on the path that led to the stables off the main road.

On the way, he passed the form of a woman bent over on the grass near the road. His eyes widened when he recognized Honoria.

"Easy, boys." He pulled his reins and slowed down. "Honoria! Are you ill?"

She looked up in surprise at the sound of his voice and put the back of her hand to her mouth. She looked positively ill, although he could see a smile appear as she dropped her hand. Her face was white with droplets of sweat on either side.

"Very ill," she said with a feeble laugh, "but nothing that six more months will not cure."

"What's this?" Theo laughed and climbed down from the carriage to give her a brief hug. "I'm to be an uncle! Or some sort of an uncle—whatever a cousin is. Where's Phil?"

"He's at the spa overseeing the work of putting in the borders around the thermal baths. I was to join him there, but I abandoned the idea when I felt too unwell."

She shook her head as he went to take her arm. "No, do not fret about me. I am accustomed to it. Go see Philip. He will want to know that you have arrived."

Relieved of this concern, Theo hurried to do just that when

she called out again. "Wait—why *are* you here? Is it for Arabella?"

He turned in his seat, holding the reins firmly. "Yes, for her. Do you have any news?"

"Some. She is not able to leave the house. She can receive visitors, and Christine thought it wise to act as though we supported the marriage. It seemed to be the right thing to do, for it has caused him to relax his vigilance around her. I witnessed this myself when I visited her yesterday—although his relaxing his stance did not extend to leaving us alone to be able to speak on anything of a confidential nature."

Theo's lips tightened, and he prepared to drive off, but Honoria held up her hand.

"There is just one other thing, and right now I know more about this than Philip, since Christine and Gus have just left the house. You will want to hear this." She had his full attention.

"Arabella was able to secret out her late husband's snuffbox, so that Christine could take it to the apothecary to have it examined. He thinks it was poisoned with hemlock. The smell is too similar, though it's a perfumed snuff variety, which partially hides it. Her husband was getting older and apparently had something of a heart condition, and this would have played on that problem, worsening it. As of now, there is no way of proving Northwick was the one to poison his brother, but we can have the mode of death changed and turn this into an investigation of murder"—she sent him a satisfied smile—"which should effectively hinder his wedding plans."

Theo's heart began to beat with excitement. Between Vincent's man, who had Northwick's associate, and his cousin and friends who had proof of poisoned snuff, they might really have something against him that would stick. He grinned—the first one in as long as he could remember.

"I cannot thank you enough for this. Do you think you can pass along a note to Arabella for me? I doubt I will be allowed within a stone's throw of her estate." He would tell her of his news after he saw Philip.

"Easily done," Honoria answered, looking healthier by the minute. "I promised Arabella in Mr. Northwick's hearing that I would come back and finalize the plans for the wedding breakfast, so I have a good excuse to go. I am sure I can pass along your letter without Mr. Northwick's being the wiser for it."

"Excellent. I'll come back to write something as soon as I can." Theo prepared to drive on. "Make sure you go home and rest. Your baby—and Philip—will need you in the best of shape."

She lifted her hand in a wave. "I am on my way. You've saved me the effort of going to tell my husband what I've just told you."

Theo drove on, suddenly eager to see Philip. He wanted to congratulate him on his happy news, and he had just the smallest glimmer of hope that he might have some good news himself, if all went according to his plan.

The mine had been drastically transformed, even since their wedding. The outside of it no longer looked like anything resembling its former eyesore. A façade had been built with cut limestone, and the entrance had been widened with windows installed. When he walked inside of it, he no longer had to blink in the darkness. Gone were the carved-out dirt walls. Now everything was paneled in wood and either whitewashed or left in varnished pine. He turned around, and blew out his admiration in a whistle.

"Theo!" Philip's sleeves were rolled up from the heat inside, and he walked toward his cousin, a smile on his face. "I am mighty glad to see you. Let me have a word with my foreman and we can go outside and talk there. The smell in here is still a bit strong. We're working on ventilation."

When Philip had finished relaying his instructions, they went outdoors in the cooler autumn air that reminded Theo of his stay a year ago—before marriage was even a thought in Philip's head.

"A lot has happened in a year, wouldn't you say?" he observed.

"I would indeed." Philip clapped him on the back. "I am the happiest of men."

Theo smiled. A week ago, he would not have been able to hear such grating optimism, but now he was more hopeful. "Allow me to offer you my sincerest congratulations. I passed Honoria on the way here."

Philip grinned broadly. "Our good news is becoming obvious, I must suppose?"

"I hadn't noticed," Theo said, chuckling. "It was rather her green tint that gave her away."

"Oh, that." Philip groaned. "She hasn't had the easiest time of it. But tell me about you. What brought you here?"

He had worded the question delicately, but Theo would be more blunt. "I've come to stop Arabella's farce of a betrothal to that man. On the way here, Honoria told me the apothecary has determined that the snuff old Northwick used had been poisoned."

"We were expecting that, even before we received his assessment," Philip replied. "'Tis a shame we cannot prove it was him."

"There is reason enough to search his belongings, however," Theo said. "Arabella's husband kept a journal about his extensive smuggling practices—stupid thing to do, if you ask me—and it appears that Northwick is still involved, because I just received word from Trudy's husband that his associate has squealed."

Philip whistled silently. "When a man is bent on evil, it's bound to come out. It looks like his day of reckoning is near." He rested a hand on Theo's arm. "Wait here while I give instructions for my servant to bring my horse to the stables. I'll ride with you."

When that was done, Theo and Philip climbed into his carriage and rode along the fields containing Philip's irrigation project.

Theo lifted his hand to shade his eyes. "You've got a harvest to bring in soon, I believe."

"We have to bring it in this week before it's too late. I am pleased to have enough to occupy me, but at times running the estate is hectic. I have only to set one thing in motion, and another—"

He broke off suddenly, his eyes alight. "By the bye, I've acquired another stud horse. My name is starting to reach the right circles."

"I'm happy for you," Theo said, and meant it, despite his own uncertain situation. They rode some before he spoke on the topic that consumed him most.

"It is likely wrong of me, but I don't even care overmuch if Northwick gets condemned for the death of his brother. I am not in the business of revenge, although every man should make it his duty to see justice done. It is only that I want to free Arabella from his grip. That is all that concerns me now. I will do anything to achieve that."

"We will start with what we have," Philip said. "The apothecary can write up his findings, and Trudy's husband will not rest, I imagine, until he has followed up every lead on the smuggling. Let's focus on arranging a way for you to see Arabella in the meantime."

"I am to understand she cannot leave her house," Theo said, not without a pang.

"Perhaps not." Philip grinned suddenly. "But I once climbed up the wall and into Honoria's window, when her father forbade me to see her."

A laugh was startled out of Theo. "Did you? I don't suppose you got caught?"

Philip shook his head, his lips pinched together as he smiled. "But it gave me an idea. Perhaps we might arrange for a night meeting. I will tell Honoria to visit her and see if it can be done."

Theo put his arm around Philip and clapped his hand on his shoulder. "I could not ask for anything more."

CHAPTER 21

A rabella sought out the drawing room, knowing her brother-in-law was closeted in the study. It was not Mr. Weald this time, but someone of coarser appearance. She had not seen Mr. Weald since Rose's disclosure.

Mrs. Billings had already chased her from the nursery. She'd then sat through Cook's suggestions for a wedding breakfast menu, which Arabella needed to show interest in if she was to continue the charade of appearing eager for the upcoming nuptials. The wedding banns had been read twice already, both in Thimbleby and in the London parish in which she had grown up. Mr. Northwick was taking care of all these details, despite being surprisingly vague about setting an actual wedding date.

A knock sounded on the front door, bringing her to her feet with excitement. When she went into the corridor, it was just as she'd hoped. Honoria and Christine stood at the entrance and were in the process of removing their bonnets. Arabella's hope was cut short, however, when the door to the study opened and Mr. Northwick exited, ushering out his new associate at what she noted was an accelerated pace. It was either because he did not think his associate reflected well upon him...or he did not want her to spend time alone with her friends.

"Good afternoon, Mrs. Townsend. Miss Grey." Mr. Northwick stopped to greet them with a perfectly cordial bow, not bothering to introduce his associate.

As he brought him to the door, terminating their conversation in a hushed manner, Arabella smiled at her friends and showed them into the drawing room. They had no reprieve there, however, for a maid was dusting the mantelpiece. It was one of the maids she liked the least, for she was always putting herself forward.

"Missy, you may leave us now," Arabella said.

"The master said I was to dust this entire room today, ma'am," she replied without glancing at her mistress.

Perhaps if the maid had said so apologetically, Arabella would have been inclined to forgive her. Mr. Northwick was an exacting master. She saw Honoria's face harden at this sign of insolence, but she did not need her friend this time.

"You will leave at once and finish when my guests have departed," she said, facing the maid squarely.

The girl looked at Arabella, then dropped her feather duster to her side and walked to the other end of the drawing room at a slow pace that made Arabella want to scream.

As soon as the maid's back was turned, Honoria slipped a letter to Arabella, who folded it and wordlessly tucked it into the sleeve of her dress. She had nothing else with her in which to conceal it, and the sounds of Mr. Northwick's footsteps increased in volume as he approached the drawing room. She'd had no time to find out who the letter was from before Christine slipped her arm through Arabella's and walked together with her toward the chairs in the center of the room.

"We have been working on the flower arrangements for your wedding breakfast but wanted to discuss some of the place settings with you. It would be simpler if you came to us," she said conversationally, surely aware that Mr. Northwick had come in behind them and would have been listening. "That way you can approve our ideas yourself."

"Of course," Arabella replied, wondering if this public invitation would alter Mr. Northwick's determination that she not leave the premises. She was desperate to have more than a few stolen minutes with her friends and to be strengthened by their unabated support. The wedding was drawing too close for her comfort.

Mr. Northwick cleared his throat. "Arabella, my dear, why don't you see to the tea tray?"

Arabella almost choked at the sound of the endearment on his lips. It was the first time he'd called her such a thing publicly. Pinching her lips in a polite smile, she stood and went over to the bell pull but was stopped by his voice.

"I think it is better that you see to the tray yourself, as any good hostess must wish to ensure that nothing will be lacking."

Arabella flicked her eyes his way then glanced at Honoria, who seemed to be sending her waves of strength through her regard. What Arabella *wished* to retort was that any good hostess must have already spoken to the housekeeper about what was to appear on the tea tray whenever guests arrived. But it was clear Mr. Northwick wanted a few minutes in which to converse with her guests. To what aim, she did not know. But if she tried to thwart him, he would likely find some way to bring it back down on her head—and she did trust her friends.

She hurried downstairs and had a few quick words with the housekeeper, who put on the tray exactly what Arabella expected she would, and then returned to intervene in the *tête-à-tête* Mr. Northwick was inflicting upon her friends. The letter chafed against her arm as it rested inside her gathered sleeve, but she would not take it out until she could be sure of her privacy.

"It is a shame you must leave us so soon," Honoria was saying when Arabella entered the room. "We had all hoped you might be married here so we would be allowed to share in the celebration."

"Alas, my business in London awaits. Therefore, we are obliged to be married there," Mr. Northwick replied smoothly. He looked up as Arabella walked in. "I was just telling our neighbors that we will be traveling to London tomorrow for the wedding. Therefore, the plans for a wedding celebration will have to await our return."

Arabella felt the blood drain from her face. Why was he taking her from Lincolnshire? All of her friends were here. She had no support in London. And did that mean the wedding would happen sooner? As she regained her seat, she focused all of her strength on removing any reaction from her face. When she was sure of herself, she met his gaze.

"I was not aware of this change in plans. But...then we will have to postpone our wedding, it seems, for we made plans with the parish to have the ceremony here." Perhaps it was good news after all.

"Does that sadden you, dear?" he asked with a tenderness that sickened her. "I am glad to hear it, for I am quite distraught over the delay, myself."

Sad was not the word Arabella most identified with in this instance. It was more akin to disgust. And the accompanying despair stole her tongue. She sat quietly, and after an awkward pause, Honoria smoothed her skirt.

"This is terribly sudden, but I daresay the wedding will be delightful. I hope we shall have the pleasure of your company once you return to Lincolnshire." She pasted on a smile. "Perhaps we might assist you with packing for your trip?"

"I have the servants to see to that, of course, Mrs. Townsend, although it is kind of you to offer," Mr. Northwick said firmly.

There wasn't much more to say after that, and Christine and Honoria were collecting their belongings by the time the tea tray arrived, apologizing for their rapid departure but excusing it based on the notion that the Northwicks must need to ready themselves for their journey.

Numb, Arabella nodded. Her delight in seeing them had turned so quickly into utter hopelessness. Earlier, the height of her ambition had been to receive callers to break up the monotony of the day—and hopefully bring her word of the apothecary's professional opinion that the snuff had been poisoned. Now she was utterly alone. Her friends left without a further word and her only consolation was that she had a letter from them that might offer something in the way of good news. It was amazing how a person clung to small tokens of mercy, even when all hope seemed to be lost.

She was not yet able to escape, for when Mr. Northwick returned from seeing her friends to the door, he resumed his seat across from her, his eyes settled on her in a way that brought a tingle to her spine.

"Surprised? If you had met me for dinner these past nights or attempted to cross my path this week, I could have informed you of it. But you are never to be found. How was I to let you know I had decided we would be married in London?

"You had best oversee your maid's packing of your trunk if we are to have an early departure. Mrs. Billings has taken care of everything for David."

Her brother-in-law had given the nurse instructions before he'd informed her of their journey?

He left the room without another word, as though he expected total obedience. Too tired to move, Arabella removed the letter from her sleeve, smoothing out its folds. The front was blank, so she pulled at the seal, ripping the paper. At the bottom of the note was Theo's name, and she sat up with a sharp intake of breath, suddenly aware of how reckless she had been to read the letter in public.

Dearest Arabella,

I have come to Lincolnshire and am staying with Philip. I could not bear to be away from you. I have not ceased my attempts to free you and David from the grip of your brother-in-law. This time, I hope to have met with some success. Come meet me tonight after midnight, if you can. I will be standing outside of the western wall waiting for you. I must see you.

Yours forever,

Theo

A sound in the corridor caused Arabella to fold the paper in haste and stuff it back into her sleeve. She stood and went to her room, where Rose and another maid were already in the process of packing her trunk. She did not need to direct them as they appeared to have received orders without her help. Rose sent her a sympathetic look, then continued her task.

Suddenly, Arabella had to see David.

In the nursery, Mrs. Billings was directing the maid as to what she should put in each trunk and how to arrange the items. David was left to himself and was pulling out toys, unhindered for once by his nurse. Arabella ignored Mrs. Billings's muttered greeting that sounded more like a reproach, and went over to her son, who lifted his arms to her. She held him tight, drawing strength from the embrace. She buried her face in his hair as one thought seized her and gained in resolution.

I must not subject David to Mr. Northwick for the rest of his life. I must not subject myself.

As this new determination turned over in her mind, she sat with him on the floor, talking to him and listening to his mostly incomprehensible babble as he played and showed her his toys. Mrs. Billings sniffed once or twice and made a vague reference to mistresses who did not know how to allow servants to see to the packing. This was one of the milder criticisms she had dished out upon Arabella's return, relishing, it seemed, in how little resistance her mistress offered up. This time, Arabella ignored her entirely. Her mind was busy grappling with how she might convince Mr. Northwick to put an end to this farce.

She could not flee again with David. She *would* see Theo— the desire was too great to refuse—but she already knew they could not run together. Theo could never live his life in such a furtive way. Her only hope was to reason with, threaten, or cajole her brother-in-law into leaving David's care to her—and without sacrificing herself. When she'd made her decision at last, she stood.

"Nurse, I will come back and put him to sleep tonight." She turned to David without waiting for an answer and smiled at him. "I will return after you've eaten, all right?"

David seemed inclined to fuss when she left, but she put her finger to her lips and smiled. "Be a good boy. I will be back."

Then she went downstairs and knocked on the study before she lost her nerve.

"Come in." The voice was curt. He was likely expecting a servant.

Arabella opened the door and walked in, coming to stand before his desk. Mr. Northwick did not betray his surprise at seeing her with so much as a flicker of his eyelid. "Yes?"

"I am not going to leave for London tomorrow, and I am not going to marry you, George," she said. The silence following her declaration seemed to ring in her ears with her heartbeat.

He paused, narrowing his eyes at her, as she breathed slowly in and out. She must not lose courage, but must see this through.

"You are willing to abandon your son, then?"

"I will not be abandoning my son. He will remain with me here at Penwood. You can serve as guardian without having to live with him, but a young boy's place is with his mother until he goes off to school. I shall oblige you by not marrying anyone else."

She kept her head high and held on to her dignity. It was all she had. This was the best she could put on the negotiating table, although it would cost her the only man she had ever loved.

He stacked the papers on the desk and stood. "I will think it over and give you my answer later this evening."

Her eyes widened at this unexpected victory, and for the first time she smiled at her brother-in-law with sincerity. She had not expected him to capitulate, and he had not quite—but the fact that he was considering her request was beyond anything she could have imagined from him.

"Thank you." Impulsively, she reached out her hand, but when he did not offer his in return, she dropped hers to her side, suddenly afraid at the hard look in his eyes. She dropped her gaze and turned to go up the stairs to the nursery.

Mrs. Billings appeared to have finished packing and was sitting with David, feeding him. There were no other maids nearby. With a quiet breath, she steeled herself against weakness.

"Mrs. Billings, I will finish feeding David."

The nurse shot her an unfriendly glance as she pulled a piece of bread out of David's hands that he had been mangling.

"He has finished his meal and now needs his bath. I will ready him for bed, and then you may put him to sleep as you suggested."

Arabella hesitated. As soon as her brother-in-law had left the premises, she would be relieving Mrs. Billings of her post in short order.

"Very well."

Arabella turned and left the nursery, hardening herself against the cry that David let out at seeing her go. She regretted not having gone to caress him, but she had been too focused on the battle with his nurse. Never mind. Victory was not far—at least she hoped it was not. True, Mr. Northwick had merely said he would think about it, but she could not contemplate that just now. She *had* to achieve her purpose.

Once in her room, Arabella went over to the bed and lay down on it, her shod feet hanging off the side. She pulled out the note from Theo and straightened its wrinkles now that she was free to read it again at her leisure. Her eyes lovingly took in the masculine scrawl. She could not wait to see him tonight.

She had promised Mr. Northwick she would not marry. Perhaps that had been hastily done. But time could do many things to repair impossible situations, and she would remain hopeful. Christine and Honoria had fed her with a mountain of determination and hope simply by their solidarity in friendship. She kissed the worn paper and laid it against her breast—a foolish gesture if anyone were to see it.

As the tension faded from having stood up for herself before both Mr. Northwick and Mrs. Billings, Arabella began to relax and eventually to doze. A sharp sound of metal on metal outside of her door woke her up with a start. The evening had settled in, and her room was in near darkness. She was bewildered from sleep, but the sound alarmed her. Her mind had already whispered what it was.

She got up and hurried to the door. There, she lifted the latch and pulled, but it was stuck. Groping underneath the latch for the key to her door, her hand came up empty. A tendril of dread curled inside of her, causing her to rush and light a candle to illuminate her room. She shone it on the door and saw that no key lay in the keyhole, nor had it fallen to the floor. Setting the candle down, she rushed back to the door and tried it again. But no—it had been locked from the outside.

Raising both hands, she slammed them on the door, beating it and calling out. "Can someone hear me? I have been locked in! Come at once!"

But there was no response. She continued beating on the door and calling out until her hands were raw and her voice hoarse. At last she sat down on the bed and stared at the door, the reality hitting her. Mr. Northwick had not capitulated, as he'd appeared to do. But then what did he plan to do with her? What did he plan to do with David?

It was nine o'clock before she had any answers. She had grown weary from crying, and when the sound of the key in the lock reached her, she wiped her tears and sat up, clutching her hands in her lap. Mr. Northwick entered the room, carrying a tray that contained a simple dinner. He set it down on the side table that stood near the door, then remained at the entrance.

"I see you are not unaffected by your confinement. I am glad to see you can be reasoned with." He looked at her for a longer stretch than she could bear. "I do not appreciate shows of independence such as you displayed today. It is not fitting for a woman, who should look to her male superior for wisdom. Perhaps you will learn the lesson before you truly do yourself harm."

Arabella remained mute as he spoke, waiting to see what the end of his lecture would be.

"Therefore, I have decided to teach you a lesson that I hope will need to be taught only once. I will remove to London with my heir, leaving you here. Do not fret. You shall be freed as soon as we are gone. I have given instructions. When you arrive in

London, I shall expect your complete obedience, and we will be married without delay. If you deviate from this plan in any way, I can assure you of this: you will never lay eyes on your son again."

With those words, he slipped out of the room, turned the key sharply in the lock, and Arabella was alone.

CHAPTER 22

When the clock struck half past eleven, Theo rode to Penwood Estate, stopping on the public road and slowing his horse to a quiet walk as he left it to take the private path. He circled around until he reached the western edge of the property and dismounted close to the stone wall. Leading off the wall was a field that dissolved into a line of trees in the distance.

The night sky was bright from a full moon, but a panoply of clouds stretched across it, and few stars could be seen. The full moon might make it more dangerous for Arabella to come to him, but he sent up a quick prayer that she would not be hindered and settled down to wait.

It defied reason, but he felt like the happiest of men because he was going to see Arabella again. He would hold her in his arms and remind her of his love for her, despite what the future might hold. He had already sent off letters to both Vincent and Anthony to let them know of their findings with the poisoned snuff. If they could attack Northwick from both ends and have him found guilty of smuggling on one hand, and of murder on the other, nothing would prevent him from facing justice. And the end result was that Arabella would be free.

Philip's gelding nibbled at the grass at its feet and betrayed their location only by an occasional soft wicker. Theo did not expect Arabella to be timely, for it might not be possible for her to come when he expected. However, as the minutes ticked into an hour and passed it, he began to grow restless. He walked along the side of the house and saw no lights in any of the windows. There was no movement from anywhere on the estate, either. Everything appeared to be shut down for the night. He would not give up hope, though.

When the horse grew tired of standing, he walked him quietly up and down along the wall, but the gelding eventually settled down as though he, too, knew it was the hour for sleeping. One hour turned into three, and although Theo had decided he would wait as long as was needed, he had begun to lose hope. When the faint signs of a breaking dawn met his weary eyes, he knew it was time to give up. He climbed on the saddle and turned toward home.

The position of the house off the public road and its adjoining stables gave him access to only two and a half sides of the façade where a candle in the window might alert him to someone awake and waiting for him. He had seen none on his arrival, nor during his wait. And although there was a chance Arabella's window was tucked into the back of the house, he had to admit there was also a chance she had decided not to come. Perhaps she had felt merely irritation over his attempts to keep pursuing her—as though he were asking her once again to choose between him or her son. He was not—he was trying to free her.

Theo's thoughts were too beleaguered either to cling to hope or to argue with Arabella in his head. He had to admit defeat. He had perhaps lost her forever, but he would still do her the kindness of ensuring she was free of her enslavement to Mr. Northwick.

Back at Boden House, a sleepy stable hand came to take the horse to rub him down, and Theo went inside with plans to sleep. But the morning was now well underway and the hens had begun clucking and running under foot on his way to the kitchens. Rather than sleep right away, he would drink a pot of tea and eat an early breakfast in the kitchen, if the housekeeper would permit it.

She did not permit it, but insisted on serving him properly in the breakfast parlor, promising to go and rouse Cook, who had gone to bed the night before with the headache. Theo obeyed, now questioning his decision not to take himself off immediately to bed.

He was sitting in one of the chairs, his legs stretched forward and crossed, and his arms folded, eyes shut, when his cousin entered the room and nudged him awake. Honoria entered an instant later. He should have known she would turn his cousin into an early riser.

"I had expected you would sleep in your own bed last night. I didn't expect you to remain at Penwood all night. Even *I* had the good sense to leave Honoria enough time to sleep when I went," Philip joked.

"Philip," his devoted wife warned.

"She didn't come," Theo said shortly.

They stopped and gaped at him, Philip in surprise and Honoria in sympathy. She went toward the door just as a footman was bringing in the breakfast contents and a maid followed with a silver teapot. The mistress of the house took the teapot and directed the footman where to put the food. She laid out the breakfast provisions within reach of the men. Then she sat and began pouring tea for all three of them as another servant followed carrying more food. Theo was so tired, the tea was like nectar, and he was grateful when Honoria took over, filling a plate for each of them.

When the servants had gone, Honoria handed him a plate of food.

"She was hindered from coming. I am sure of it. It is impossible that she would receive the letter—and I put it directly into her hands—and not have done everything possible to see you. I know her feelings for you, despite how little she talks of them."

Her words soothed him, but Theo could not deny the facts.

She had not come. And this morning, she was to leave for London. He had felt despair the day she left Newark-on-Trent, driven to it by Northwick, but it was nothing to this, for her wedding was imminent. He was not certain he could save her. He was not even certain he would see her again.

They ate in relative silence, with Philip and Honoria keeping up a light conversation about estate matters. He knew they were doing this for his benefit, to take his mind off the disastrous night. All he wanted now was his bed, and when he finished his meal—feeling better, despite himself—he stood, prepared to tell them so.

An urgent knock came from the front entrance, the sound reaching them from the drawing room. They all looked at each other in surprise as the possibility of who it could be struck Theo.

"Honoria! Philip! Please help!"

It was Arabella. Theo knocked his chair over backwards as he left the room and ran into the drawing room where the front door was located. He threw it open before a servant could arrive, with Philip and Honoria right behind him.

There stood Arabella, her hair falling in long curls down her back and with no carriage in sight. He threw his arms around her and pulled her into the house and into his embrace. She was freezing cold, and that was when he realized she wore nothing but a day dress. She trembled violently in his arms, and as he met Philip and Honoria's stares above her head, he whispered soothing words and held her as long as he dared.

When he felt she had the strength to talk, he led her over to the sofa where Honoria flew to her side and rubbed her hands. Philip went to the door and ordered a passing maid to bring the tea as quickly as it might be done.

"Mr. Northwick has left for London with David," Arabella said. "Yesterday, I informed him that I would not be marrying him, and that I would be keeping David. He gave me false hope, for he told me he would think it over and tell me of his decision that night. Instead, he locked me in my bedroom and told me he

240

was teaching me a lesson not to interfere with him again. He warned me that any future disobedience would cost me my relationship with my son—said I would not lay eyes on him again if ever I were to repeat the offense."

She looked at the three of them, adding, "I truly fear he means to kill David. After all, he has nothing to gain by keeping my son alive. Mr. Northwick will inherit, after all."

Honoria put her arm around her shoulder as Arabella sent a pleading look to her and Philip.

"I must go to London. I must try. But I do not have a carriage left at Penwood, and none of the servants are loyal to me, except Rose—but she is powerless to help. I have come to beg you to lend me your carriage and the means to go to London. I promise to pay you back as soon as I might."

Theo's gaze had not left Arabella's face as he listened to her with a set jaw.

"I will take you there in my carriage. I don't want you to go alone. That monster needs to be stopped, and I will make sure the deed is done."

"I will go with you," Philip said, then added wryly, "Someone has to protect you from rash decisions."

"I am coming as well. I will go pack our things." Honoria turned to leave.

"No!" The outcry was simultaneous from all three parties in the room. She turned in surprise, staring at each of their faces.

"I am sorry to state the matter baldly, but you are with child and not in the best form," Theo explained.

Philip went over and put his hands on his wife's shoulders. "I have never once asserted my authority as a husband, but I am doing so now. You will be staying here."

Honoria looked at him, her chin rising a notch. She put her hands on her hips.

"I would never forgive myself if something were to happen to the baby," Arabella said softly.

Honoria looked at each in turn, then capitulated with a loud sigh. "Very well, although I think you are all being ridiculously overprotective. However, we must inform Christine and Gus. They will want to know."

"And Gus has the proof from the apothecary, for whatever that may be worth," Philip added. "We should bring it with us. I will ride over now and tell them of this latest development."

"Proof?" Arabella asked, wrinkling her brow.

"Your husband's snuff had been tampered with. It is just as we thought," Theo said.

Honoria did not allow for a reply but helped Arabella to her feet. "And I will have a hot bath drawn for you. Philip, ask Christine to bring some warm clothing. She and Arabella are of the same size."

She then rounded on Arabella, sounding much like the mother she was soon to be. "The journey will be long, and you need to be refreshed. Theo, please bring her to the breakfast parlor and give her something to eat, while I take care of these preparations."

Both Honoria and Philip went their separate ways, and Theo brought Arabella to the breakfast parlor. When she was seated, he went to the end of the table that held the spread of breakfast. "Would you care for tea or coffee?"

"Tea, I suppose," she said. He felt her eyes on his back as he poured her a cup and brought it over with the sugar nips and the milk. He went back and filled a plate with bread and eggs and a slice of ham, which was still warm, though not steaming.

She was stirring the milk and sugar in her tea and emitted a weak laugh. When he raised his eyebrows in question, she shook her head wearily.

"It is nothing. It is only that I remember when we were in Lincoln the day after the Stuff Ball, and Philip served Honoria breakfast. I had never been served a plate of anything by a gentleman, and I thought it was the kindest gesture I had ever seen."

He set the heaping plate in front of her and smiled. "And now you have been served by a man, although he is a merchant and not a gentleman."

242

She would never be able to finish what was on her plate, but she would have a selection. She did eat, and not timidly, he was gratified to see. Although he had many questions for her, he remained silent while she ate enough to satisfy her appetite. At last she looked up.

"I did not dare to eat what Mr. Northwick brought into my room last night in case it had been poisoned. I had to be sure I was well enough to go after David."

"How were you able to leave your room this morning?" he asked her.

"One of the servants had been given orders to open my door. I suppose he did not want a coroner's inquest when a fully clothed skeleton was found locked in a Penwood Estate bedroom," she replied in what he thought was an attempt at humor.

Theo grimaced. He found no comedy in that image. "But they did not hitch up a carriage for you to ride here. How did you come?"

"No, they did not. They ignored me, except for the one maid who is sympathetic to my cause, but she could do nothing. For the rest, it was as though I did not exist."

Arabella stopped and put her hands over her eyes. When she opened them, she was blinking away tears.

"I followed the same steps as when I fled to Newark. I stopped on the public road, although this time I flagged someone going in the opposite direction toward Horncastle. I managed to find a kindly farmer who worried over my state of undress and made me promise that I would get help. I told him merely that I was in distress, but that I had faithful friends living in the town of Horncastle."

"You do indeed," Theo said. He took her hands in his, which were now warm. "You have friends—many friends. I can promise you that you will never have to fight alone for anything again in your life."

Now the tears spilled over in earnest. "But why? What am I that you should care for me?"

Theo swept her to her feet and pulled her into his arms in one fluid movement. He buried his face in her soft curls that smelled of soap and the outdoors, feeling strength course through him from their closeness and from the depth of his love for her. He felt she was waiting for an answer, but he had none he could give that would make any sense.

"You are you," he said at last. "It's your... Oh, how can I say it? It's your soul that shines so very brightly that makes people want to care for you. I am sure the others would agree. But then for me, it's more."

He pulled back to look at her, noting with great tenderness how beautiful she was when her hair was in disarray like this.

"Who can put words to love?" He smiled, almost sheepishly. "Not I! I am no poet. I only know that I would go to the ends of the earth for you—and am prepared to do so now."

Honoria came back into the room and did not even blink twice at the sight of their embrace. Theo was slightly more satisfied—as if he had taken the edge off his hunger—just from being able to hold her in his arms and tell her what he felt for her. He was glad to see a glimmer of Arabella's smile return.

"We have not a moment to waste," Honoria said. "If I know our friends, the Greys, they will not need any convincing to aid us in our journey. And they will not tarry in coming."

At a look from both Theo and Arabella, she amended, "Aid *you* in *your* journey. I dare not disobey my husband, now that he has given me my very first order."

Her eyes twinkling with amusement, she put her hand on Arabella's arm and led her to the grand staircase outside of the library so she might freshen up. Theo let them go. As much as he was anxious to be off and to wring that man's neck for the pain he had caused Arabella, he knew she needed to be warmed up in the very real sense and clothed. Honoria would do that better than anyone.

It was not until over an hour later that the sound of horses pulling up to Boden House woke Theo from where he had been dozing on the sofa. He rubbed off his sleep and opened the door to greet them.

Gus and Christine climbed down from the carriage. Their groom sat at the front of the coach, and Gus's pair of bays stood in the harness. Theo leaned against the door frame and folded his arms, giving them a tired, welcoming smile.

"I have what Arabella needs," Christine said, wasting no time in going past him into the house with a wrapped parcel.

Theo looked at Gus, wondering what he was thinking. He knew from Philip that Gus had not been entirely happy to lose Honoria's youthful admiration for him, and that he had been tempted to close off from Philip at the time. This could only have come as an even stronger blow, for Gus had been in active pursuit of Arabella. Theo had wondered if he could rely upon him to help, but the presence of his best horses indicated that he would. Gus would never let the pair of them out of his sight.

He needed to hear it from the man himself, however. "You're coming to London?"

"Northwick deserves whatever he will get for treating Arabella in such an abominable way," Gus said, his gaze not quite meeting Theo's. "Besides, friends stick together. I can't let you go there alone. You and Philip are far too nice to be effective."

Theo ignored his friend's attempt at humor and replied from the heart. "Thank you."

Gus shrugged and looked down at his feet, kicking the stone post at the bottom of the stairs. "She never so much as glanced my way. I should have seen that before. I wish you happy."

"Thank you," Theo said again, touched. He knew Gus had a heart, or they wouldn't have been friends for so long, but it seemed that Gus was growing somehow—becoming more aware of the feelings of others. It was not easy to change one's nature. Not easy, but not impossible. Theo should not be surprised.

In little more than ten minutes, the women came downstairs, heralding a freshened Arabella, properly clothed for more warmth and hair pinned up neatly. She smiled at Theo, and then her glance rested on Gus, a little more uncertain.

"Morning, Arabella," he said, doffing his hat. "Let us go and retrieve your son for you."

She gave him a trembling, grateful smile, and he held out his hand for her to clasp.

Then there was a flurry of deciding who would go in what coach. They settled on the women riding in Gus's carriage with whatever luggage they carried. Gus would drive, and the groom would sit beside him. Philip and Theo would ride in Philip's curricle, with the footman on the back seat; as this was the lighter carriage, they would change horses between vehicles to prolong the ride. The footman would arrange to have the horses sent back to Horncastle at the first stage.

The preparation for the journey, and starting off—not without Honoria at the doorway waving a handkerchief—was achieved with simplicity when everyone in the party was of a like mind. Theo could only be glad to be moving at last, and he was determined to wrest Arabella and her son firmly from Northwick's control. He would not lose this time.

The only thing that hindered his satisfaction over the efficient start to their journey was that he was not allowed to be the one riding in the coach with her.

CHAPTER 23

A rabella listened to Christine's unusually voluble conversation as they started on their journey to London and knew her friend wished to distract her from the unpleasant thoughts that were lurking, ready to plague her as soon as there was silence. But Arabella quite thought they would achieve their aim this time. She was afraid for her son, yes, but she held on to the hope that her brother-in-law would not have had time to perform any of the evil designs he might be contemplating. Besides, never before had Arabella been surrounded by true friends, who had her best interests at heart as she was now. It could only fill her with a sort of optimism that was as much a surprise as it was a novelty.

Despite that, the doubts did creep in at times, especially when they stopped for the night and she turned in her bed, trying to fall asleep. Would Mr. Northwick be in the London house when she arrived? Would she have access to the house to retrieve David from his clutches straight away? Or would they need to undergo a long legal process to prove he was not a fit guardian? She could not think of all the possibilities they might face. They were too great for her, and too much was at stake. She would simply need to go on trust.

It took them three days of hard travel to reach London. Christine and Arabella spoke little between them about what they would do upon arrival, but when they met with the three men over dinner each night, their collective plan slowly began to take shape. The first thing they would do was to go to her London house and try to get David. Gus surmised it would only be possible if Mr. Northwick was not on the premises to hinder them.

Theo said that after they'd retrieved David, he must meet with his brother-in-law to see if they'd found any more leads. He would give him the snuffbox, along with the apothecary's findings. But they would need something to connect the two. Arabella regretted not insisting that Rose join them. She was almost certain she would have come had she been asked.

Having a plan could not remove every trace of anxiety, however, as a great deal rested on chance. It was more likely than not that something would hinder Arabella's attempts to retrieve her son, as Mr. Northwick would absolutely prevent any such an attempt, and his servants were highly unlikely to disobey his orders. Beyond that, pinning any criminal activity on her brother-in-law would surely take time and much more discussion than they could do while on the road.

Stress and discomfort were Arabella's constant companions. But every time they stopped for a pause or to take shelter for the night, Theo would seek her out to offer words of encouragement or to press his hand in hers. This constant attention added to her hope and steeled her determination.

At the end of the third day, the sight of smog enveloping even the church spires let her know they had at last reached their destination. Despite everything she must face, the familiar odors and bustle reassured Arabella, for the return to where she had grown up was bringing her near to her son. As she watched the passing buildings from the window of the carriage, she began to tremble with anticipation and nervousness. Christine reached over and held her hand without a word. Gus had been given the directions of her London residence, and the two carriages made their way directly there. It was approaching evening.

Her house was located on Chancery, and the lane was quiet enough that there was room for the two carriages to come to a halt in front of the residence without blocking another coach. Arabella sent an anxious glance at Christine, and clutched her fingers together as Gus jumped down from the box seat and opened the door.

This was it. Her limbs shook as she alighted, but she felt a force inside of her that had not been there before. It allowed her to face with readiness the marital home she had lived in when in London. She might have been feeding herself on illusions—and her brother-in-law might appear at any moment and quickly slam her back into reality—but she would not give up without a fight.

They were all standing by the coaches now, and Theo made a sudden movement and held up an arm for all to be quiet. Without a word, he pointed to a phaeton that pulled out of the mews several feet ahead. The driver did not turn and see them, but drove toward the far end of the street. Arabella recognized him at once as her brother-in-law. As soon as he neared the corner and was out of earshot, Theo grabbed the reins from Philip and climbed back into the curricle.

His friend did not hesitate to follow his lead. "James, I will need you to stay here with the horses while the women go inside to get Mrs. Northwick's son."

Gus grabbed something from his coach and climbed onto the box seat behind Philip and Theo, then addressed his groom.

"Mort, you will accompany the ladies inside to retrieve David. Christine, we will meet you at The White Hart afterwards."

Theo sprang the horses, who were still fresh enough. One of their last pair of rented horses had lost a shoe—they had been sluggish anyway—and Gus had been obliged to change them once again right before they entered London. This pair was surprisingly strong. Arabella watched them go, sending a prayer up that they would find him...but then wondered if that was best. He had proven to be dangerous. She prayed her friends would be safe.

"Ready?" Christine asked.

Mort nodded at his mistress, and then to her. He seemed more than able to defend them against any unwilling servants inside. Arabella squared her shoulders and took a deep breath as she stepped forward.

"Ready."

She marched up the stairs, her heart pounding and her mouth dry, on the wings of courage forged by her friends. If ever she could reclaim her son and his inheritance, it was now. She refused to think about the alternative.

Grasping the bronze knocker in the shape of an angry Greek god, which she had always hated, she gave a firm *rap, rap, rap.* Within a short time, the door opened, and the butler raised his eyebrows in surprise at seeing her. His attention then went behind her to Christine and Mort.

"Mr. Northwick did not inform me that you would be coming to London, Mrs. Northwick," he said, and was forced to step aside as she pushed her way in, followed by Christine and the groom.

"He was not aware of it, Timor. You will not be needed," she added as she moved forward and gestured for Christine and Mort to follow.

She walked the familiar path up to the nursery. It was a narrow house, and the stairs were built on the east side of it. She climbed them with determination, hearing the reassuring echo of footsteps behind her.

There was a murmured conference at the foot of the stairs as two maids and a footman came to confer with the butler, but she ignored them. All of the servants had taken their cue from their master and had treated her with the same disrespect that he showed. She would soon be rid of them all.

It had occurred to her that it would be difficult to physically remove her son from the house with all the servants in place, but she felt they would be less likely to make a fuss with another lady accompanying her, not to mention the burly groom.

As though she knew this, Christine slipped her arm through Arabella's at the top of the stairs as they advanced down the third-floor corridor toward the nursery.

A sudden wail from inside the room brought Arabella's heart to her throat, and she quickened her steps until she was almost running. Christine and the groom kept pace with her, and Arabella threw open the door as Mrs. Billings was dressing David for bed with sharp, punishing movements as he stood in front of her. Arabella's heart began to thud. Had Mrs. Billings always treated David this way when out of the sight of others?

"You will step away from David, Mrs. Billings. I will dress my son." She went over and put her hand on David, who threw his arms around her neck in complete trust. It utterly transformed Arabella into a fierce, protective mother who would no longer let anyone come between her and her son.

Mrs. Billings did not comply but gripped David's arm, pulling him back until Arabella was afraid he would be hurt and allowed the nurse to take him. She would have to try a different way, for she was not leaving this house without her son.

"Mrs. Northwick, I have my orders," the nurse said. "You are not to come anywhere near the boy until Mr. Northwick returns and gives his permission."

Christine came over, ever practical, and took David easily from Mrs. Billings, who did not seem as inclined to fight a woman who was not Arabella. Christine perched him on her hip so he could look at his mother. David's lip was trembling, and he seemed indecisive about whether or not he would cry.

Arabella turned and faced Mrs. Billings. "You are relieved of your post."

She left the nurse standing in the middle of the room and began throwing articles of clothing and small toys and blankets into a cloth bag she'd found folded on the side of the room.

"You are not mistress here," Mrs. Billings retorted when she found her voice. "Mr. Northwick is guardian of the boy, and as such he owns this house and manages the servants until the boy comes of age. He hired me to watch over him, and that is exactly what I intend to do until he returns."

She hesitated only briefly before walking around the table to try to remove David from Christine's arms.

Christine raised an eyebrow at Mort, and the groom came over and inserted himself between her and Mrs. Billings.

"I don't think ye'll be doing sech a thing." He folded his arms, his face stoic. Mrs. Billings took a step back.

"You will regret this day's work," she said, her lips white with anger. "When Mr. Northwick returns, he'll send the law after you for kidnapping."

"Mr. Northwick is in league with a ring of smugglers, and the noose is closing in around his neck. He also murdered my husband, and very likely others. He will not be returning, and if he does, it will only be until he is carried out of this house in chains."

Arabella threw the last few items in the bag—she hardly knew what she was packing—then turned to face the nurse.

"I understand following orders. I can even respect it. But you delighted in making me cower. You took pleasure in making me feel as though I was an inadequate mother. That is something you will have to live with when you attempt to find another position after having been turned off without a character. Meanwhile, I am going to raise *my* son into a man who knows how to treat women with respect and dignity."

She turned to leave and saw from the corner of her eye that Christine and Mort were following. When they were in the corridor, Christine said, "Let me hold him until we get out of the house. I promise you it will take the wind out of the sails of those servants who are likely congregating below and planning mischief. They will not dare to take him from me."

Arabella had wanted the satisfaction of sweeping out of the house with her son in her arms, but she saw the wisdom in what Christine said. What she wanted even more was to actually leave the house with her son in her possession, so she gave a quick nod and then strode toward the stairs. She couldn't get out of this house fast enough.

Christine had been right. When they rounded the last part of the stairwell, there was a bevy of servants standing at the bottom of the stairs, with Timor standing in front.

"Now, Mrs. Northwick, do be reasonable," he said, moving to intercept her, but not—she noticed—Christine who was holding David.

Mort stepped neatly in between her and the butler and, without pausing for thought, decked Timor on the chin and sent him reeling. Arabella gasped and almost laughed as the pompous, hostile butler collapsed in an undignified heap. She turned shining eyes toward the groom. *This* was what it was like to have a loyal servant.

The maids stepped back, and Mort looked at the two footmen in turn. "Anyone else care for a little more home-brewed?"

They glanced at each other and both stepped aside, raising their hands in surrender. Mort kept his eyes on them while Christine and Arabella left the house, before he stepped outside himself.

As they exited into the night air, their breath coming out in thin clouds, Christine reached for the bag holding David's clothing with one arm, and Arabella turned to catch David who was already leaning toward her. In front of the narrow house, the footman waited by the horses' heads, and as soon as he saw them, opened the door for them to climb inside. Christine and Arabella swept into the coach, with David safely tucked into her arms. He closed the door, and the carriage rocked as he and Mort climbed on the box seat in the front, and the groom clicked the reins.

They moved forward and Arabella breathed out. She was too stunned to do more than look at David, who had begun to suck his fingers. Suddenly he reached forward and put his wet hand on her cheek.

"Mama."

"That's right, I'm your mama," she said, her throat closing with emotion. She smiled at him through her tears, then gave a laugh of sheer relief.

"That you are," Christine said, the corners of her lips stretching wide as she watched them both. "And none finer."

CHAPTER 24

Theo drove the hired pair down the street at a spanking pace with Philip at his side and Gus standing behind. It said a lot about his friends that they allowed him to drive although it was not his carriage, nor was he the most skilled. But it was his fight. The sun had begun to set above the buildings, which blinded him to what was ahead, but the street was nearly deserted and they were not at great risk of having a run-in. When they rounded the corner, they spotted Northwick's carriage up ahead turning down Farrington, and Theo urged the horses forward.

"He's heading to the dockyard, I daresay," Gus called out from behind.

"Do you think so? At this hour?" Philip leaned forward, squinting, trying to make out the outline of the carriage.

"The deeds of darkness are better done in the dark." Theo gripped the reins. They were so close. He had no very clear idea of what he would say to Northwick when they found him. It had been pure instinct to follow him, but he was questioning the wisdom of that decision.

As though he'd read his thoughts, Philip lifted his voice from the clatter of the curricle riding over the paving stones. "Do we have a plan when we find him?"

"We just need to see what he's about. Anything we can get on him might be useful," Gus answered, and they fell silent again.

Theo focused on the driving, his jaw set. If they could catch Northwick at smuggling, it would give them the proof they needed to set the law after him, but it was not done in the matter of an evening. And then there was his brother's death to prove. They had much on their side, but they would need a stroke of good fortune for it to all come together in a successful resolution.

They followed his carriage, and as they left the finer part of the city, there was more activity on the street to hide their pursuit. This was a relief, as Theo had begun to fear Northwick would turn back at the sound of their carriage. Then they would lose the chance to see what he was up to.

They were nearing the Thames, and shouts came from the dockyard in front of them along with the smell of fish. On their left, a fishmonger called out what he had on offer from behind his crates; ahead, the squeaking sounds of boats docking, along with the wheels of carriages that came to transport the fish, absorbed all other noise.

"He's gone to the right after that last building." Gus pointed ahead from where he stood.

Theo slowed the carriage as they approached the dockside and pulled up near the water's edge without turning to follow. Philip seemed to sense what was needed and jumped down to peer around the corner of the building, holding his hand up to Theo and Gus as he watched what was happening there. Theo tied the carriage to an iron hook in the side of the building.

After a minute, Philip returned. "He's there. He's examining the contents of a shipment, and I saw him fingering something and lifting what looked to be tobacco to his nose."

"Before nightfall?" Theo said, his brows furrowed as he glanced up at the darkening sky. "He can't be so stupid. This must not be the smuggled stuff. Or they have two amounts—one for the customs officials, and one for themselves as his brother's ledger noted."

"I don't think he's capable of doing anything above-board," Philip replied. "What I think we should do is go to Bow Street and hire someone there so they can catch him in the act."

Gus shook his head. "We'll never have time. He won't stay around long enough to be caught, not if he's got anything in his brain box. He's examining the snuff and collecting his money before he heads off to the club and pretends to be a gentleman."

"We'll have to confront him ourselves then," Theo said, unwilling to wait another day before setting Arabella free from Northwick's power.

Philip put his hand on Theo's arm. "We cannot take the risk. If he's willing to poison his own brother, you may be sure he has not come unarmed."

Gus walked around the coach and leaned over into the seat. "Well, my friends, neither have we." He lifted a box containing dueling pistols, which he opened, and took one out. "I grabbed it from my coach before we left. Here, help me load the other one."

Gus handed one to Philip, but before either could do anything to the purpose, a movement ahead caught Theo's attention, and he turned toward the river. Mr. Northwick had appeared and was advancing toward them, his demeanor casual, except for the pistol he held in his hand.

"I would advise you to drop that," he said.

Theo, Gus, and Philip looked at each other, and in wordless agreement set the unloaded pistols on the seat. They outnumbered Northwick—and he wouldn't have time to reload before they overtook him—but it still wasn't a risk they could take. If he was a good shot, one of them would lose their life before the others could react.

"I wondered who was spying on me from around the corner," he said. "I should have known it was you. How long have you been following me?"

"Give yourself up," Theo said. "You are outnumbered three to one, and we know everything about your activities. If you are not hanged for smuggling tobacco, you will be for poisoning your brother's snuff. We have the proof on both counts."

Northwick's face hardened. "As you say, I will be hung for any one of those things you imagine me to have done—*if* I have done them. So why should I give myself up? Especially if I am the one holding the gun?"

From behind him, three more men stepped around the corner, one of whom was brandishing a second pistol. Northwick added, "And especially if I am not outnumbered."

"Now would have been a good time for those Bow Street Runners to arrive," Philip murmured.

Northwick walked forward, trailed by the three men. With a jerk of his chin, he gestured for them to advance upon Theo and his friends.

"Tie them up," he said. "It will give me time to put a bullet in one and reload at my leisure to take care of the other two. Anyone who struggles will be the first to die."

Theo had been on high alert since he took the reins and followed Northwick, but now his muscles were on edge as his thoughts raced. Should they run and risk Northwick getting away? Should the three of them put up a fight, as he couldn't kill them all? No, one of them would surely die before they could accomplish anything.

The men advanced, their fists raised in a show of determination, and Theo decided he could not go down without a fight, come what may. He exchanged a look with Philip.

Before he could open his mouth, the air was rent by a loud "hiya" on the other side of the carriage. Gus lifted an arm, and the two horses bolted toward the river with the carriage in tow, heading straight into the path of Northwick, who pulled the trigger in his panic. The flash of white was immediately followed by a sting on Theo's ear.

Northwick was down, and Theo wasted no time in running to retrieve the gun, which had slid across the pavement. It would be useless until reloaded, but he was not taking any chances. He stood over Northwick, covering him.

Philip ran over to the two men, who had fallen in the commotion, and he grabbed the ropes from one of them. They were still outnumbered, however. He risked a glance at Gus and froze in alarm. His friend had both his arms in the air, and the remaining man was holding a pistol level at his head.

Northwick laughed from his position on the ground. "It was a nice show. My gun, if you please?" he said to Theo as soon as he'd gotten up from the ground. When he hesitated, Northwick held out his hand, adding, "If you don't want to witness your friend killed before your very eyes."

Theo ground his teeth as he handed over the pistol. It had been a valiant effort. However, now it was too late even to run— not when Gus had a pistol to his head. He wanted to roar with the frustration. Everything he had tried to do to win Arabella was in vain, and now he would not be able to free her. He would not even live to protect her as he had promised.

"Gentlemen," Northwick said, "the ropes."

The men were clearly not gentlemen in any sense but what a free trader would use. The largest one grabbed the rope from Philip as the other took hold of Theo's arm. He surrendered to his fate. He would not be the cause of Gus being shot first.

Despite his noble intentions, a shot rang through the air, sending shock through to Theo's entrails. He covered his face with his hands, unwilling to see one of his oldest friends lose his life in such an ignoble, dastardly manner.

After a split second's consideration, he lowered his hands. No, he would face everything bravely until the end. He followed Northwick's gaze to where the shot came from, but Gus was still standing! To Theo's amazement, it was the smuggler who had held a pistol to Gus's head that was face-down, taken out with one bullet.

Gus jumped to retrieve the pistol and aimed it in Northwick's direction as Theo sent a confused look ahead to the Thames. There, an armed patrol of customs officers stood assembled near the dock, and some of them already had a few men in their grasp. The river had masked the sound of their arrival, and the building had blocked them from view.

Northwick turned to see them and went white as he grasped his fate. He bolted in the opposite direction, but Theo was ready for him and received the full force of his flight, tumbling to the ground with him and holding his torso. In moments, chaos erupted as the officers whose hands were free of prisoners ran and took the rest of the smugglers into custody, most of whom had been out of view near the smuggled goods. Theo's head hurt like the devil from hitting the pavement, but he kept an iron grip around Northwick, determined that he should not escape.

The weight of him was lifted at once, and Theo blinked, surprised to see Trudy's husband standing in the void.

Vincent reached his hand down and clasped Theo's to pull him to his feet. Keeping hold of his hand, he grasped Theo's other arm, his face full of deep affection that his usual reticence would not allow him to show.

"Mighty glad to see you hale and hearty," Vincent said.

Theo reached back to the bump forming on his head and gave a weak laugh. "Almost hale and hearty." Then he grasped Vincent's arm in return.

"How in the world did you know?" he asked as soon as the whirl of events allowed him to form the question. It seemed fantastical that his brother-in-law should know where to find him.

Vincent smiled. "Anthony sent word to his friend—the Mr. Earnest Fairgood over there, who appears to have just planted a facer to the man still struggling—that he should come find me if Northwick returned to London. He did so yesterday, and with that knowledge, we began to watch his every move. The shipment coming in was scheduled, so it was not unusual to have a few customs men on site. But we needed to prove that there was additional cargo that had not been declared before we could move in. When we heard the shot, we took no more chances and just rounded up the men and came to your aid."

Theo watched Earnie, who looked like he was thoroughly

enjoying his part in the adventure. "I suspect he's going to have no shortage of news when he sees Anthony and vastly raise you in my brother's esteem," he said with a chuckle.

He felt weak as the rush from their fight left him. He looked around and saw only Philip assisting the patrol. He hoped Gus was all right, but considering he had escaped being shot, he figured nothing else posed much of a risk. He and Vincent watched the officers shouting orders and tying up the men. In a short while, he saw Gus leading the carriage and harnessed pair around the corner. Of course. He would have been concerned about the horses, who fortunately did not appear to have suffered any harm.

"How did they hide the tobacco in the shipment?" he asked Vincent. It didn't matter much, since it seemed they had the proof they needed at least to keep Northwick in custody. But it had been a surprising development, that he would attempt anything so openly.

Vincent smiled. "Jenkins accompanied Weald down to London—Northwick's associate who turned on him. He's the one who told us about the shipment this evening, and it was from him that we learned about the secret compartments."

He stopped and gestured with his hands. "You see, all the casks have holes for the officers to stick a cane into to see that it's not being used for anything else but for what it was intended. However, a cane cannot touch all sides of a round barrel, and the smugglers came up with a way to hide tobacco in the compartments that the cane cannot reach."

Vincent paused and glanced at Northwick, whose face was unreadable as he stood with his hands bound behind his back.

"I guess Northwick thought this would be a simple run and a matter of bribing the land customs agent, but we've been working too hard to shut this down to trust it to a man who was not one of ours."

One of the agents came up to him to report the number of men and smuggled goods in their possession, and Vincent turned to Theo.

"I had better go oversee this. My position does not usually require me to be in place to seize the goods, but this one held personal significance." He signaled to the officer who was waiting for him, his eyes still on Theo. "Will you be all right from here?"

Theo nodded, causing a dull throb to his head, and smiled weakly. "Better than all right. I'll see you back in Newark when you get there."

Gus was still soothing the horses when Theo went over, and Philip came and squinted at his ear. "Got hit, did you?"

Theo lifted his hand to his ear and felt it sticky with blood. It didn't seem like any piece of significant size was missing, but he did not want to examine it too closely right now.

"Appears so."

"Good thing your ear sticks out," his cousin pointed out kindly. "Served as a sort of target to draw Northwick's aim from your head."

"My ear does not stick out," Theo said with dignity, as Gus waved them over.

"These horses are spent, and although they're a hired pair, they've done well. Haven't you, boys?" he asked, patting the side of the one nearest him. "Shall we bring them back to the stable near the inn and let them be rubbed down?"

"And get cleaned up ourselves," Philip added. "Theo, you can hardly present yourself to your ladylove covered in your own blood."

Arabella! Theo perked up as he remembered that the evening was not over. Just as quickly, he remembered what challenge had lain ahead of her that evening. She would not have had to contend with Northwick. But had she been successful in retrieving her son?

CHRISTINE HAD the groom drive them to the inn they had agreed upon, and fortunately there were available rooms, so they did not need to try their second choice. Time was spent settling into the rooms and ordering a dinner, but Christine took care of most of that so Arabella could spend time with David, reassuring herself that he was indeed alive and with her. She treasured the victory of the moment, but her sensation of wellbeing warred with her worry for Theo and their friends.

They would come as soon as they had seen what Mr. Northwick was up to. But her heart was in her throat as she imagined a more dreadful outcome—that Mr. Northwick had been able to overpower Theo. He would waste no time scouring London for her and ripping David from her arms once again. She could flee, but she was tired of fleeing, and then what would Christine do without her to accompany her back to Lincolnshire?

But she had to remain hopeful. Surely they would succeed at getting Mr. Northwick arrested. If only she *knew* what was happening. If only she could be sure that Theo would not be hurt. Christine reentered the room where she was bathing David and informed her that the dinner would be set out in the private parlor as soon as the gentlemen returned. She appeared to have no doubts about them getting through the entire ordeal unscathed. Arabella would draw strength from her friend's faith.

It was a full two hours later, a stretch during which Arabella could not boast of having kept her faith as strong as Christine's, that she gasped and lifted her head. The noises of men's laughter and conversation reached them as they mounted the stairs— voices she recognized. She and Christine shared a startled look, and Christine ran to open the door.

"We cannot come in like this. We look a mess," Philip was heard to say.

David had fallen asleep on the bed, and Arabella left him there, running to the door. "No, you must not say that. We are eager to hear the news."

Her eyes fell on Theo, who was covered with dried blood on the side of his head.

"Oh!" She ran over to him and cupped her hand around his face. "You've been hurt. Allow me to tend to it."

"I'll go and get more hot water," Christine said. "And I'll order baths for you three. You will need it."

Arabella did not wait, but pulled Theo into the room and gently pushed him into a chair. Nearby was the basin of water she had used to clean David, and she took the cloth inside of it to gently rub at his face. She stood as near to him as she dared, and he closed his eyes during her ministrations, which made her breath suddenly go unsteady.

Before she became lost to the sensation of caring for him, she turned to look over her shoulder. "Tell me what happened, please."

Christine reentered the room at that moment. "The baths will be prepared in each of your rooms, although it will take a while to have them all ready at once. Then we may eat."

They murmured their thanks, and began to recount the events of the evening. When Arabella heard about the horses bolting—which Gus proudly announced had been his idea—and the gunshot which ended up missing Theo's head by an inch, she felt faint. She must have looked it, because Theo stood from his chair and pushed *her* gently into it.

"There is no need to faint," he said, smiling at her fondly. "As you can see, he did not achieve his aim of ridding the earth of me. Not that I think he meant to aim at my head at all. He was in the process of being bowled over by as fine a pair of rental horses as I've ever seen."

"Indeed," Gus interjected. "I've a mind to purchase them if the owner will sell."

Theo placed his hand on her arm. "And he has not achieved his aim of forcing you into marriage, for he will be busy getting acquainted with his new cell mates in Newgate."

She looked up at Theo fondly, still feeling weak at the thought of losing him. "And he will not get out? There is enough evidence to hold him?"

"I'll say," Gus said. "There's enough evidence to get him sentenced three times over. He might have been granted passage on a ship to the new world if he had not been directing the activities against the Crown. As it is, he is more likely to hang, especially when they finish gathering evidence on the two men who were poisoned—three, if we count your husband."

Arabella's whole body was weak. She did not want to contemplate such things. Of course, people must pay for their evil deeds, but it was all so horrible to think of. Why could people not simply choose to be good?

Theo's regard was full of concern as he studied her face, then he glanced at the others.

"Would you all give me a moment alone with Arabella?" He then added, "You may keep the door to the room open for propriety's sake, but I require a private interview with her."

The others exchanged a glance and murmured their agreement, before filing out. Christine was the last one out, and she did keep the door open...by a hair.

Theo knelt in front of Arabella as she sat on the chair. "I should have waited until I was presentable before I asked you this, except that I find I cannot wait a minute more. Will you do me the honor of becoming my wife?"

She blinked at him, her thoughts rushing from the awful fate of Mr. Northwick to the decidedly blissful notion of accepting his hand in marriage. She opened her mouth, then shut it, hesitating only because the strength of her emotions seemed to have left her bereft of speech.

Theo waited. He swallowed and waited longer, his eyes not leaving hers.

"Yes, Theo. I will." She raised her eyes to his, her chest flooding with a sensation of lightness that seemed too spiritual, too pure to belong to this earth.

His face broke into a smile of relief. He stood then, and drew her to her feet, caressing her cheeks as he devoured her with his gaze.

"You honor me. I promise to make you happy. And I promise to protect and honor *you*. From here on in, that is all you need to concern yourself with—today and every day. I will shoulder the rest."

EPILOGUE

Arabella had the team of new servants, directed by her head maid, Rose, throw open the shutters in Penwood Estate at an early hour. She was up as early as any of them, and she wandered through the drawing room, then the corridor, the dining room, the library and study, the sunny breakfast room, checking each room to ensure that everything was perfectly in order. Only then did she go upstairs to the nursery.

Felicity was installed there with David, and as soon as she saw Arabella, she jumped to her feet. "Good morning, ma'am. Do you have need of David? I've only just fed him, but I've not dressed him yet."

"No." Arabella smiled at her newly hired nurse, whom Trudy had graciously sent to her as soon as she learned of her brother's forthcoming marriage. "We have hours yet before everyone comes. I just wanted to see my son."

David had been playing with a carved set of wooden soldiers, and he came toward her now, holding one up for her to inspect. She swept him up into her arms and planted a kiss on his cheek. His blond hair was getting long, but it had a curl to it that she found charming. She was not in a hurry to trim those locks.

"In one week, you are to have a new papa. And he adores you

just as much as your mother does. You are the luckiest of boys to walk about this earth on stout little legs."

She leaned in and made a buzzing sound that vibrated on his neck just underneath his chin. He giggled and pulled away. Still smiling, Arabella set him down.

"You may bring him down when our guests are here. In the meantime, he might like to spend time outdoors. Dress him warmly, for there is a chill to the air."

An hour before the guests were to arrive for a pre-wedding celebration, a knock sounded on the door and Arabella came out of the drawing room as the new footman went to answer it. She hoped it was Theo, for she would love to have time with him and be reassured of his affection before everyone arrived. She did not need it, but she had grown used to the comfort of his presence.

It was Honoria. "Philip is bringing the carriage around to the stables. I am early, but I hoped I might be of help."

Honoria was showing through her skirts, and she admitted she'd had to let some of them out. Being with child caused her to glow with joy and good health, especially since her father had seemed to forget all signs of his former animosity against Philip with the impending arrival of his grandchild. Honoria's brother and his wife had not yet been blessed with a child, but it was too soon to give up all hope that it might happen.

"You are always welcome here, whenever you wish." Arabella smiled brightly at her friend. "Come see how I have decorated the table."

One benefit of Arabella's former marriage—and there was only this, besides the crowning gift of having been blessed with David—was that her son had inherited a beautiful house located on the edge of a decently sized estate. And she was to live here, now that she had been granted temporary guardianship until she married Theo, after which it would be shared.

This was a gift, too. Vincent used his connections in the Court of Chancery to push through David's case. Although Mr. Northwick had not yet been tried, he had been deemed an unfit guardian for David, and the court had decided in favor of Theo based on their betrothal. Theo told her that the speed in which the court rendered the decision was practically unheard of, thanks to Trudy's husband.

The table was set. There were three vases of hothouse flowers on its center, and the plates were all Limoges with dark pink flowers, nestled in between the silverware. The napkins were of a finely woven cloth, once embroidered with North-wick's initials that Christine had already picked out with the pearl-inlaid scissors Arabella had given her. She promised to re-embroider them all with a D for Dawson, plus a T on one side for Theodore and an A on the other for Arabella. But it would be bad luck to set the newly monogrammed napkins at the table before the actual wedding had taken place.

"You've set everything beautifully. You have a gift for table decoration, although I hope you will still allow us to assist you for the wedding breakfast, if only for our own amusement," Honoria said. This brought a flush of pleasure to Arabella's cheeks, and she nodded her agreement.

The fire crackled in the dining room fireplace, and Honoria crossed over to the doorway where she had dropped her basket.

"I thought you might like some of my almond cakes. I am sure your new cook is very good, but I could not resist baking some in celebration that at last you are to marry Theo."

"You are the best friend a woman could ask for. You and Christine. I could never have imagined as a young girl that I would have such good friends." Her eyes grew bright with unshed tears of happiness. "And Philip, and Gus."

She left Theo's name unspoken, for he was so much dearer to her than a friend and would become even dearer still when they were married.

There was nothing left to do to prepare, and Honoria admitted laughingly that she had come early for nothing as Philip joined them after having seen to the horses. In a short time, Christine and Gus arrived as well. As this was only an inti-mate gathering among friends, it was of no consequence; there would be more people for the wedding itself. Theo's entire family would be arriving in Horncastle the next day.

In addition to Theo's family, their wedding would be attended by the Bassetts, Honoria's parents, as well as her brother and his wife Barbara. Also in attendance would be the Mercers and the Reids, in addition to some of the newer members of Arabella's circle. Christine and Honoria had not wasted any time presenting her to the women of their town, who had all welcomed her as one of their own. Arabella could hardly believe such happiness could be real. That there existed such a large group of well-wishers who had no desire to gossip about her, shut her out, or speculate on her shortcomings.

At last Theo arrived, looking more handsome than she had ever seen him. He must have been measured for new clothing, for he appeared in surprisingly modish attire. His pantaloons were a crisp ivory color, the threads of which seemed to shine in the light streaming in from the windows. His waistcoat was a pristine white, and he wore a snowy neckcloth tied in a style she learned was called the waterfall. His coat was of a stiff blue superfine, molded to a set of shoulders that were rarely idle. And something had been done to his usually disordered hair that made him look very well indeed. Her breath caught at the sight before her eyes registered the arrival of Anthony behind him.

His brother, who always dressed in the height of fashion, was likely behind Theo's transformation. Not that he'd needed any transformation at all, for Theo was nearly perfect in her eyes. Yet she could not help but appreciate the effect of a talented pair of hands behind his attire. Theo kissed her on the cheek and rested a lingering look on her lips before going over to greet the others, and Anthony came up to her next.

"I have given you a wedding gift in the form of a valet for Theo," he said with a grin. "Even if he swore to me that you didn't think he needed it, the ton must differ with you on that point. The sight of him offended."

Arabella laughed. She held out her hand for him to clasp, her soon-to-be little brother. "I do *indeed* thank you, Anthony. For this, and for running the mill so that Theo can come and live at Penwood, and for sending Trudy's husband to save Theo's life, and oh—for any number of things."

Anthony blushed hotly and stammered something about it all being of no great consequence.

Once Theo had announced he would be handing the mill over to his brother, Anthony had not stopped coming up with improvements and new ideas for textiles that brought in more streams of revenue. He had even mentioned an interest in the daughter of a local rival that hinted at the possibility of one day joining the mills to compete against the others even more, although such a thing was a ways off, Anthony had assured them. He wanted to marry for love and not for a possible alliance.

They sat to an early dinner, their intimate number of nine including Honoria's brother Samuel and wife Barbara, plus Anthony, in addition to their usual circle of six. Arabella noted with pride that her new servants were capable of setting out an elegant dinner, despite being so new to their roles. When the three courses were finished, tea was served in the drawing room, along with the almond cakes Honoria had brought. Four of the men set up a game of cards, and Barbara, Christine, and Honoria gathered around the table, discussing ideas for decorating the church on the day of the wedding and shooing Arabella away with laughter when she came to listen.

"Leave it all to us," Honoria said.

She smiled at them, surrounded by the warmth of acceptance and love, and turned to Theo, who had been shut out just as effectively.

"It could only have been by design, but I do not regret it," Theo said, holding out his arm for her to take. She smiled at him and slipped her hand under his elbow, allowing him to lead her to a small sofa by the window.

The thin windowpanes let in the cold, and it was far from the fire, so Theo whisked her to her feet again to draw nearer to the chimney.

"I cannot have you catching a cold before our wedding, for I intend to marry you at all costs, even if it means I must bring the rector to your bedside. But I cannot think you would like that."

"No, for my nose is certain to be an unsightly red," she teased back.

He led her to a small sofa near the fire that was not so far from the card table or the group of women planning the decorations. It would not allow for much of an intimate conversation, but she did not mind.

He leaned in and murmured in her ear, "I had hoped to steal a kiss, but I am beginning to suspect it won't be possible."

"You may have one in a week's time," she whispered back. "More than one, even, for I am generous."

"I must be very strong then and steel myself for the wait," he replied, holding her gaze, his eyes crinkling in the warmth of his smile.

She loved the way it felt to be near him, the way her heartbeat picked up, the way she wanted to float about the room—how she wanted to laugh, if only to relieve the happiness when that sentiment threatened to bubble over.

Honoria caught her attention. "Where is David? I had expected to see him by now."

"His nurse told me he fell asleep right before we began eating. He must be arriving at any time," Arabella answered, just as a shout came up from the table of cards at an unexpected hand that stole the game.

Christine went over to inspect the winning hand, and the door opened, revealing her son and his nurse. Felicity trailed behind David, whose little legs hurried into the room before he stopped short at the sight of all the faces. Arabella stood to catch his attention, and Theo stood beside her.

"David," Honoria called out to him, smiling.

He walked toward her, but when he saw Theo, he made a beeline for him instead, and Theo lifted him up high. Perched in Theo's arms, David looked around the room, subjecting each visitor to his serious gaze. Arabella stepped up to Theo, and

David leaned over to be transferred into her arms, so Theo put his arm around Arabella's waist instead.

Their friends returned to their cards and conversation, allowing Arabella a moment with her son and her intended. She held David, enjoying the warmth of Theo's arm around her as she cast her eyes about the drawing room, full of the people who mattered most to her in all the world. It did not signify that they had become a part of her life so recently. It only mattered that they would be part of her life for all the rest of it.

Theo seemed to read the fullness of her thoughts, for he pulled her closer to him and stole a quick kiss on her cheek, then planted one on top of David's head. Her inquisitive son reached up for his neckcloth, but this one was too fine to destroy and Theo intercepted his hand, then pretended to bite his fingers, causing David to laugh.

It is in this moment—Arabella thought, standing at Theo's side—*and in moments like these, where happiness resides.* She laughed as another cheer went up from the card table, and Gus threw down his hand in mock defeat.

It is found here when you are kept occupied with the gladness of your heart.

ACKNOWLEDGMENTS

I want to thank Rod Stormes, once again, for coming to my aid for many of the details in this book. Your wealth of knowledge of Lincolnshire and of England in general—including a wealth of historical details—has saved me from many embarrassing blunders. (Not to say that I still haven't made any—you just saved me from making *more*.)

I credit all my knowledge of smuggling to the book *Smuggling in the British Isles* by Richard Platt, including the unfortunate officer whose head was shoved down a rabbit hole. It was a stroke of luck—considering I chose my location in the first book, before I had decided to include smuggling—that there were indeed smuggled goods coming in through Horncastle, primarily tobacco which was then processed in Lincoln. The "farmer" who carried Arabella to the stagecoach in the middle of the night was likely one such land smuggler.

Thank you, Jess Heileman for being an amazing critique partner, as well as Emma Le Noan and Genevieve Dousson for your early reads. A huge thanks to my assistant, Marilee Merrell, who —besides her numerous other talents—possesses the talent of unabated encouragement. To my editors, Jolene Perry and Theresa Schultz, you're the best! This book would not be what it is without you.

What's next? Christine Grey's story is told in the book *A Presumptuous Hope*, but because of my publishing schedule, it will not be out until autumn of 2024. As such, it is too early to put on preorder. My sincere apologies to those who *haaate to waaaait*.

BOOK CLUB QUESTIONS

1. This novel is called *A Stroke of Good Fortune*, and there were many "chance" events that contributed to a successful resolution. What, for you, was the ultimate stroke of good fortune that made the story deserve its name?

2. Arabella's growth in the story was clear. She learned to believe in herself and stand up for what she wanted—to depend on other people instead of believing she was not worth their time. Theo also had his own character arc. Did you spot it? How would you say he grew throughout the story? How did his growth compare to Arabella's?

3. Mr. Northwick was a particularly heinous villain for the narcissistic way he belittled Arabella and kept her under his tight control. How did his part in the story affect your overall enjoyment of the book? Did it make you uncomfortable and long to skim over those parts? Or were you eager to see how he would be vanquished?

What in your own life—to the extent that you feel like sharing—do you think caused you to react that way to this particular villain?

4. If you are a mother—or even if you are not—what did you relate to the most in Arabella's way of caring for David? There were times she stood up for herself and other times she thought

it better to cede to the stronger authority. What would you have done differently and what would you have handled the same?

5. There is an overarching theme of friendship, family, and "found family" and how they serve both Theo and Arabella over the course of the book. Theo's family members are also his friends, and Arabella's friends become her found family, although she has to gain self-confidence and win over Trudy before it can happen. How does this theme manifest itself in your life?

6. Some parts of the book might feel heavy to read for some people. What were the things—if any—that made you laugh?

ABOUT THE AUTHOR

Jennie Goutet is an American-born Anglophile who lives with her French husband and their three children in a small town outside of Paris. Her imagination resides in Regency England, where her best-selling proper Regency romances are set. She is also author of the award-winning memoir *Stars Upside Down,* two contemporary romances, and a smattering of other published works. A Christian, a cook, and an inveterate klutz, Jennie sometimes writes about faith, food, and life—even the clumsy moments—on her blog, aladyinfrance.com. But if you really want to learn more about Jennie and her books, sign up for her newsletter, on her author website: jenniegoutet.com.

* Photo Credit : Caroline Aoustin

Printed in Great Britain
by Amazon

27143417R00162